What the critics are saying...

"It's one of the rare books where my husband actually turned the telly up ~ to drown out my bursts of laughter! I will never look at Mondays the same way, ever again!" ~ *Euro-Reviews*

"About Monday is a fun and fresh romantic comedy with a paranormal twist which will enchant readers everywhere! Written with style, verve and a wicked sense of humour, Sydney Laine Allan's story is a gem which you should not dare miss!" ~ *ECataRomance Reviews*

"I will definitely be on the look-out for more from Sydney Laine Allan in the future!" ~ *Joyfully Reviewed*

Sydney Laine Allan

About Monday

Cerridwen Press

A Cerridwen Press Publication

www.cerridwenpress.com

About Monday

ISBN #141995430X

Edited by Sue-Ellen Gower.
Cover art by Syneca.

Electronic book Publication September 2005
Trade Paperback Publication February 2006

Cerridwen Press is an imprint of Ellora's Cave Publishing, Inc.®

About Monday

ꩻ

Trademarks Acknowledgement

~

The author acknowledges the trademarked status and trademark owners of the following wordmarks mentioned in this work of fiction:

Lexus: Toyota Jidosha Kabushiki Kaisha Corporation

Godzilla: Toho Co., Ltd.

Ben & Jerry's: Ben & Jerry's Homemade Holdings, Inc.

DC-10: McDonnell Douglas Corporation

Bud Light: Anheuser-Busch, Incorporated

Meijer: Meijer, Inc.

Jockey: Jockey International, Inc.

Red Wings: Rochester Community Baseball, Inc.

Honda Accord: Honda Giken Kogyo Kabushiki Kaisha

Evian: Societe Anonyme des eaux Minerales D'Evian

Manolo Blahnik: Blahnik; Manolo

Twinkies: Continental Baking Company

Gucci: Gucci Shops, Inc.

Honda: Honda Giken Kogyo Kabushiki Kaisha (Honda Motor Co., Ltd.)

Lycra: E. I. du Pont de Nemours and Company

Lamborghini: Same Deutz-Fahr S.p.A

Rolodex: Insilco Corporation

Mack: Mack Trucks, Inc.

Wonderbra: Canadelle, INC

Nyquil: Richardson-Merrell Inc.

Chapter One

ഗ

Sometimes it stunk being second best. Especially when first best was five-foot eleven-inches of all-American blonde beauty named Monica Starke.

The years 1990 through 1994 at Ferndale High School, Monica had been the "It" Girl. Cheerleader, captain of the debating team, president of the National Honor Society, the lead in the play and valedictorian. She dated the captain of the football team and was the envy of every girl in school.

Jenny Brown, barely five-foot tall with mousy hair and unremarkable features, was the salutatorian—something to be proud of for sure—but otherwise relatively invisible. After graduation, Jenny waited tables at a Coney Island to pay her tuition at the local community college. Two years later, after enduring umpteen million pick-up lines from married, middle-aged men on the prowl for their midlife crisis trophy, Jenny graduated with an associate's degree. She landed a starting position for just above minimum wage at a small advertising company in Southfield.

In contrast, nothing changed for Monica after she graduated. She still lived a blessed life. Daddy paid her tuition at U of M Ann Arbor and she had a riot playing sorority sister. Monica and the rest of the Gamma Kappa Chis partied morning, noon and night until she finally decided it was time to graduate six years later. At graduation, she proudly displayed her certificate for her bachelor's degree in graphic design and then enjoyed her small graduation gift from her father—a trip to Europe.

After landing stateside again, she snagged a job at the same small advertising company—for quite a bit more than minimum wage. She dated a billionaire jewelry broker who bought her a house in Birmingham for Christmas and a Lexus for her birthday. On the weekends, they played golf at Oakland Hills and hung out with his rich friends.

Gee, what a rough life.

Jenny heard about their weekend plans every Friday morning at work and although she tried to pretend that it didn't bother her, it sometimes did. Life was unfair. Some people got things the easy way and some people struggled for everything they had.

Never the whiner, and normally grateful for everything she had since she'd busted her butt to get it, Jenny didn't complain, and she didn't sit around and ruminate the injustice of it all. She liked her studio apartment. It was cozy, cheap to heat and all hers, and her subcompact didn't have leather seats or a built-in game system, but it started every morning and got her from Point A to Point B.

But every now and then, when Monica was bemoaning her latest tragedy, Jenny indulged in a guilty pleasure and daydreamed of when she would be best, when she would land the dream account or date a multi-zillionaire. Monica would learn how it felt to be second.

Naturally, Jenny knew it would take the act of some god for that to happen, but like dreaming of winning the lottery on Friday nights before the numbers were drawn, it was occasionally fun to think about.

And today was one of those days.

It was Friday, not Jenny's favorite day of the week but not her least favorite either. It didn't start out bad. She woke up feeling rested and ready for the work, her shower was hot—something that didn't happen too often—and she'd managed to avoid all the major traffic snarls on the way to work. Yet the moment she walked into the office, her Friday took a turn for the worse.

"Do you have a minute?" Monica asked the second Jenny stepped in the door.

She knew what those words meant, and frankly she wasn't interested in ending her week by playing Monica's therapist. "Wow, you're here early. I didn't expect anyone… I have a lot of work—"

Monica pressed her palms together and held them in front of her chest as if she was praying. "Please? You're the very best friend I have in the whole world and I need someone to talk to. It's important."

Liar. She says that to everybody. Jenny held back a sigh, walked to her cubicle, dropped her purse and lunch on her desk and sat in her chair. "Okay. But five minutes. That's it. I'm setting a timer."

"You're the best!" Monica pulled up a chair to Jenny's desk and plopped in it. "It's about the Kelly's Yogurt account. I was supposed to finish up the coupon layout this week and turn it in today by five, but I had a major personal crisis and didn't get the chance to work on it. Today's the two-month anniversary of my breakup with Jason and I was so depressed all week long I couldn't concentrate on anything—"

Oh boy, Jenny could see where this was heading. "Uh-uh. I can't. If I do your work then my stuff won't get done and I'll look bad. Again."

"Pretty please? It would mean everything to me. I'd owe you big." Her bottom lip started trembling and the whites of her eyes turned a pretty shade of pink that matched her lipstick and coordinating nail polish. "You have no idea what I've been going through."

Yeah, like no one else on earth has broken up with their boyfriends. "You have my sympathy, really. I'm sorry you're…suffering…but I can't afford to be late with this project. It goes to print tomorrow—"

Monica leaned forward and caught Jenny's hand, gripping it tightly until all circulation was lost to her fingertips. "Look, I'm desperate. What'll it cost me? I'll pay anything."

"It's not about money." She tugged, trying to free her hand before suffering any serious damage. Her knuckles were grinding together. "Let go. You're hurting me."

"I can get you backstage passes to any concert at Pine Knob."

She gave her hand another sharp tug but Monica still didn't release it. "Not into concerts, sorry."

"Box seats at a Red Wings game?"

"It isn't hockey season. Besides I hate hockey." Accepting the fact that Monica wasn't going to voluntarily release her hand, she started prying Monica's fingers loose, one at a time.

"What born and bred Detroiter hates hockey?" Finally releasing Jenny's hand, Monica dropped her face in her hands and turned on the tears full blast.

Her shoulders shuddered, her breath came in raspy bursts. It was a pathetic sight. *Good grief, I've seen better acting on those old Godzilla movies. She'd better not quit her day job.*

"I can't take it anymore," Monica moaned, sounding like something between a dying cow and an overwrought teenager. "I just can't. You don't know what it's like to be me."

Oh God.

"I don't have anybody. I'm all alone. No one to help me."

You expect pity? Where's your zillionaire boyfriend? Where's Daddy? He'll take out his checkbook and everything will be rosy. Jenny forced herself to pat Monica's shoulder in a show of support. "I'm sure everything will be all right. Mr. Kaufmann likes you. You're his top star. He'll give you an extension and everyone will be happy."

"I can't ask him for another extension. He threatened to fire me the last time."

"Fire you? He'd lose fifty percent of his business if you left and he knows it. He won't let you go."

Monica fished a CD jewel case out of her designer briefcase and set it on Jenny's desk. "I'm telling the truth. Please? I'm begging. I need this done by today. It's half finished. It'll only take an hour or two."

"Then what's the problem? You have all day."

"I have something else to do. Something vitally important. Please. I won't ask you again. I'll give you all the credit if you want. You're probably due for a raise, aren't you?"

Past due by, oh…about two years. "Well…"

"See? It'll be good for both of us. I saved the file on this CD." She slid the plastic case across the desk, closer to Jenny. "Come on. You'll get a raise and I'll get a break. No one loses."

She would probably regret this, but what the heck? Only an hour or two wouldn't kill her. She'd still have plenty of time to finish the layout for the car wash newspaper ad she promised this afternoon. "Okay. But just this once. Don't ask me again."

"Oh, I promise I won't. Thank you! You're the best friend I've ever had. I owe you big!" Monica leapt to her feet, swept up her briefcase and as Jenny watched, charged out of the office, waving over her shoulder just before going out the door. "See ya Monday," she half said, half sang. "Wish me luck."

Where the heck was she going?

Dread gnawed a hole in the pit of Jenny's gut. She had a feeling an hour or two was a gross understatement.

* * * * *

Late. She was late. Then again, why should that surprise him?

Jason Foxx lobbed his head from side to side, cracking his neck as he waited impatiently in his car for Monica to return home. *I don't have all day for this. Damn it, why does she have to be fashionably late for everything, including an argument?*

If he didn't need the stuff he'd left in her house when he'd hastily moved out a couple of months ago, he wouldn't have bothered. Especially knowing she'd think his return was some kind of half-hearted attempt on his part to reconcile.

No way that was going to happen. He'd had enough of self-centered, high-maintenance Monica Starke to last a lifetime. The next woman he dated would be different, the complete opposite, right down to the color of her hair.

He glanced at the clock on his dashboard again. Damn it! He was going to be late for his appointment. He looked up the phone number of the gentleman he was scheduled to meet and punched it in his cell phone, apologizing profusely and rescheduling for later that afternoon. Just as he hit the end button, Monica pulled in the drive, grinned and waved, and shut off the engine.

"Sorry. I had to take care of a few things first. You look great, by the way."

Not in the mood to listen to her compliments or excuses, especially since they'd rescheduled this simple task at least a dozen times because she'd had a scheduling conflict, he grumbled, "I had an important appointment this morning. You said you'd be here an hour ago."

Hands on hips, she stood defiant, her chin lifted just enough to get on his nerves. "Would you let it go? I said I'm sorry. What more do you want me to say?"

"Nothing. Please, do me a favor and say nothing. Just let me get my things and we won't have to talk about anything anymore."

"Fine." She teetered to the front door on her high heels and unlocked it, pushing it open and motioning for him to go in first.

He shook his head and waited for her to enter then followed her. "I'll only be a minute."

"Don't you dare take any of the artwork. It stays with the house."

"I promise I won't touch a single knick-knack." He shook his head. The woman was selfish right to the bitter end. "I just need a few personal things. I forgot about some stuff I left in the spare bedroom closet."

"Fine." She followed him through the foyer and up the stairs. "But I cleaned that closet. There wasn't anything in there but old junk."

He spun around to face her, panic and rage threatening to burst more than a few vital blood vessels. "What are you saying?"

"I'm saying the closet's empty."

Desperately hoping she was lying, he rushed into the room and pushed open the doors. "Damn it! Those were my family's heirlooms! How could you?"

To her credit, she looked a little surprised and remorseful. "I thought they were just trash. Some old, crusty-looking coins and ugly dishes and pottery. I sold the whole shebang to a dealer for a few bucks. Why would you leave it here if it was important? Why wasn't it in storage somewhere?"

"You know I don't trust those storage lockers. They aren't secure. Wait a minute, you said a few dollars? How few?"

Her face paled. "Please tell me those old pots weren't worth anything."

"How few?" he repeated, wondering if there was a legal defense for strangling an ignorant person who'd basically given away a priceless collection of art deco art glass.

"Is it insured?"

"Yes, against damage or theft, not against them being sold for pennies on the dollar by some—" He didn't say the rest. Insulting her wouldn't do a damn bit of good. "You should have called me before you did anything. You knew those things weren't yours."

"You're right, I should have. I just assumed you didn't care since you left them."

He bit back a cliché about the hazards of making assumptions, figuring it would fall on deaf ears anyway. He'd never met a more irresponsible human being in his life. "Who'd you sell them to and how long ago?"

"About two weeks ago. I don't remember the man's name. I found him in the paper." She hurried toward the stairs. "Maybe his ad's in yesterday's *News*. I have it down in the kitchen."

His anger receding slightly, replaced by hollow grief, which hardly suited him any better, he followed her. "By any chance, he didn't give you a receipt…or a card…or anything?"

"No. Should he have? He paid me cash."

And made off like a bandit before she figured out what she'd done. Goddamn thief.

She hurried into the kitchen and rifled through the newspaper sections. "The ad was in last week's classifieds. Here! This is the section." She ran her brightly polished fingertip down the columns.

He wondered if the proceeds from the sale of *his* precious heirlooms had paid for her manicure.

"I'm looking. Give me just a minute."

His energy spent, the hope of finding his grandmother's possessions nearly dashed, Jason slumped against the counter. "Okay."

"It isn't here." She looked up, genuine regret in her eyes. "I'm so sorry. If I'd known they were valuable I wouldn't have done that. Honest. You know I'm not that vindictive, don't you?"

Mute, he just nodded and walked toward the front door.

"Please forgive me. I know you think I'm a cold bitch, but I didn't mean to give away something precious. I swear. I'm very sorry. Can I make it up to you somehow? Do you want the money?"

"No. What's done is done. Goodbye, Monica. I hope you have a very happy life."

She looked tired as she watched him exit. "Goodbye, Jason."

* * * * *

Monday, thanks to Monica's supposedly almost finished project—which naturally hadn't been remotely close to complete—Jenny got a tongue-lashing from Mr. Kaufmann for missing the deadline for the car wash ad.

Monica got a raise for the fantastic job *she* did on the yogurt coupon then disappeared for the rest of the day.

It plain didn't pay to be nice.

Giving herself a mental ass-kicking for believing Monica would keep her word and give her credit, Jenny left work that day angry and frustrated. She deserved that raise! The yogurt coupon that her boss raved about was her work. But there was no way to tell Mr. Kaufmann that. He knew only one thing—she was late with the car wash layout and the ad would have to run in next week's Sunday edition of the newspaper. The owner of the car wash, a long-term client, was furious and about ready to find another agency for their future advertising. With so much at stake, a petty argument between employees was meaningless to him, the last thing he wanted to hear about.

So, Jenny told herself, she'd learned her lesson the hard way. She wouldn't be stupid next time—and she was sure there would be a next time. Monica's tears could fill the whole office, the whole building for that matter. She wouldn't budge. Monica could take care of her own problems.

Jenny had enough of her own, thank you.

That night, she sat in her pajamas—an ancient pair of sweats and oversized T-shirt—on her tiny balcony with a pint of her favorite Ben and Jerry's ice cream and watched what few stars she could see, the ones too brilliant to be faded out by the bright city lights.

As she filled her mouth with creamy, calorie-laden sin, she again wondered what it would be like to walk in Monica's three-inch stiletto heels. How would it feel to have men practically falling at her feet? Doors opening, people crawling over themselves to do her every bidding, money wired from Daddy whenever she wanted? Monica Starke was as close to a big New York socialite as Metro Detroit had.

She was something Jenny would never be, wasn't even sure she'd ever want to be—although a few of the perks would be nice, like Daddy's bottomless bank account.

As Jenny dug into the bottom of the container for the last bite of ice cream, she caught a bright flash in the night sky from the corner of her eye. She looked up. Maybe an airplane landing at the little airport down the street, or a traffic helicopter? Did radio stations have traffic helicopters patrolling after nine on a Monday night?

It soared in a broad arc from left to right. And then several more followed.

A meteor shower. Cool.

She hadn't heard anything about a meteor shower on the news but that had to be it. Enthralled, the ice cream all but forgotten, she watched more brilliant flashes blaze across the sky. It was a regular heavenly fireworks bonanza. Gorgeous.

And as she watched, that kid's rhyme about stars and wishes echoed through her mind. She'd never wished on a falling star before. Who knew, maybe they were magic.

Okay, so that sounded pretty dumb, but today had been a rough day. She deserved a little silly fantasizing. It couldn't hurt anything.

"Star light, star bright. First star I see tonight. I wish I may, I wish I might...have the wish I wish tonight." She focused on one particularly bright star then closed her eyes and thought—assuming of course it would never come true—*I wish I was Monica.* Before she opened her eyes, she added, *for a little while. Not forever.*

Content with her wish, she nodded and opened her eyes.

The meteor shower seemed to have stopped. In fact it looked like there had never been any unusual activity at all. The sky was its usual semi-dark blue with a band of orange hanging low to the west. A handful of faded stars peeked from behind a thin cover of wispy clouds.

Sleepy, she went inside, tossed the ice cream container into the trash and settled into bed. Tomorrow would be another day. Barring any unforeseen disasters, it was bound to be better than today.

Chapter Two

ℌ

Even semi-asleep, Jenny sensed something was different. The bed felt unfamiliar, softer, and it smelled like perfume. The scent burned her nose.

As she drifted closer to complete wakefulness, she realized there was no traffic noise rumbling through the open window. No trucks roaring down the freeway or angry motorists on the verge of morning rush hour road rage blaring their horns. It was peaceful. Serene.

What the heck? Was the freeway shut down?

She blinked and opened her eyes and immediately realized why she didn't hear the traffic and why the bed felt different.

This wasn't her bed or her bedroom. Where the hell was she?

Her heart immediately shifting into triple-pace as panic wound its way around her insides and clamped down tight, she sat up and looked around the room. It was a fancy place. All the furniture matched. The bed, a massive dark wood piece of furniture with a gorgeous brocade canopy gathered at four ceiling-height posts, sat positioned in the middle of one wall. The window, dressed in curtains to match the canopy, was directly opposite.

She ran across the room, not completely unaware of how soft the carpet felt under her bare feet, and pulled the curtain aside. She stared into a lush green lawn full of mature trees.

No clues there.

Turning slowly, she scanned the room again for a sign of where she was. Why would anyone kidnap her and bring her to a place like this? It made absolutely no sense.

She ran to the door and gripped the knob, fully expecting it to be locked. It turned without a problem.

Why would someone kidnap her and put her in an unlocked room? Had to be the dumbest kidnappers in history. She opened the door just enough to poke her head out and took a peek. There wasn't an armed guard standing in the hallway.

Weird. Gotta do some more investigating but I need to take care of one minor problem first.

Feeling like her bladder was about ready to burst, she spun around, pushing the door closed as she turned. But as she took a step forward, something caught, yanking her backward.

Her nightgown was trapped in the door. She opened it, pulled the filmy material free, closed it again and…*nightgown*?…and freaked out!

Someone had changed her clothes? Where were her sweats and T-shirt?

Exactly how far down had they undressed her? Surely they hadn't stripped her nude, had they?

How embarrassing. I wasn't wearing my good underwear last night. She untied the lace at her throat and peered straight down. Yikes! She had no underwear or bra on.

Sheesh, with boobs like that I don't need a bra…

Wait a minute! Oh God!

"There is a boob fairy!" she said to the air before looking down to admire her new breasts again. "I was expecting you about fifteen years ago, but I suppose it's better late than never." Those had to be at least thirty-four Cs or maybe Ds. She'd never seen anything that large up close and personal. Up until now she'd been blessed with barely-there thirty-two As.

Someone kidnapped her, gave her plastic surgery and then brought her to this fancy place to recover? Funny, she didn't feel a twinge of pain. Her friend Janice got a boob job and moaned about the pain for months. Wimp.

Yippee! What rich fairy godmother did she have to thank for this? Or was it one of those reality shows? Was there a hidden camera in the room somewhere? She nervously glanced around, eyeing artwork on the wall with suspicion. Maybe it was hidden behind that busy floral print over there… It's too ugly to be there for any other reason. She walked over to get a better look.

Didn't seem to be any peepholes for tiny camera lenses. No, the reality show idea was losing credibility quickly.

The fairy godmother theory was too—at least a real human fairy godmother—since it couldn't be legal to perform plastic surgery on someone without their knowledge or consent.

That left her with no logical explanations. This was getting stranger by the second.

Now, hardly able to catch her breath, thanks to equal doses of confusion and panic, as well as a spasming bladder, Jenny ran across the room and tried a door that looked like it might lead to a bathroom.

As she found herself in the middle of a well-stocked, walk-in closet, she realized her bladder wasn't the only part of her in an uproar. Her empty stomach was clenching and unclenching and she was about to retch.

Luckily, the second door she tried led to a bathroom. She dashed inside, grabbed an empty trash can to catch anything coming up, yanked up her nightgown and sat on the toilet to catch anything going down. And settled in for the long haul.

When she finally had herself collected, she stood up and looked into the mirror to see if anything else had been surgically altered…

…and nearly fell over.

Her hands gripping the smooth polished stone countertop, she screamed, "Oh my God!" One hand rose to her face, her fingertips searching the lines and curves of familiar features, but ones that definitely didn't belong to her.

"I'm...Monica? But how?" Even her voice sounded different. Could a surgeon change a person's voice?

Immediately she recalled last night's wish but dismissed it. That was a silly, childish rhyme, not magic. Real magic didn't exist outside of fairy tales and movies, everyone knew that. Those fancy magicians who made DC-10 airplanes disappear used illusion.

This had to be some kind of illusion too.

She pulled her hair back and gathered it into one fist, then felt along her hairline for some kind of seam, figuring someone had put some of that special makeup on her, like the rubber mask Robin Williams wore in that old movie, *Mrs. Doubtfire.* But after searching thoroughly, she concluded either there was no makeup or it was applied so well it couldn't be detected.

Maybe a shower would wash some of it away.

She turned on the water—no easy task, considering the number of gadgets and gizmos in the glass enclosed cubicle—and stepped inside, scrubbing from top to toe with soap. When she stepped out and scrutinized her face in the mirror, she still found no signs of makeup, no seams or smears.

Okay. Running out of steam fast, she sat on a cushy bench in front of the mirror and stared at herself. There had to be a logical explanation. Didn't there?

Whoever was responsible for this crazy event evidently wanted her to play Monica for a day or two for some reason. Why, she couldn't begin to guess. But she figured she had two options—either she could hide out until someone showed up to explain it to her, or she could make the best of it and do what she'd secretly dreamed of doing—see how it felt walking in three-inch Manolo Blahniks and driving a Lexus.

Wrapping her—correction, Monica's—body in a luxurious bathrobe, she padded into the bedroom, rummaged through drawers until she found the necessities she was looking for, then went to the wall-to-wall closet to find an outfit that suited her.

So many choices! Good God, the woman owned enough garments to clothe a small nation. Heck, some of them still sported their price tags. She pulled out a black skirt, tag still attached and read the price. Three hundred bucks? For a little black scrap of material? It had better do something special for that price, like clean itself.

Stepping into it, she immediately recognized how terrific it fit. It seemed to have been made for her—correction, Monica. There wasn't a bit of extra room anywhere, nor did it fit too tight, even around the hips. "I guess for three hundred dollars you should get something that fits perfect." She ran her hands down her upper thighs, smoothing the fabric. It felt nice.

Next, she found a white button-down shirt with subtle gray stripes. It, too, fit her like a second skin. And a silky cashmere sweater finished off the outfit. Cashmere felt like heaven. Now Jenny could appreciate why it cost so much.

After slipping her feet into a pair of high-heeled pumps, which were extremely comfortable—unlike the cheap plastic pairs Jenny regularly bought at the discount shoe outlet in the mall—she walked down the hall to the kitchen to find a bite to eat. Unfortunately, the fridge was empty. The woman kept no food in her house?

So that was her secret! Made sense. You can't get fat if you don't have any food to eat.

Heading for the front door, and hoping to run across a purse and some keys, Jenny vowed to do the same at her place when she returned. She could stand to lose at least ten pounds. The Monica Starvation Diet would do the trick.

Yes, she was learning some valuable stuff already—how to lose a few pounds and the value of a good cashmere sweater—and she hadn't even left the house yet.

She found a purse, briefcase and a set of keys lying on the console next to the answering machine with the blinking red message light, then went back through the kitchen, hoping the door leading to the garage would be somewhere in there. They usually were, weren't they?

After taking a tour of the butler's pantry and a half bath, she found the door in question, exited but didn't arm the house's alarm system, and pushed the button to kick-start the automatic garage door. Then she got in the car.

Like the clothes, the car's leather seat fit like a glove. The padding wrapped around her derriere and gently cradled it like a loving mother. The motor sung a soft lullaby. And, as she first backed out of the garage then drove down the street, she realized it glided smoothly, almost floating above the street's surface.

It took her a while to find her way out of Monica's twisty-turny subdivision, and Jenny had the forethought to not only write down the address but also keep track of how she got out so she could find her way back in if she needed to. Who knew how long she'd be stuck living this farce, so she figured she'd best be prepared.

When she finally arrived at work, almost two hours late, she headed straight to her cubicle to see who or what was there. Maybe Monica had taken her place.

It was empty. No sign of anyone. Darn! That meant she'd have to finish both her own projects and Monica's! Grumbling, she plopped into her chair and turned on her monitor, figuring she'd get her stuff done first before trying to figure out what Monica had on her plate.

"Ms. Starke, what are you doing here?"

Startled and feeling like she'd been caught doing something she shouldn't be, Jenny spun around to face her boss. She tried to look nonchalant as she shrugged and said, "Working."

"I can see that. But why are you at Ms. Brown's desk?" He motioned toward the picture of herself she'd tacked on the bulletin board behind her monitor.

"Oh! I'm…finishing up the Muffin House project."

He didn't look satisfied with her answer. "The Muffin House is Ms. Brown's account. Why are you working on that?"

Good question. "Um…because…she asked me to take a look at it for her?" she rambled, adding, "As a favor. I owe her."

"Really? That's very interesting." He tipped his head, looking as intrigued as his words suggested. "Can I ask why you owe her a favor?"

You can but I don't know if I can answer. Wait a minute. Duh! I couldn't have planned this better if I'd tried. At her feet was the perfect opportunity to tell him about the yogurt account. Maybe that's why she was changed into Monica. Some kind of supernatural opportunity to correct an injustice. That was the first logical explanation she had found.

"Well," she began. "Last Friday I got into a bind and I didn't have time to finish up the yogurt ad. Jenny was kind enough to finish it up for me, even setting aside her own projects and putting her job on the line for me. I promised to give her credit for the fantastic job she did but it kind of slipped my mind until now." She tried to look remorseful, hoping that would make her speech somewhat believable. Just about everything she'd said sounded so unlike the real Monica that she wondered how he'd ever buy it—outside of the obvious, what he saw.

Mr. Kaufmann's eyebrows rose high on his forehead and he crossed his arms over his chest, shaking his head in disbelief. Nope, he wasn't buying it. Not at all. "Ms. Brown designed the yogurt ad?"

"I know it's hard to believe—a girl with an associates from a community college for God's sake," she added hoping that sounded more like Monica. "But it's true. She did the entire thing. I started it, but frankly my original design was worse than garbage. I've seen better stuff in an elementary school's hallway. She threw it away and started from scratch."

"When was the last time you spoke to Ms. Brown?"

"Uh. Last night. Why?"

"Because this morning she came in early, finished everything she had for the week and took the rest of the week off, paid."

"Paid? She used my—er, her—vacation days? Four whole days? You saw her?"

He nodded. "I did."

"She turned in everything?"

"I have it all, including the Muffin House project. And it's perfectly acceptable. So I suggest you get to your own work."

"Okay." She punched the power button on her monitor, swept up her purse and briefcase, and walked back to Monica's office. As she settled in Monica's comfy leather chair, she sighed. Oh yes, the perks were nice. She glanced around the room. Perks like four walls that reached the ceiling and a real door that could close. Monica's office afforded her space to move around as she brainstormed. She spun around in the chair, facing the door, and ran her hand over her U-shaped desk's smooth work surface. "Oh yeah, I could definitely get used to this." Then she glanced up and caught Mr. Kaufmann watching her through the open doorway. She answered his puzzled expression with a silly grin then turned toward the computer to see what Monica had to work on.

Good God, the girl had a load and a half! And everything was due by next Monday. Despite the obvious advantages, this part of walking in Monica's shoes—designer or not—wasn't looking so great. Resigned to late nights and early mornings for the next several days, and possibly no time during the weekend to try out Monica's hot looks at Jenny's favorite hangout, Jenny set to work on the first project—a full page spread for a pet store.

* * * * *

Twelve hours later, stiff, sore and starving, Jenny shut off Monica's computer, threw her purse over her shoulder, fisted her keys and locked up the office. Weary and wobbling on her high heels, she trudged out to the parking lot.

As soon as her liquefied gray matter registered what she saw, she was wide awake.

Someone was towing her—or, Monica's—car! Kicking off her shoes, she ran toward the man operating the winch that was slowly dragging the flashy gold car up on a flatbed truck. "Stop! What do you think you're doing? This isn't a no-parking zone, for God's sake. It's a parking lot."

The grizzly-looking character who resembled a bouncer at some local biker bar gave her a quick once-over then grinned. "I know that. But I have orders to repossess this car. I have a court order, signed by a judge. It's all legal." He pulled out a bundle of papers from the truck's cab and waved them at her.

"Orders from whom? There must be some mistake."

"Orders from the gentleman who owns this car, miss, and the judge who signed this." He gave her another up and down assessment then unfolded the documents and scanned them. "I'm guessing Mr. Foxx's not so pleased with you anymore." He folded them and tucked them under his meaty arm and returned to operating the winch.

"What? I…" Oh, she was so steamed she couldn't speak. "I own this car. It was given to me by my boyfriend."

The man waved the papers again. "The papers I have say it don't belong to a woman. It's owned by a fella and he wants it back."

"Let me see that." She lunged forward but he quickly pulled it out of her reach. "Uh-uh. You can't look at this. It's confidential."

"But it's my car!"

"The State of Michigan says otherwise." He gently pushed her away as he walked toward the rear of the truck. "Now, be a good girl and move aside so I can finish up here." As he secured the car, he set the papers on the truck bed. "I don't want no trouble. I'm just doin' my job, miss."

She saw the opportunity and ran with it, quickly swiping the papers before the thug could stop her, and made a mad dash back toward the building. She read the name and address as she ran, trying hard to ingrain it in her foggy, overwrought brain until she had a chance to write it down. Fortunately, the address wasn't difficult to memorize. And neither was the name, Jason Foxx, 388 Harding Lane, Franklin.

Maybe it was time to pay Monica's ex-boyfriend, Mr. Nasty—what kind of man would repossess a car given as a gift?—a little visit and talk some sense into the man. Fearing being tackled, she dropped the papers on the ground and went inside to call a taxi, hoping Monica kept a decent amount of cash in her purse. Otherwise, it would be a long, long walk to Franklin.

Chapter Three

ꕥ

After stopping at a third gas station and having every credit card in Monica's wallet declined again, Jenny knew things were looking bleak. The first time, she'd assumed it had been a computer error. The second time, she grew worried but still held some hope. But now…no, there could be no mistake. Every card Monica possessed was maxed out.

No car. No money. As Jenny, she'd never been in such a fix, no matter how tough she'd thought things were. Right now she couldn't even afford to buy a twin pack of Twinkies.

Cold—she hadn't thought to put on a jacket this morning, she'd been driving a car with heated seats for God's sake and wearing a snuggly sweater—starving and exhausted, she sat on the curb outside the gas station and fought to keep it together. She wouldn't cry like a baby! No way. Nor would she panic. Home, warm but with an empty refrigerator, was miles away. And Jason's house was miles away, in the opposite direction.

Would a man who was cruel enough to repossess a car from his ex-girlfriend be willing to feed said ex-girlfriend if she asked nice? Or would he simply laugh in her face?

Did she have any other options?

She inhaled sharply as a patron exited the gas station, savoring the scent of coffee as it wafted out the open door. Her stomach grumbled.

That was it. Desperate times and all that. She'd take her chances and pay Jason Foxx a visit, beg for a scrap of bread if that was what it took. Now was not the time to be prideful.

As she sat and rubbed her numb toes to try to return circulation to the blood-starved appendages before setting off—evidently there was a time limit on comfort even for designer shoes that cost a small fortune—an elderly woman stopped and smiled at her.

"Do you need some help, dear?"

Jenny shook her head. "Oh no, thanks."

The woman lowered her walker over the curb and shakily stepped down. "A ride, perhaps?"

Undecided, but tempted to take the woman up on her offer, despite the gruesome stories she'd been told as a kid about the dangers of accepting rides from strangers, she eyed the frail-looking woman. What kind of danger could a woman who could barely keep herself erect possibly pose? Guns were the great equalizers, but would someone like this kind-looking elderly woman carry one?

"I don't have any money or valuables, outside of what I'm wearing. Unless you like Gucci bags." She motioned toward Monica's purse. "The plastic inside it is worthless."

"I'm not looking to rob you, dear. You won't rob me, now, will you? Since you're broke."

"Oh, heavens no! I wouldn't know how to be a crook." Laughing, and grateful for this unexpected lucky break, Jenny slipped on her shoes and followed the woman to her car. "Thank you," she said as she helped the woman fold up her walker and put it in the backseat, and then settle herself behind the steering wheel. "It would have been a long walk, and frankly I don't think my feet are up to it."

"I'm glad to help. I've been where you are once, you know. Did he throw you out for some young hussy?"

"He? Who?" Jenny took her seat.

"Your husband." Not waiting for Jenny to close the passenger side door, the old woman started the car and hit the gas, racing toward the road and showing no signs of stopping for traffic.

Jenny quickly slammed the door and braced herself against the dashboard. Petrified, she closed her eyes, fully expecting the car to slam into some poor unsuspecting soul driving down the road. But before they hit anyone, the woman slammed on the brakes. Jenny flew forward, her chest landing square on the dashboard, the force knocking the wind out of her. She opened her eyes, checked to see where they were—sitting at the end of the driveway—then glanced at the old woman.

She grinned. "My grandson says I should have my license permanently revoked. He says I'm a menace on the road. Can you believe it?"

Jenny gulped as she tried to reinflate her lungs and secured the seat belt, pulling it as tight as she could. "No."

Without looking, the old woman gunned the engine again and sent the car careening into traffic, narrowly missing an SUV and a subcompact that looked much like hers. Finally turning her attention to the road, she said, "I've been driving since 1932. Do you know what it's like to drive a thirty-two pickup truck? Compared to that, this little beauty's a piece of cake. It has power everything. And it's very zippy. By the way, where are you headed?"

"Franklin? Will that be out of your way? You could let me out sooner if you like."

"Hell, no. I'm going that way myself. I live on Woodbridge Street."

"Is that close to Harding?"

Running a red light, but seemingly unconcerned, the woman nodded. "Right around the corner. By the way, I'm Mabel." Obviously deaf to the sounds of car horns as she jetted through traffic leaving near-crashes in her wake, she smiled. "What's your name?"

"Jen…er, Monica."

"Never heard of a name like that. Jenermonica? You young people are always trying to come up with clever names for your kids. Whatever happened to simple names? Like Martha or Mary or Erma?"

"No, it's just Monica. Jenny's my…middle name. Some people call me that."

"I see." She took a corner at thirty, sending Jenny slamming into the passenger side door, despite the seat belt.

She double-checked the door's lock. God forbid she get thrown from the car. Then again, she thought as she held her hands forward to stop from splitting her face on the dashboard, that might give her a better chance at survival. The way Mabel drove, she'd be dead long before she reached Franklin. And that was only a couple of miles away.

"You said Harding Street? Do you have family living there? I know just about everyone in my neighborhood."

"No, just a friend." Curious to see what Mabel had to say about Jason, she added, "Do you know Jason Foxx?"

"Foxx, you say? I sure do. Very nice young man. He mows my lawn for me. I used to pay that company—bunch of moneygrubbing thieves they were—but he offered to take care of my lawn, and I cook him a nice dinner once a week in return."

"Really?" That didn't sound like the kind of man who would leave his ex-girlfriend stranded at nine o'clock in a parking lot. Was there more than one Jason Foxx living on Harding Street?

"Yes, and last Christmas he bought me a lovely sweater and pants set. And he always asks if I need something when he goes to the grocery store. He's a very sweet boy, says he needs to take care of me since I'm all alone. He's a bachelor, you know. Broke up with his girlfriend a month or so ago, she looked a lot like you. Could be your double, come to think of it. But she sure didn't act like you. Very uppity, that one was. Didn't give me the time of day. I told him she wasn't right for him. He deserves a nice girl. Someone like you."

Jason Foxx was sounding less and less like the demon she'd imagined him to be. But Mabel's description of Monica didn't surprise her. The only time Monica was nice was when she needed something. "You mentioned you have a grandson. Does he live far away?"

"He lives in Ohio. I've been trying to convince him to move here but he won't. I even offered to leave him my entire estate. I've been doing okay by myself, thanks to your friend, Mr. Foxx, but I know I can't live alone much longer. And once they take my driver's license, then I'll be homebound, forced to rely on someone else to chauffeur me around. I hate the idea of losing my freedom."

"I can understand that. Until tonight I'd forgotten what it's like to be dependent on other people." Jenny relaxed as they turned onto Fourteen Mile Road. Only a half-mile or so to go.

"What happened to you?"

"An old boyfriend had my car towed away. And I'm a little short on cash until payday."

"Well, isn't that despicable! What kind of man would do that to his girlfriend, broken up or not? You should pick better men to date, my dear." She patted Jenny's hand. "Though if you ask me, there aren't too many worth a second thought. Except that nice Mr. Foxx. Take my word for it, he's something special. I've been married six times. I should know." She pulled the car up a long, winding, wooded driveway and stopped in front of a gorgeous Greek revival colonial. "Here you are. This is Mr. Foxx's home. Good luck, dear. Hope to see you again sometime."

Jenny smiled at Mabel, not only grateful for making it to Jason's house alive but also having genuinely enjoyed the conversation. "Thank you. I do too. It was wonderful meeting you."

Mabel nodded and gave her a conspiratorial wink. "I'll put in a good word for you with Mr. Foxx. If he knows what's good for him, he'll listen to me." Then with a wave, she turned the car around and drove away, leaving Jenny hacking from the dust her tires kicked up, and standing in front of the most impressive, most intimidating house she'd ever seen. As she climbed the front stairs, she told herself it looked like a mansion in Beverly Hills, California.

But when she reached the door, she couldn't convince herself to ring the bell. What the heck would she say to him, a man she'd never met but a man who'd think she was someone else, someone he'd been intimate with for who knows how long? "Excuse me, but can I please have the car back?" sounded like a good start. Problem was she didn't know why he'd had it hauled away in the first place.

She spun around, wishing the porch lights weren't so bright and hoping no one had seen her, and descended a single step. "God, I've made a mistake. I should have just gone home to my empty refrigerator. What am I doing here?"

"I'd like to know the same thing," a distinctly male voice said behind her. Its tone was deep and sexy but she also sensed a sharp, icy undertone.

Anxious to see what a multimillionaire jewelry broker who had old girlfriends' cars repossessed looked like, she shivered and turned to face the source. "How did you know I was…?"

The multimillionaire jewelry broker looked too good for words, she realized the minute she'd turned completely. His last name was far more descriptive than she'd guessed. Jason Foxx was a mega-fox, an ultra-fox. The epitome of fox.

Her tongue glued itself to the roof of her mouth as she stood mute, taking in the sight of the most gorgeous man she'd ever met in person—starting at about mid-chest level, which was eye level to her since he was standing several steps higher, and rising slowly, following a nice bumpy ride over a completely nude, smooth-skinned chest and wide, well-developed shoulders. His skin was the color of her morning coffee—lots of cream, light on the coffee, and glistened slightly with sweat suggesting she'd caught him during a workout. He mopped his forehead with the white T-shirt he held in his fist.

Monica was one lucky girl! Very tall, handsome, and built like a tank, he was the kind of guy Jenny had dreamed of marrying all her life. He even had her dream man's dark, curly hair. Heck, he was better than her dream man. With picture-perfect features that were neither too pretty nor too rugged, he could easily be a model or a movie star.

"...here?" she squeaked, recalling she'd stopped speaking mid-sentence some time ago.

The problem was he didn't look happy to see her. His stubbled jaw was tight with pent-up tension. His dark eyes were narrowed into tiny slits. Nope, he wasn't thrilled in the least.

"Security camera." He pointed up. "I should have known you'd come here. The answer is no." He started pushing the door closed.

Without thinking, she ran up the stairs and thrust her arm forward to catch the door before it shut. "Now, just wait a minute!"

He didn't look surprised or thrilled as he pulled the door open again. "What?" he asked, not trying to hide the exasperation in his voice.

"Aren't you at least curious to know how I got here?"

"No. Why should I be?"

Wow, he's one cold son of a... "If you'll notice, there isn't a gold Lexus in the driveway." She motioned toward the drive like one of those models on *The Price is Right*. "And why, you might ask, would that be? Because you had mine towed away!" Her model act forgotten in her anger, she put one hand on her hip and poked his chest with the index finger of the other one. "That was a rotten, underhanded thing to do. Did you know I was stranded in a dark parking lot miles from home, cold, hungry, alone? Anything could have happened to me. I could have been kidnapped or raped." When he didn't respond she added, "Aren't you the least bit sorry?"

"Sure I am," he answered slowly, his voice lacking its previously icy edge. He lifted his arm to comb his fingers through his hair. The motion made all kinds of muscles bunch and flex. It was a yummy sight even if she was trying not to notice. "But didn't you know?"

"Know what? Of course I didn't know it was going to be towed. How would I?"

"I left several messages on your machine last night. You didn't call me back this afternoon, so I assumed you were prepared."

The fight left her in a loud huff. "Oh. The machine. I didn't think to check messages this morning."

"Come inside before someone calls the police thinking there's a problem." He caught her hand and pulled her inside, and while she should have been ohhhing and awwwwing at his incredible foyer, all she could do was stare into two impossibly deep, dark eyes and enjoy the buzz of instant arousal his innocent touch sparked.

"Did you say you're hungry?" he asked.

"Among other things," she heard herself answer.

"Come on. I'll get you something to eat. What're you in the mood for? The usual? I had a dinner party last night. Have some leftovers."

Her hand in his, and feeling vaguely like she was floating above the ground rather than treading upon it, she followed him down the hall toward the kitchen, asking, "What's the usual?"

"What do you mean?" Reaching for the refrigerator, he glanced over his shoulder.

She shrugged. "Just making small talk, I guess."

"You're acting weird tonight."

"I am? How? I've hardly spoken."

"Well, that for one. And…I don't know. Besides the food thing, something's different."

"Well, I did just suffer a scare from finding my car on the back of a flatbed truck, walking several miles to a gas station and then risking my life in Mabel's car to get here. That might have something to do with it."

"Mabel's car? How'd you end up with her?"

"Bumped into her at a gas station."

"What was she doing at a gas station? Her tank's full. I filled it this afternoon."

She shrugged. "I don't know. She didn't carry anything out of the store, at least not that I saw."

He pulled out a plate covered with foil and set it on the counter. "Are you thirsty?"

"Yes. Do you have any diet cola?"

"Diet cola?" He slowly turned and studied her with narrowed eyes again. "Looks like you, and sounds like you…but it can't be you. Do you have an identical twin?"

"No, why?" Trying to appear casual, she lifted the foil from the plate to get a peek at the food. It didn't look appealing at all—kinda resembled slimy fish parts with green unmentionables, like something she'd seen those poor schmucks eat on Fear Factor—but she didn't want to seem ungrateful. "Oh, this looks fabulous," she lied.

"I have an Evian. Will that do for now?"

Wow, the fancy water. I've never tried that. "Sure. Thanks."

He pulled out a chilled bottle and handed it to her then unwrapped the plate and carried it to the snack bar at the end of the natural stone counter. "Enjoy. I'll be back in a minute."

She plopped on a swivel stool, spinning around to face him. "Where are you going?"

"Be right back." He patted her hand like she was a little insecure kid—which she was not, thank you very much—and left the kitchen, leaving her to investigate the clammy food on her plate. Evidently it was either meant to be eaten cold or she didn't rate the extra time it took to heat it in the microwave.

Figuring explanation number one sounded the most reasonable, since he had bothered feeding her in the first place—after all what was another couple of minutes—she lifted the friendliest-looking piece, some kind of rolled up thing, and held it to her nose.

Gag! It reeked! *Must be spoiled.* She set it down and reached for something else…and then another…and another.

Despite the fact that she hadn't eaten all day and was ready to gnaw on the artificial vegetables in his table centerpiece, nothing on the plate smelled edible. With Jason still missing, she went back to the refrigerator to see what else she could find.

Ah ha! Now this was better! Thin-sliced roast beef, whole wheat bread, Swiss cheese and honey mustard would make one superb sandwich. In the cupboard she found some nacho chips. Before starting work on the sandwich, she ripped those suckers open, packed a handful into her mouth and chewed, and refilled every few seconds as she stacked the meat and cheese on the bread. Sandwich completed, she lifted it to her mouth, inhaling the scent of meat and mustard, then took a bite.

Now that was good eating! Relishing the flavor, she closed her eyes in ecstasy.

"What are you doing?" He sounded annoyed.

She opened her eyes and realized he wasn't so much angry as he was confused. Swallowing first, she motioned toward the plate with the slimy, stinky food and said, "That stuff didn't smell right. I hope you don't mind I made myself a sandwich."

He wrung an article of clothing in his hands. "Um…you don't eat red meat. Haven't had any in almost ten years."

"I do today." She took another bite to illustrate and smiling, chewed and swallowed. "I've forgotten what I was missing. This is delicious. Dead cow is good." She watched as he continued to twist the fabric in his hands. "What are you destroying there? If you don't stop, it'll be nothing but rags."

"Destroying?" He looked down at his hands. "Oh. I found this for you, since you said you were cold." He dropped it next to her on the counter, leaning just close enough to give her a minor case of the warm fuzzies.

Cold? I'm not cold anymore. With a hot bod like yours so close how could a girl be cold? "Thanks. That's very sweet."

"It's just an old sweatshirt, but it'll keep you warm." He looked like he wanted to say something more but didn't.

"What?"

He took a step backward and shook his head. "It's…nothing. Do you need a ride home?"

"Wow, anxious to get rid of me so soon?"

"Kind of."

His honesty floored her and she didn't know what to say. What had happened between them, she wondered. What had Monica done? It had to have been Monica's fault. Jason seemed much too kind and considerate to be the guilty one. "At least you're honest," she finally managed to say before taking another bite of sandwich. "Do I have time to finish my food first? I didn't eat all day. I'm starving."

"Sure."

"Will you drive me home or will you get someone else to do the dirty deed?"

"Yes, I'll drive you. Who else would?"

"Oh, I don't know." Evidently he didn't have a chauffeur. "I thought maybe you'd get Mabel to do it," she said, deciding to make a joke out of it.

"So that's it!" he slapped the countertop with his palm. "Where's it hurt?" He rushed forward and inspected the top of her head.

"Hurt? What?"

"Your head. Did you hit it on the dashboard riding with Mabel? I know what kind of driver she is. You must have a concussion. You're acting so different. Either that or…you wouldn't…would you?" He stared into her eyes, which made her uneasy, like he could see it wasn't really Monica he was talking to.

"Would what?"

"If you think this sudden metamorphosis into a decent human being is going to change my mind about you…about us, you're wrong."

Aha! It had been Monica's fault. Why didn't that surprise her? It seemed for all Monica had, she didn't appreciate any of it, hunky, rich boyfriend included. Shame on her!

"I'm not trying to convince you of anything— Well, it might be nice if you'd give me back the car—"

"So that's it! All this to convince me give back the Lexus? You little, conniving—"

"Whoa, before you start throwing insults, at least let me explain. Yes, I came to ask you why you had the car towed away but I'm not putting on an act for anything. I was hungry, so I ate. I wasn't going to eat some smelly, slimy raw fish guts or whatever that stuff is so I raided your refrigerator for something that looked edible, which just so happened to be the product of a land-dwelling species. Shoot me. Sheesh! Who would've thought a sandwich would cause such an uproar." Disgusted with how things were progressing, wishing he'd toss aside his need to figure out why she'd changed and just kiss her, she shoved the plate away. "I'm finished. Will you take me home now?"

"It's not just the sandwich."

"Whatever." Now that had to sound like the old Monica he knew. Maybe being rude would set him at ease. She walked across the kitchen toward the front door.

"Where are you going?"

"Out."

"That's the wrong way."

"It is not. This is the way…" She looked up and down the hallway, certain she'd seen that painting and those doors before…hadn't she?

He caught her shoulders in his strong hands—she liked men with big, strong hands—and stared into her eyes again. "Do you have amnesia?"

"I don't think so..." Was this the opportunity she needed? He wanted some sort of logical explanation. Amnesia sounded logical—at least a whole lot more logical than a wish on a meteorite. "...well, maybe. I am feeling a little funny."

"I've heard about stuff like this. Do you remember what happened?"

"No. Nothing. I just woke up this morning...uh...not feeling myself. I mean, I looked in the mirror and I knew who I saw, but it was like that wasn't me."

"That doesn't sound good at all. Maybe you should go to the hospital."

"No way. And sit there all night just to have some doctor tell me nothing's wrong? Uh-uh."

"I'll stay with you."

"No, I'm not going. I hate hospitals. I'm sure I'll be fine. I'm probably just a little stressed out."

"Fine, then I insist you stay here tonight so I can keep an eye on you. You never know what might happen. You probably shouldn't be alone."

Never know what might happen? She liked the sound of that. "Well...if you insist..." Would he sleep with her? Her body tingled at the thought of curling up alongside that very masculine, very sexy body she suspected hid under the baggy sweatpants and loose T-shirt he was wearing. What was he doing putting more clothes on? She wanted him to take what he'd had off.

"You can stay in any room you like."

How about yours?

"I promise I won't try a thing."

Bummer!

"What do you think?"

She feigned indecision. "Oh I don't know. Do you think that's such a good idea, considering, you know? Besides, I really should go home. I don't have any of my things here and I need to go to work in the morning."

"I'll drive you. I can take you home early so you have time to dress then drop you off at work when you're ready."

"That's awfully nice of you, Jason." She smiled, sensing a bit of chemistry as she leaned closer. "Thanks. For being so great about this. I mean, you were a jerk for having my car hauled away, but at least you didn't throw me out and leave me to find my own way home. Why'd you do that anyway? Take the car?"

"Insurance. You let the policy lapse again. I told you the last time I can't afford to have you driving the Lexus without insurance. It's like driving a billboard that says 'Sue me, I have money'. I've already paid out two settlements and those had been for tiny fender-benders in parking lots. I can't imagine what I'd have to pay if you hit someone hard. You and your reckless driving are putting me in the poorhouse."

"Oh." Sheesh! Who could blame him if that was true? "I understand."

"If the insurance is too steep, how about we find you another car? Something that's cheaper to insure?"

"I guess that makes sense." She nodded and stepped into the hallway, shuddering as he rested his hand on the small of her back.

"Good. I think you should call off work tomorrow and we can go car shopping."

"Oh no. I can't. I mean I'd like to..." Climbing the stairs, she turned around to face him and got instantly lightheaded. With her standing one stair higher, they were almost nose-to-nose. She could easily lean just a bit and kiss him. And it was encouraging to see him looking as tempted as she felt.

Was this the reason she'd changed places with Monica? Maybe it hadn't been about work or that silly yogurt ad. Maybe she was supposed to make things right with Jason, right whatever wrong the real Monica had done.

All in all that didn't sound like a bad deal. In fact, it sounded like a whole lot of fun…if she could remember why she was doing this and keep her heart out of it.

Falling in love with another woman's boyfriend was not a good idea. Nope, not at all.

Chapter Four

ꕥ

Who the hell was this woman?

Jason pulled back the instant before their mouths met and stared into her eyes. It was Monica on the outside. No doubt about it. Same traffic-stopping smile, blue eyes and long blonde hair. Same body with surgically altered boobs and lipo-sculpted hips and tummy. Same long legs that made every guy on the planet drool when she wore a short skirt.

But inside there was something different. Could amnesia be the cause? Would it change her into a completely different human being? He highly doubted it.

Monica was still Monica.

It might be close to impossible, but somehow he had to remind himself of her more devious side. The one that had tricked him before, taken advantage of his impulses to take care of the women in his life.

Monica would not wiggle her way into his heart again!

He shook his head, trying to clear it, and hoping the motion might send some much-needed blood to his brain. She'd come very close to seducing him, but he'd make sure she didn't succeed. While he nursed his guilt for having had her car hauled away, even if for a valid reason, he'd keep an eye on her until she had a means of transportation she could afford to maintain on her own. After that, he'd cut the ties. No need to cling to her any longer.

Just one night. Come hell or high water, by tomorrow he'd make sure she had a car. She wouldn't need his help any longer.

He just had to make it through one short night. Eight, maybe ten hours.

Unfortunately, based upon the expression on her face, she wasn't about to make it easy for him. If there was one thing Monica knew, it was how to play him. Damn her for being so good at it!

They were over, he reminded himself. She'd sold his grandmother's collection of pottery for peanuts, for God's sake. She'd treated him like a convenient ATM for the past year, pushing a few buttons until he paid out. It had gotten to the point where he'd been disgusted with himself every time he succumbed, but damn it, he couldn't seem to help himself.

Weak. He'd been weak. But not anymore!

Gathering up what remained of his wavering will, he gently nudged her forward. "Let's get upstairs before one of us falls." *Both literally and figuratively.* Damn, he wanted her. Something fierce. He wanted to taste her, to feel her, to hear her sigh his name as she climaxed. He wanted to hold her until morning. He wanted to serve her breakfast in bed and lie next to her, smoothing her sex-tousled hair after she ate. *Stop it now or you won't be able to resist.*

"Jason?" She reached forward and rested a palm against his cheek. "Would you believe me if I said I was truly sorry?"

I want to believe that but I can't. I've heard it too many times before. "No."

"I wish we could start over again. Pretend like we were complete strangers and do things right."

Why are you telling me this now? Damn it, stop! I can't listen to this. "I can't. We were never right for each other. We want very different things in life."

"Well, maybe I've changed my mind."

He gave her another gentle nudge and she took several steps up before stopping and turning again to give him another imploring look, batting eyelashes and all. "No way. It's too late for that now. We can't go back. We can't change who we are, although you seem to be making one hell of an effort. You're you. I'm me. And together we make a mess."

She smiled and her eyes glittered playfully. "A mess. I like that." Turning, she climbed the rest of the stairs and walked straight to his bedroom door. "Can I stay in this room?"

"No. That's my room. You know that."

"Even so, you said I could stay in any room I wanted."

Shit. I should have known she'd do this. "Fine, but I won't be sleeping in there with you." He opened the door and followed her inside.

"Will you stay for a little while? Can we talk? I'm still a little shaken from earlier. I don't think I can sleep."

"I have cable TV. Watch a movie." He pulled out a pair of sweatpants from a drawer and handed them to her then walked back toward the hallway and safety. He was confused, didn't know his mind. While her outside—her physical beauty—did nothing for him anymore, the mystery of what she seemed to have become inside absolutely fascinated him. He could spend all night talking to her, trying to discover who she was. It was as if someone else had taken over Monica's body. Of course that was impossible!

"Please?" She walked across the room and opened the bathroom door. "I promise we will just talk. Nothing more."

He felt his resistance draining.

"Pretty please? You can stay way over there," she said pointing at the love seat positioned in front of the fireplace. "And I'll stay over here on the bed. I won't do anything naughty. We can just talk."

"Fine."

She beamed. "Thanks. Be right back. Gonna go change." She went into the bathroom.

Feeling both defeated by his lack of willpower and intrigued by the opportunity to talk to the woman who had overnight become a fascinating stranger, he dimmed the lights, lit the gas fireplace and sat in the loveseat. Then he prayed to God for strength and turned as he heard the bathroom door open.

She bounded out with far too much energy considering the hour and flopped on her stomach on the bed.

"What do you want to talk about?" he asked.

"Do you have any ice cream? Late night gab sessions aren't the same without Ben and Jerry. Oh, and nice fireplace. It's very romantic."

"It was chilly in here," he offered as an excuse, feeling guilty as if he'd done something wrong. He decided not to take a stab back by pointing out the fact that she never ate ice cream, always lectured him about how bad it was for him. She had to know what she was doing by acting like her antithesis. "I might have a little bit left. Want me to go down and check?"

"I'll go with you." She rolled off the bed and followed him down the hall. "Chocolate Therapy is my absolute favorite. You don't have that flavor by any chance, do you?"

Of course I do and you know it. That's my favorite. "I might."

They walked through the kitchen and, leaving the lights off, Jason dished out two bowls of ice cream. Monica stood waiting by the French doors, staring out into the back yard. "Can we eat out there?"

"It's cold. You'll freeze your butt off. You freeze when it's eighty."

"I'll be fine with these warm sweats. Come on." She opened the door, stepped out on the deck and looked out onto the yard. "Wow, this is gorgeous. I like those lights. Just enough so you won't walk into a shrub or fall into the pool. But not too glaring."

"You have always hated this backyard, called it The Jungle."

"I did? Well, it is very lush, but now that I see it again, I think it's lush in a good way. I like all the green. I feel like I'm on vacation on some tropical island. Can we sit over there? Oh! Is that a hot tub?"

He handed her a bowl. Of course she knew it was the hot tub. Why was she acting this way? "Yes."

She ran across the deck, plopped onto her behind at the rim of the sunken tub and, setting her bowl aside, pulled up the sweatpants above her knees and dipped her feet into the steamy water. "Oh, this is heavenly." Picking up her dish, she spooned some ice cream into her mouth.

"Glad to see you're enjoying yourself."

She patted the wood deck next to her. "Come and sit with me. Promise I won't bite. My mouth is busy at the moment."

He couldn't help grinning as he sat and took a bite of ice cream.

"Do you still appreciate how spectacular this place is? I mean, sometimes when we've had things for a while we take them for granted."

He glanced around the yard and nodded. "Yeah. I guess I do kind of take it for granted. I don't get to enjoy it much. Don't have the time."

"If you're too busy working to keep it, then what's the sense in having it at all? If you ask me, you should consider simplifying your life, cutting back. You'll be a whole lot happier if you do. Who wants to live for a house? It may be straight out of a House Beautiful magazine, but if you have to work twenty hours a day to keep it, what's the point?"

Just last week Monica had made a comment about him needing to buy a bigger home, something more showy.

"I'll keep that in mind. Thanks. So, does that mean you're okay with a smaller, more economical car?"

"Oh yes. I'm perfectly fine with that." She ate another bite of ice cream, licking the spoon before dipping it back in the bowl. "I mean, I love the Lexus. It is total class. But I don't need it. I'm through trying to put on airs for people. I'm not what I drive or where I live. I'm me."

"That..." *Sounds nothing like the Monica I know.* "...sounds like a change for the better."

"Are you surprised?"

"A little. You're acting very different from yourself tonight. I wonder if tomorrow when you wake up you'll be back to your old self or not."

"Me too. Though I'm enjoying myself this way."

"So am I," he heard himself say before he could stop.

She smiled again. "You're a straight shooter. I like that."

"I appreciate honesty too."

"And you're generous. It wasn't your fault I didn't pay my insurance and it wasn't your fault I didn't check my answering machine this morning. Yet you fed me, let me stay here tonight, and you're treating me so nice—even letting me polish off the last bit of ice cream. I don't deserve it. Heck, you're buying me a new car. What guy does that for his scatterbrained ex-girlfriend?"

He finished his ice cream in one big bite then swallowed, welcoming the chill as it cooled his throat and stomach. "I didn't mean for you to be stranded."

"I know. You did what you had to." She scooped more ice cream into her mouth and licked the spoon again. "I completely understand. You don't owe me. You don't have to pay my insurance."

"There was a time—not too long ago—when you claimed I did."

"Well, that was mighty greedy of me." She set her empty bowl aside. "Now I'm cold."

"Told you."

"Mind if I take a dip in the whirlpool?"

"No. Be my guest."

"I don't have a bathing suit."

"What's that matter? It's not like you haven't skinny-dipped in the hot tub before."

"Oh…yeah…right." She visibly swallowed, showing an unexpected glimmer of uneasiness he hadn't expected. He couldn't begin to count the number of times he'd seen her nude before. Never once had she been self-conscious, not even the first time they'd made love. Why the sudden case of embarrassment?

What the hell was going on?

* * * * *

Jenny knew it wasn't her body she was bearing, and she knew Jason had seen it all before—or so she assumed—but that didn't ease the burn on her cheeks or the sudden case of shyness threatening to extinguish the sex kitten alter ego she'd adopted. Being Monica hadn't proven to be as carefree as Jenny had expected, but it still had its advantages. The long legs, big boobs and beautiful face, for example. So why couldn't she find the nerve to flaunt them?

Jason was absolutely to die for. Handsome, nice—she had no idea a guy who looked that good could be nice—and rich. What a package!

And speaking of package, the lump in his sweatpants looked mighty promising.

Determined to take full advantage of the situation, despite her fear, she drew in one of those deep yoga cleansing breaths and stood, caught the bottom of the sweatshirt in her hands, and knowing she'd taken off everything she'd been wearing under it earlier, including her bra, when she'd changed, she drew it over her head and looked to Jason for a reaction.

He looked unimpressed! The nerve of him! What male doesn't appreciate the sight of perky, surgically enhanced 34Ds?

Figuring she had nothing to lose now, she yanked down the sweatpants and stood completely nude—a huge turn-on that was making her hot and achy all over—in front of him.

Unfortunately, it didn't appear to have the same effect on him. He might as well have yawned in her face. Nothing stirred. He didn't even bat an eyelash.

"Are you getting in or not?" he asked, looking a little smug, which made her uneasiness that much worse.

She couldn't feel any stupider. "Yes." She stepped down into the hot bubbly water and sat on the bench. Okay, so he wasn't impressed with what Monica had. That wasn't easy to comprehend. She was the picture of female perfection. Was he gay? "Won't you join me?"

"No, I think I'll just watch."

"Okay."

She decided to go for broke, since she seemed to be striking out completely. "Don't you find me attractive anymore?"

"I don't want to talk about that right now."

"Why not? We're two adults. We should be able to talk about anything, shouldn't we? I can accept the truth."

"You cannot. Once you asked me if a bathing suit looked okay. I told you it wasn't the nicest bathing suit I've seen and you fell apart, refused to eat for a week."

"That was before. Try me. Do you find me attractive?"

He looked thoughtful, and she sensed he wanted to answer but feared hurting her feelings.

"I promise I won't cry or starve myself or anything too drastic."

"Why are you asking me this now?"

"Because I need to know. I want to know where we stand. If there's hope—"

"Absolutely not. There's no hope. We won't get back together, no matter who you act like. You could pretend to be Mother Theresa and I wouldn't change my mind."

"I'm not pretending to be anyone."

"No one changes this much overnight."

"I have."

"How?"

"I'm not exactly sure how it happened, but it did."

"Yeah, and the minute I take you back you'll change into the old Monica again. No thanks. I've had enough."

He didn't sound as sure as his words suggested.

"Can I ask a stupid question?"

"I guess."

"What exactly did I do to you?"

His mouth fell open in an exaggerated show of exasperation. "Bullshit! Now you're going to suggest you don't remember?"

"Humor me. I want to hear it from you."

"We've had this conversation once. Frankly I don't want to go there again."

"Please. I won't ask again."

He crossed his arms over his chest and stared at her, clearly expecting her to acquiesce.

"Please," she repeated. "What happened between us? You sound bitter."

"I have a right to be. You've been a conniving bitch."

Feeling mighty exposed sitting naked in the water while he insulted her, she squirmed and moved closer to a jet, hoping the bubbles would completely hide her body. "Specifics, please."

"You used me. You only dated me for my money. Otherwise you pretty much treated me like trash. And speaking of trash, when I stopped handing out the cash by the fistful, you dumped me like yesterday's leftover pizza. You refused to pay your car insurance, even after costing me tens of thousands of dollars. You shamelessly flirted with all my golfing buddies until they refused to play with me and their wives threatened divorce. You stole things from my home and did God knows what with them and the last few weeks you showed absolutely no affection toward me. To sum it up, you are a stone-cold bitch. Then, after we broke up, you sold my grandmother's art collection to a junk dealer to get even with me."

"Wow."

"Have you heard enough yet or do you want me to continue?"

"There's more? No, I think I've heard enough. Considering all that, I'm shocked you didn't break up with me ages ago, or at least slam the door in my face tonight."

"I tried, remember?"

"Yeah." She didn't know what else to say. To Jason, she was the woman who'd done all those terrible things. He believed what he saw, like most people did. There was no convincing him of anything else.

"I didn't say those things to make you feel bad. You wanted to hear it."

"Yes, I did. Thanks for being honest. I think I'm ready to go to bed now." She started to stand up but hesitated, wishing he'd avert his gaze while she dressed.

Thankfully, he seemed to sense her discomfort. He turned around and started walking toward the house. She got out of the tub and quickly put on the sweats, not caring that she was still dripping wet. Being soggy beat being nude, hands down.

In silence, she followed him inside and up the stairs. He escorted her to his room, said goodnight and left her to toss and turn, fearful of falling asleep yet hoping this experiment…or curse…or whatever it was…would end.

Maybe being plain old Jenny wasn't so bad.

The next morning was awkward and uncomfortable as Jason drove Jenny home and waited for her to dress for work. Before they left, she listened to her messages, hoping she hadn't missed anything else important.

Monica's answering machine tape was full of calls from angry bill collectors threatening lawsuits, utilities threatening to shut off services, and creditors threatening everything but bodily harm. As she listened to the last one, she peered around the corner, hoping Jason hadn't heard.

Monica made tons more money than Jenny. There was no reason why she should be in such financial straights. What was she doing with her money?

Jason dropped her off at work, promising to return at noon to go car shopping during her lunch hour.

She hurried through her work and took half the day off. She needed some time to sort out some things and was anxious to get her hands on Monica's bank statements and checkbook to try to straighten out the mess she'd gotten herself into.

Clearly being Monica Starke was not the cakewalk Jenny had expected. Yep, being plain old Jenny with the little apartment and ugly but reliable car wasn't looking so bad anymore. It sure beat people screaming for money, angry, bitter—if positively delicious—ex-boyfriends, and a workload that would keep at least three people working full-time.

Monica, the woman who had it all, didn't have much of anything. It was all show.

What a shocker.

That afternoon, Jason gave her a polite smile as he drove her to the car dealership down the road. "I want you to pick a car that'll hold its value and be reliable as well as inexpensive to insure."

"I know exactly what I want." She chose a sharp-looking, black Honda Accord, and thanks to Jason's financial clout, had it in her possession by later that afternoon. He sent her on her way with a wave, a couple hundred dollars cash, and a "Good luck". She responded with a "Thanks", and headed back to Monica's house to tackle the bills.

Regardless of whether she remained Monica forever—something she hoped wouldn't happen since she was beginning to miss her old life—or they eventually switched back, that was one thing that had to be straightened out, no matter how difficult it might be.

Pain in the backside or not, Monica deserved to live better than this.

Chapter Five

ꙮ

Jenny finished out the workweek as Monica, and was exhausted by Friday night. She didn't know whether to be grateful for the fact that the phone didn't ring off the hook that night with a truckload of offers to go out on dates or to parties, or be disappointed. From the way Monica had made it sound, every weekend had been an adventure. Local celebrities and hotshot business owners vied for her attendance at their gatherings.

More fantasies, she supposed.

Oh well. Maybe tomorrow night she'd venture out.

She wrangled with Monica's checkbook for a few hours, finding a lot of unexplained checks written for exorbitant amounts that made no sense, then went to bed early and got caught up on her sleep. The next morning, refreshed, and possessing a small amount of cash after paying the most important bills—like the rent—she ventured to the grocery store and stocked the cupboards and refrigerator. That night, when she received no calls from friends with impromptu invitations, she dressed in a sexy little black dress and heels and headed to her—Jenny's—favorite nightclub for a drink and some dancing. She wasn't in the mood to be alone.

For one thing, she couldn't stop thinking about Jason.

When she walked into the bar, she got a kick out of all the guys staring at her. She'd never experienced that much attention from men before. They didn't try to hide what they were thinking as their gazes wandered over her body lustfully. It was a bit unnerving, made her feel like she was a prime piece of meat hanging in the butcher's window, but for the most part she found it amusing.

More than one offered to buy her a drink but she refused, knowing what price she'd be expected to pay. She'd never picked up a man at a bar as Jenny and she wasn't about to start as Monica either.

One-night stands were not her thing…but she might consider it with Jason if he'd give her the chance.

Like that was ever going to happen!

"Excuse me?" a familiar female voice called from the end of the bar. "Can I have a Bud Light?"

Jenny turned her head to see who it was, knowing she recognized the voice but unable to place it. She knew who it was the instant she saw her. Beth worked in the front, answering phones, and she'd often confided to Jenny that she despised Monica. At work she acted reasonably polite but not over-friendly. "Hey, Beth! I didn't know you came here."

Beth shifted her eyes nervously when she realized who'd spoken to her. "Oh! Hi…Monica. I don't usually but I'm a personal friend of the lead guitarist in the band playing tonight. Remember? I told you about him."

"Oh, that's right." Jenny sipped her diet cola and tried to pretend she knew what Beth was talking about. "The rock star."

"Hardly. But hopefully some day." She paid the bartender then picked up her beer and walked toward Jenny. "Look, I'm sorry I didn't call you back. Tonight was kind of a spur of the moment thing and I assumed you were busy. You're always so busy. If I'd known you were still free, I would have called you. Honest."

Why was Beth befriending Monica when she'd made it so clear she couldn't stand her? Was it out of pity or was there another reason?

Beth glanced over Monica's shoulder, clearly looking for someone or something. "Where's your boyfriend…what was his name?"

"Jason?"

"No, I don't think that was it. I'm talking about the radio guy you were talking about last week. I was hoping he'd be here tonight to hear my friend's band. I gave you their CD, remember? You promised he'd take a listen. Do you know if he did?"

Aha! The truth comes out. Beth was using Monica.

Jenny wondered if there even was a radio DJ boyfriend. Knowing Monica, Mr. Radio was probably as much a figment of her imagination as so many other things had proven to be.

"I'm not sure. I haven't spoken to him in a few days. But I'll let you know as soon as I do."

"That's fine. Do you want to go backstage and meet everyone?"

"Oh, I don't know. I'm not much of a groupie."

"Come on. They're great guys. It'll be fun." Beth tipped her head toward the back of the bar and the currently empty stage and smiled. "They're getting ready to go onstage now. I'll introduce you to them."

Jenny wasn't buying the let's-be-friends act. In fact, it was making her a little sick. "No thanks. I think I'll stay here."

"You get to drink for free."

"Then what are you doing buying your own beer?"

"I don't care much for wine. That's all those guys drink." Beth tugged on Jenny's arm. "I'm not going to take no for an answer. Besides, it'll be fun to hang out during sets when they're playing. Do you like to dance?"

"Love to."

"Well, there you go." Beth looked around again. "That is, unless you're meeting someone else here tonight."

"No, I don't think that's going to happen."

"Good! Then you're mine for tonight." Full of boundless energy, Beth yanked harder on Jenny's arm until she relented and slid off the stool. Her diet cola in one hand, the other gripped firmly in Beth's, Jenny wound through the crowd toward the rear of the bar. And only after they slipped through a hidden door next to the stage did they find a little bit of elbow room.

"They're this way." Beth led Jenny down an ugly, dim hallway to a cramped, smoke-filled room full of mangy-looking, rock star wanna-bes and women wearing way too much makeup and too little clothing.

The men clearly appreciated what Jason hadn't a few nights ago. Every one of their gazes settled first on her boobs before venturing anywhere else. And they took the roundabout, indirect route—down her legs and back up again—to her face.

"Hey, everyone, this is Monica. She's the one I told you about—the one dating what's-his-name on WDTL."

"Cool." One guy who looked like a throwback to the eighties—big hair bands and grotesquely tight spandex and all—grinned like the cat about to eat the canary. "A hot chick with connections. They're always welcome. Want to do a line?" He motioned toward a card table in the far corner of the room. Another guy was bent over inhaling white powder off a mirror through a rolled-up dollar bill.

"No thanks. I don't care for coke…at least not that kind."

"No problem. Just trying to be hospitable. What about weed? Someone here's got a joint burning."

So that's what I smell. Sure hope I don't fail my next drug screen just because I'm standing in here inhaling secondhand smoke. She fanned her face with her hand. "No thanks. I'm fine. Really. Beth insisted I come back here and meet everyone and I have so maybe—" With one thing in mind—escape—she turned to find the door.

One of the guys caught her wrist and held her tight. "Sure hope you aren't planning on going anywhere yet. We haven't had a chance to get acquainted."

She tipped her head to look at him.

He was a scary-looking character with hair longer than she'd ever worn, and more Lycra than you'd find in a sporting goods store. His face was pocked with acne scars and, as she glanced down at the hand gripping her tightly, she saw his fingers were stained from smoking. Definitely not her type. Not even close.

"Sorry, gotta go. I'm meeting someone outside. I just remembered."

"Yeah? Your radio boyfriend?"

"Yes, that's it. My famous radio boyfriend who can get your CD played on his station during morning drive-time." When he released her, she made a beeline for the door, ignoring Beth's insistent shouts as she left.

Dragging in a few non-drug-laden breaths in the hallway, she nearly collapsed from relief then headed out toward the main part of the bar.

The minute she walked out into the large room, she caught a glimpse of him. It was Jason.

He stood casually resting a shoulder against a wood pillar chatting with a cute brunette. His smile flashed bright in the dim light and his eyes sparkled with the look of piqued interest. Immediately, the sting of jealousy burned her stomach.

He hadn't looked at her that way, even though she thought Monica's face and body were far more attractive than the brunette he seemed to fancy at the moment.

That woman was almost ordinary, reminded her of herself—when she had been plain old Jenny. Sure, he might not want to revisit what he'd had with Monica—for good reason—but she couldn't imagine he'd find someone like that woman, someone like Jenny Brown, attractive.

That kind of thing didn't happen—at least not outside of the movies. In the real world, rich, good-looking guys like Jason went for the beautiful women with tight butts and perky boobs and perfect hair.

As if he sensed her staring at him, he stopped smiling and glanced her way. She immediately felt foolish, yet couldn't stop gawking, couldn't move. Like a deer caught in headlights, she stood frozen and gaped at him.

But a swift and unexpected swat on her ass broke the spell quick enough. Angry, shocked, flabbergasted, she spun around to see who or what had done such a thing.

Mr. Lycra Pants gave her a crooked grin, handed her something, whispering, "Here, love, hold this for me, will you?" then climbed on stage, and blew her a kiss before taking a seat behind a massive drum kit.

Ewww… She shuddered and stuffed the grimy, wrinkled cigarette pack he'd handed her into her purse.

"I see you've made some new friends." Jason said from behind her.

She turned to face him, noticing his wrinkled nose which she assumed was because he didn't exactly understand her attraction to Mr. Lycra Pants, not that she could blame him. "No, they're not my friends."

"Well, I'd say he thinks so," Jason said, pointing over her shoulder.

Knowing exactly who he was pointing at, and guessing what kind of gestures the gentleman—and she used that term loosely—was making at the moment, she didn't bother turning around. "He's on drugs."

"Speaking of drugs…" Jason sniffed. "I smell something…marijuana? You weren't smoking pot, were you?"

"Oh, gosh no!" Frantic, Jenny waved her arms up and down like some deranged bird trying to take flight. "I smell like weed? I was only back there for a few minutes. Beth insisted." She thrust her arm forward toward his nose. "Do you still smell it?"

"Back where?" He shook his head then bent to sniff her neck. "No, it's coming from somewhere else."

"Shoot! That's what I get for playing groupie to a bunch of heavy metal hair band wanna-bes." She waved her arms up and down again. "It was so smoky back there. It must have soaked into my clothes. I wish I had some perfume with me. You know I don't do drugs, don't you? I swear I didn't touch the stuff."

"Easy! I believe you." He caught her wrists. "Now stop that before you hurt somebody." He smiled over her shoulder and holding her hands, drew them together in front of his chest. "Sorry, she's just showing me something she watched on Animal Planet last night."

Jenny turned to see whom he was talking to.

"Monica, who's this?" Beth asked as she stepped around her. "Aren't you going to introduce me?"

"Er…Beth, this is Jason. Jason, this is Beth. Beth and I work together."

Jason released one of Jenny's hands to shake Beth's. "Nice to meet you."

"You too," Beth said, almost falling over herself. The girl's tongue was practically skimming the floor. "What do you do? All of Monica's friends have interesting careers. Let me guess. Are you a lawyer? Doctor? Local politician?"

He released Jenny's other hand and stuffed both of his in his pants pockets. "No, nothing that…exciting. I buy and sell jewelry."

"Oh. Cool! Next time I want some new earrings, I know where to go." Beth gave Jason an ear-to-ear grin and twisted her hair with her fingertips. What a flirt!

To Jason's credit, he didn't seem to be biting, at least not this time.

"Sure," he answered. "Monica can give you my number if you ever need it. She has my card."

Evidently, Beth caught Jason's subtle but definitive shutdown when he didn't eagerly dole out his number. Her smile faded considerably. "Sounds great."

Earsplitting music bellowed from the speakers as the band started playing.

Beth started gyrating to the beat, resembling a pole dancer without the pole. "Well, gotta go. Monica, are you coming?"

Jenny stood between Beth the pole dancer and Jason the bitter ex-boyfriend, wanting to stay and talk to Jason—if that was possible with the loud music blasting from those speakers—but knowing he was probably looking for a reason to leave.

She glanced at him to see if she could read his expression. It was rather indifferent. "I don't suppose there's any chance you want to dance with me?" she yelled, hoping for a yes but expecting a no.

He wrinkled his nose and shook his head. "This isn't exactly my kind of music."

She shrugged, shouting, "Mine either."

"And the whole mosh pit thing is a little too dangerous for my blood. I'd like to avoid a trip to the emergency room tonight."

"It's not that wild out there. 'Course it's not like they're doing the waltz either." A silly thought struck her and she smiled. "How about we make total asses out of ourselves and slow dance?" The thought of his body pressed snugly against hers made her hotter than hot.

He chuckled, and even with the bass making mincemeat of her eardrums, that wonderful sound found its way to her ears and her heart.

"Yes?" she yelled, motioning toward the dance floor, which was filled to capacity with jumping, shouting men and women. "Come on! It'll be fun."

"What the hell." He took her hand and led her into the crowd, stopping somewhere in the middle and gathering her into his arms.

If there truly was a heaven on earth, she'd found it. There, in the middle of mayhem, with people hopping up and down and slamming into each other, she'd found peace. Content to stay there forever, she looped her arms around his neck, pressed her ear against his chest and inhaled his scent. Her body tingled wherever it made contact with his. And wave after wave of warmth coursed through her body.

She tipped her head to look up and he glanced down at her. One of his hands pressed against her back, pushing her tighter against him while the other palmed her cheek. His thumb stroked her lower lip and she instinctively slipped her tongue out to taste it.

A spark flashed in his eyes as he tipped his head and lowered it until his mouth hovered painfully close to hers. Breathless, eager for his kiss, she closed her eyes and waited.

He didn't kiss her. Instead, he tortured her by leaving his mouth a fraction of an inch from hers. Their breaths mingled as their breathing quickened. And her lower regions burned with the need to be touched. She ground her pelvis into his leg, pressing and rubbing, furiously trying to ease the ache between her legs as they swayed. His hands dropped to her bottom and rested there, and hers slid down his chest, her fingertips tracing the lines of his developed muscles through the thin knit material of his T-shirt.

It was a magic moment, the most erotic, intense experience of her life. Their gazes locked and she could tell he too was overcome by the intensity. His tongue darted out to moisten his lips and she mirrored him. They didn't speak. There was no need for words. Everything that needed to be said was conveyed through their eyes. In his, she saw the confusion and hunger, the fear and hope. It hurt to see him that way.

Then the song ended and with it the magic. Jason stiffened, stepping back when she lifted her hands, and gave her an awkward smile. "Shit, I can't do this. My God…you…I could have…I mean, I want to…" He sighed. "I gotta go. Good night, Monica. You'll be okay here, won't you?"

"Sure. I'll be fine. Bye." She watched him as he pushed his way through the crowd then decided to call it a night as well. Being a very sexy, very available Monica—despite all the gawking stares—just wasn't what she'd expected it to be.

That didn't surprise her.

What did surprise her was finding Jason standing next to her car, his back turned, his head lowered as he scribbled a message on a piece of paper and slipped it under her windshield wiper. As he turned around to walk to his car, he saw her watching. "I...uh..." He ran his fingers through his hair as he visibly grappled for words. "God help me, but I want to talk about this."

"About what?" Jenny asked, wanting to be crystal clear about his intentions before jumping up and down with glee and making a total ass of herself. She hurried to get closer, hoping he'd forget all about talking and just get to the good part. She could only imagine what a make-up kiss would be like from a guy like Jason, especially after that incredible dance.

"Us."

She did a little celebratory skip across a couple of empty parking spots. "You do?"

"Don't look so happy."

"Sorry. I'm finding it tough to contain myself these days." She performed a little happy dance—including a shake of the tush—for his benefit then flung her arms on his shoulders and pressed her body to his. His erection was a stiff bulge that pressed against her stomach. "Looks like you're having a hard time too," she teased as she slid a hand down between their bodies toward his crotch.

"Cute." He grabbed her wrist to stop her and gently pushed her away. "Uh-uh! Not yet. We need to take this slow. I feel like I don't know you anymore. I need to know if this is really you or if it's all some kind of act."

"Oh no. This is no act. It's me." When he didn't look completely sold, she added, "You don't believe me? Then let me prove it to you. Give me a chance to show you who I am. Let's start over from the very beginning." She held her hand out. "Hi, I'm Jen—er, Monica. Monica Starke."

"Jen?"

"I…uh…that was my nickname in grade school. You see, there were two Monicas in my third grade class, so everyone started calling me by my middle name," she said, not sure what Monica's middle name actually was, and hoping he'd never read her driver's license.

"Really? You never told me that."

Looks like he's buying it! Mental note to self, check driver's license as soon as possible. "How could I? We just met."

He took her hand in his and gave it a shake, staring into her eyes as if he could see clear down to her soul. "Hello, Monica. It's nice to meet you."

"Now that we've gotten the formalities over, how about we sleep together?" she suggested, half-teasing, half-serious.

"Wow, mighty forward, aren't you?"

Feeling a little naughty, she grinned. "What can I say? That's me. I know what I want and I go for it. So what's the answer?"

He stepped back and crossed his arms over his wide chest, clearly distancing himself. "Didn't anyone ever tell you that the man likes to be in control?"

"Sure. And in bed that's exactly the way I like them. Completely in control, if you know what I mean." She winked. This teasing, flirting stuff was a whole lot of fun!

Jason's jaw dropped to his chest and then he laughed. "I can't believe you just said that."

"Do you expect me to apologize?"

"No. But that doesn't mean we're sleeping together either. I don't have sex on the first date."

"Was this a date?"

"See? We haven't even gone on a date yet. What kind of guy do you think I am?"

"A really nice guy," she answered honestly. "So when are we going to have our first date?"

"How about Friday? Seven o'clock?"

"Hmmm…I'll have to check my calendar." She smiled. "That sounds great! See you then." She plucked the note from her windshield and fisted it before getting into her car. Jason, being the gentleman he was, opened her door for her and gave her a flirty smile as she slipped into the seat.

She read the scribbled message—*Call me. We need to talk.*—then slipped it into her wallet, taking a quick peek at Monica's driver's license while she had it handy. Monica's middle name was Irene. Oh well. Hopefully Jason would forget her little fib. Closing her wallet and dropping it back in her purse, she started the car, opened the window and said "goodnight, sweet dreams", in the huskiest voice she could manage.

His laughter echoed in her head all the way home. And her dreams were sweet that night as well. Very sweet.

Chapter Six

ꟓ

Monday morning, Jenny went to work early, hoping to catch Monica before she got into the office. She sat in the parking lot, waiting for her little subcompact car and her five-foot-two, plain-Jane body to arrive.

But what she saw wasn't what she'd expected.

It seemed that Monica had made a few improvements. In fact, Jenny hardly recognized her own body!

Her hair was darker, cut with shaggy, sexy layers around her face and very shiny. And her clothes fit her just snug enough to make the most of her curves.

Gasp! Monica had made her into a babe.

That wasn't the only change Monica had made. The car was new. Fire engine red. And a convertible of all things!

All Jenny saw were dollar signs. New hair, new clothes, new car. Had Monica maxed out all her credit cards in a week? Jenny couldn't exactly kill her if she had.

"Monica!" Feeling really strange looking at her own body from the outside, Jenny dashed across the parking lot.

"Jenny!" Monica smoothed her black skirt down her legs. "We need to talk."

God, her voice sounded strange. "Yeah, we need to talk. Where's my car?" Jenny asked, pointing at the convertible.

"Where's my Lexus?" Monica pointed at the Honda.

"Long story." Jenny motioned toward the building. "Want to talk inside? We can use your office."

"Sure."

Jenny hurried inside, unlocking the door with her key. She was relieved to see that no one else had made it in yet. They'd hopefully get at least an hour to talk things through in private before the rest of the staff made it in.

They both ran to Monica's office and headed for the leather chair behind Monica's desk. Monica made it there first.

"Maybe I should sit there, just in case Mr. Kaufmann comes in," Jenny suggested.

"Oh. Yeah. I forgot." Monica shuffled around the desk and sat in the chair opposite Jenny. "What happened? Why am I you? How do we change back?"

"I don't know. All I remember doing is making a silly wish and then the next morning I woke up in your bedroom."

"This is your fault! What were you making a wish like that for?"

"That's another long story I'd like to avoid right now if I could. Besides, how do you know it's my fault? How many wishes have you had come true?"

"I guess it doesn't matter. Can you un-wish it? I'd like my body back, if you don't mind. Not that there's anything wrong with yours."

"Thanks. I think. I want my body back too but I don't know how to make it happen. Heck, for all I know it wasn't my wish that caused this. And even if it was I don't know if I can un-wish it. I never expected it to come true. I've never had a wish come true before."

"Neither have I, but you have to try something. We can't stay this way forever. You wouldn't believe how shocked I was to wake up in your sweats, in your apartment…in your body…last week! By the way, we have to do something about that little cave you live in. It's a dump. And the neighborhood… I won't even go out to check the mail after nightfall. The only good thing about it is the balcony."

"Well, it's affordable. I don't have millionaire boyfriends buying me houses in the 'burbs for Christmas like some people do."

"Speaking of my boyfriend, have you heard from Jason?"

"Yes, you could say that. By the way, I like what you've done to my hair. It looks great."

Looking very pleased with herself, Monica smoothed the glossy brown hair with her hand. "It does, doesn't it? I have a fabulous hairdresser. It was quite a trick getting him to take me, since he doesn't know who I am. But thanks to me you are now a client of the extremely talented Geoff Laroque at the exclusive Laroque Salon in Beverly Hills. He gave me the works last week. You needed it. Good grief girl, when was the last time you had a pedicure? Your toenails were gnarly. I don't know how you dared show them at all this past summer. Please tell me you didn't wear sandals or I think I'm going to cry."

More dollar signs flashed through Jenny's brain. Bells rang, lights blinked. That infamous cha-ching sound echoed in her head. "How much does the works cost at Laroque Salon?"

"Oh, I don't know. I put it on your credit card. It went through without a problem. Couldn't have been too much."

"Oh no! What else have you bought? Those clothes look new."

"They are. You owned nothing but rags. I couldn't be seen in public dressed like that. You really should have more respect for yourself than that. You're young and pretty. What're you letting yourself go like this for?"

"I have more respect for myself than you do. You spend every penny you earn and more. I know. I tried to balance your checkbook. You're drowning in red. And what the hell is Hometown? You're sending them thousands every month. That's no way to live, way beyond your means."

"Hey! My money matters are personal. I can't believe you're snooping." Monica's pout looked silly on Jenny's face and if Jenny wasn't so upset about this whole thing she might have found it funny.

"I'm just trying to help. That's more than what I can say for you. All you're doing is putting me in the poorhouse. How much is the car costing me?"

"I got you a great deal since you have A-plus credit. You got prime rates. The payment's only three hundred sixty-five."

Jenny felt sick. Monica was making a mess of her life. Somehow she had to stop her. "*Only* three hundred sixty-five? I can't afford that!"

"Sure you can. You've been saving four hundred a month. I saw it on your bank statements."

"I'm saving to buy a house. You're ruining my life! You need to stop spending my money and quit snooping."

"I didn't snoop. Your bank records were sitting right there. And I am not ruining your life. I'm making some much-needed improvements. You, my friend, were stuck in a rut. This is exactly what you needed. Now, what kind of mess are you making of my life?"

"I'm not making a mess. I'm helping you. Your finances were a disaster, and you weren't taking care of yourself properly. And Jason—"

"What about Jason?" she growled. "Tell me you haven't pissed him off. It isn't hard to piss him off."

"I haven't. We're getting along wonderfully. In fact, I'm helping you get him back. That is what you wanted right?"

Monica jumped up and screeched. "You're what!" She poked a finger at Jenny's nose. "Don't you dare touch him! That's just plain yucky, considering you're me and…you…you… I can't believe this!"

"Then you don't want him back?"

"Yes. Of course I do. I might even like to marry him someday. But I don't want you to get him back for me. I don't want you laying your hands on him and kissing him—or would that be me touching him? You touching him with my hands? Oh. My head hurts. I can't think about this right now." She started pacing back and forth, and despite being frustrated by Monica's lack of appreciation for what she was trying to do, and her anger for what Monica had done to her bank account and credit, Jenny noticed her butt looked pretty darn good in that skirt. It was weird, admiring her own butt.

"I haven't touched him...much. Say, have I lost weight?"

"Five pounds." Seeming to have forgotten their prior topic, Monica did a little pirouette. "Can you tell?"

"Yes! My butt looks smaller. And my hips. How'd you do it? I've been trying to lose weight for ages."

"You were feeding yourself garbage. It's a wonder you weren't as big as a barge. I can't believe what I found in your refrigerator! The processed meats and white bread. And pasta by the bucket. Chips, sweets... What were you trying to do to yourself? Eat yourself to death? And what was with all that ice cream in the freezer? I swear you had more varieties of Ben and Jerry's in there than Meijers."

"That was my emergency stash."

"Looks like you were stocked for Armageddon. Please tell me you aren't polluting my body with all that junk."

Jenny shrugged and tried not to look guilty. "Not too bad."

"Stand up and turn around."

Jenny stood and turned.

"Oh God! You are! Look at my butt! It has..." Monica gasped, "...bulges!"

Jenny turned back around. "It does not. Those are called *curves* and they're perfectly normal. A woman should have them. If you ask me, you were too skinny. It can't be healthy being built like a boy...with big boobs."

"I wasn't asking you." Monica pressed her hands on the stone surface between them and gave Jenny a stern look that was obviously meant to intimidate her. "Cut it out with the ice cream!"

Not in the mood for intimidation tactics, Jenny rested her hands directly across from Monica's and stared her right in the eyes. Staring in one's own eyes was kind of creepy. "You stop spending my money!"

"I'll bet you even ate red meat, didn't you?"

"Yeah? Well I'll bet you've maxed out one of my credit cards, haven't you?"

"I maxed them both out."

Jenny gasped. "Both? You bitch! You spent four thousand dollars in one week? Well, I ate a roast beef sandwich, tortilla chips and a quart of Chocolate Therapy and I'm not through eating yet! Hmmm…I think I'm in the mood for pizza today."

"Pizza?" Monica screeched. "Don't you dare!"

"Or maybe a big, juicy hamburger with extra mayonnaise and a super-sized order of French fries. I'm going to put on a pound for every thousand you spend."

Monica leaned closer. "You wouldn't!"

Jenny leaned so close their noses almost touched. "I would. Want to risk it?" Several heartbeats pounded in her ears before Monica backed away.

"No. Do you have any idea how hard it is to keep my shape?"

"And do you have any idea how hard it is to keep my credit score?"

They looked at each other for a moment, their chests heaving, their noses almost touching, their faces twisted in anger and then they started giggling uncontrollably.

"Truce?" Jenny offered, still laughing.

"Truce."

They shook hands.

"This is crazy." Jenny dropped into the chair behind her.

Monica rested her butt on the desk and nodded. "We both must be insane."

"I don't know how this happened but I'm kind of glad it did," Jenny admitted. "I've always been a little bit jealous of you."

"Believe it or not, I was always a little jealous of you."

Monica envied me? "No? Really? Jealous of what?"

Monica toyed with the Rolodex, spinning the wheel and making the cards flip over and over. "I don't know. You seemed to have it together. Your life was maybe a little boring, but it seemed predictable. Safe. Not chaotic like mine was…is. It's still a mess, isn't it?"

Jenny nodded. "A little. I honestly don't see how it got to be so bad. By the way, your car was repossessed. Just thought you should know."

"Repossessed? By whom? There isn't a bank loan."

Knowing an outburst was coming, Jenny cringed. "By Jason. You didn't pay your insurance again."

Sure enough, Monica jumped up and yelled, "He did? What a jerk! That was my car. He had no right."

"I'm very sorry but I checked it out. Legally the car belonged to him and if what he said was true, he had every right."

"What? What'd he say?"

"According to him, he's paid out two legal settlements for accidents—"

Monica crossed her arms over her chest, and Jenny noticed her cleavage seemed a little…more cleaved. "They were little fender benders."

"Did you get me a boob job too?" She pointed at Monica's chest.

"Nope. Just a Wonder Bra. They do wonders, don't they?"

Jenny nodded and stared at Monica's chest, admiring the way the bra pushed her breasts together and made them look fuller under her white button-down shirt that was unbuttoned one button too many. "I had no idea. Don't you think you're showing a little too much? I mean, I don't want to be known as a slut."

"No, I'm not showing too much." Monica looked down. "And you have nothing to worry about. You're known as a prude. By the way, I'm curious. Did you go to Catholic school?"

"Yes." Jenny felt her cheeks heating.

Monica shook her head. "That explains a lot. Are you still a virgin?"

Jenny gaped at Monica for a moment then stammered, "No, I'm not a virgin."

"When was the last time you had sex? You seem rather uptight. Maybe I should—"

"No way! If I have sex, I'd like to be there to enjoy it, thank you."

Monica laughed. "Yeah, I suppose you have a point."

"Enough about me and my sex life, okay? We were talking about you and your car situation. Your little fender benders cost Jason thousands of dollars. As long as the car's in his name, he's responsible."

Monica dropped back in the chair. "He wouldn't put the car in my name, claimed he couldn't for some legal reason. Same as the house, since the mortgage is in his name. It won't go into my name until I either refinance on my own and take his name off the loan, or thirty years from now when the stupid thing's paid off. You think it's so great having rich boyfriends give you things. But it isn't all it's cracked up to be. Nothing's really yours."

"The good news is the Honda's in your name. It's yours. Free and clear."

"Really? How'd you get him to do that? Oh my gosh!" She covered her mouth with her hands and her eyes widened. "You didn't sleep with him, did you?"

"No way! That would be a little weird, don't you think?" *I thought about it a few times though.*

"Well, this whole thing is weird. I've been showering every morning with my eyes closed so I won't see anything I shouldn't, if you know what I mean. It isn't easy shaving your legs when you're not looking."

"Imagine my pickle. You shaved *everywhere*." Jenny stifled a giggle. "Needless to say, you'll have some grooming to do whenever we switch back."

"Oh! I forgot about that." Monica laughed and Jenny couldn't help joining in. "Everyone'll be getting in soon. Should we work on our assignments together?" Monica asked after they'd both spent all their nervous energy.

"Yes, that sounds like a good plan."

"Good. I guess until we switch back, we'll be a team. What do you say?"

"I'd like that." Jenny smiled. For the first time since the switch, she felt at peace with what had happened.

It seemed that there was more to be gained than what she'd thought in this crazy, mixed-up situation. She sensed she just might get something far more precious than a raise.

She might end up with a true friend who had literally walked in her shoes.

Wanting to keep their newfound peace, she didn't mention the date she had with Jason that weekend. She wasn't exactly ready to break it to Monica how close she was to getting him back. Until it was a done deal, and there was less risk of it falling apart, she would rather keep it to herself. She didn't want Monica to get her hopes up.

But one thing was certain, she wouldn't sleep with him no matter what. As tempting as it was, it wouldn't be right. Jason was Monica's ex-boyfriend. She respected the fact that even though Jason would be sleeping with Monica's body, he would still be cheating—in a crazy roundabout way. And she knew Jason wouldn't want to be a cheater.

That Friday night, as she stood before the closet searching for just the right outfit, she repeated over and over in her head, *He's not mine. It's Monica he wants. He's not mine. It's Monica he wants.* And keeping with her vow to herself to keep things under wraps, she chose a dressy pair of pants and a V-necked blouse with long bell sleeves that was feminine but not too sexy.

Tonight she'd try a different ploy-- she'd appeal to his mind rather than his body. Really challenge him, talk to him, listen. He'd learn what a caring, attentive, intelligent person Monica was.

The doorbell rang and her heart skipped more than a couple of beats as she took a few seconds to do a final mirror check before answering the door.

She was doing this for Monica, she told herself as she studied Monica's reflection in the mirror. As long as she remembered that, she'd be okay.

After working closely with Monica for a week, and literally walking in her shoes, Jenny had developed a genuine fondness for her former rival. Now, with a more realistic view of Monica's life, Jenny was eager to fix Monica's messed-up finances and faltering romantic relationship. It was the least she could do until they switched back, whenever that might happen.

Monica was doing Jenny a few favors as well, including earning her a hefty raise and helping her lose a few more pounds. By the end of the week they both admitted the arrangement was working out far better than either had ever expected, despite their earlier difficulties.

The doorbell rang again, and Jenny rushed to the front door to answer it, finding Jason on the porch with a gorgeous bouquet of flowers in one fist. He grinned, displaying an even row of pearly whites and a cute dimple she hadn't noticed before on his left cheek, and thrust his arm forward to hand her the flowers.

Smiling so wide her cheeks ached, she took the bouquet from him and stepped to the side to let him into the house. As he brushed past her, she gazed up into his eyes. "Wow. How sweet. Thank you." A fly buzzed by her ear, and too busy staring at his dark blue—or where they violet?—eyes, she blindly fanned her hand to shoo the fly away. "They're absolutely gorgeous."

"Are you talking about the flowers?"

The pesky fly continued buzzing around her head and she waved her hand again, this time making contact but knocking it into her head instead of swatting it away. An angry buzz rattled next to her ear and then she felt a sharp sting. "Ouch!" She dropped the flowers and palmed the spot where the burning was originating. The insect to blame, tangled in her hair, wriggled under her hand. "Oh! Ouch!"

"What? What?" Jason looked alarmed. He sounded alarmed too.

"I think I was stung by a bee!" Combing her fingers through her hair to free the insect, she ran to the bathroom to take a look in the mirror.

Instantly, she realized something was wrong. The right side of her face felt funny. Tingly and hot. Her eyelid looked strange, a little puffy, and her lips and tongue were starting to feel funny too. She spun around, finding Jason behind her. "Do I look strange to you?"

"Strange? Noooo?"

"Here. My face. Does it look swollen? Should it be doing that?"

Jason scrutinized her face. "It does look a little swollen."

A very alarming thought occurred to her as she explored her face with her fingertips. Something was definitely wrong. "Am I allergic to bees?"

His eyes wide with worry, he said, "I don't know. Should I call someone?"

She turned back around to see if the swelling was getting worse. It was. Her whole right side of her face was getting puffier by the minute. "Yeah. 9-1-1!" Her heart started racing and her hands trembled. "Oh my God, I'm going to kill her."

"Her? Who?" Jason punched the buttons on the cordless and said something into the receiver.

Chapter Seven

ᘓ

Jenny was unable to be still, or give enough attention to what Jason was doing to understand what he was saying. Scared, she paced back and forth. "She can't die. I didn't know. How could I have known? Oh God! It was an accident."

"The ambulance is on the way."

Jenny ran to the bathroom again. Her throat felt tight and the skin around her eyes did too. When she looked at her reflection in the mirror, she gasped.

She looked like someone had pumped up her head with air. Her skin looked stretched to the point of splitting. "It's getting worse. Oh my God!"

Jason grabbed her shoulders, practically dragged her away from the mirror, and steered her toward the couch. "Sit down before you run into something and give yourself a concussion."

"But I can't swallow. And it sounds funny when I talk. Anaphylaxis." That wasn't easy to say with lips like over-inflated bicycle inner tubes.

He nodded and answered calmly, "Yes."

Feeling like she wasn't getting her point across, she fisted his shirt in her hands and gave him a little shake. "People die from it."

"You're not going to die. I promise." He turned his head to glance out the front window. "The ambulance will be here any second.

She felt drool dripping from the corner of her misshapen mouth and had to force herself not to begin crying.

He found a tissue in his pocket and dabbed her face, wiping away the wetness.

"Embarrassing," she mumbled.

"No. Don't be embarrassed. You can't help it. I should have checked the flowers for bees. Who would've thought? It's a little late in the season for bees." He glanced out the window again. "They're here," he said on a sigh, the sound in his voice revealing exactly how nervous and worried he had actually been. He stood to open the front door and let the paramedics in. They entered, hands full of equipment, took one look at Jenny and said, "Sir, we're just going to get her loaded and head for the hospital. Can you follow us?"

"Sure."

One of the paramedics quickly led Jenny to the ambulance and helped her up onto the gurney inside. Jason followed, and the last thing Jenny saw before the paramedic closed the ambulance's rear doors was his worried expression.

"Okay, I need you to lie down," the paramedic said as he wrapped a blood pressure cuff around her arm and inflated it.

Jenny shook her head and wrapped her hand around her throat. "Can't swallow. Choke."

"We'll take care of that right now." He released the pressure from the cuff, took the measurement and pulled it off her arm then checked her pulse. "What's your name?"

"Jenny…I mean Monica. Monica Starke."

"Okay, Monica. I'm going to give you some medicine." He quickly gathered a syringe and a vial of clear fluid, filled the syringe and stabbed her upper arm, injecting the medication into her muscle.

She winced as the medicine burned her flesh. "What's that?"

"Something to stop the reaction, I hope. It should work fairly quickly." Hoping he was right, Jenny counted heartbeats as she waited to see if the medicine would help. She got to two hundred—her heart rate was mighty quick at the moment—before he asked, "Feeling better yet?"

"I'm not sure." She noticed her speech sounded a little less garbled.

"It looks like it's working. Can you lie down now?"

Jenny took a trial swallow and was relieved when the little bit of spit she'd forced down made it past the knot in her throat. "I think so."

"Good." He helped her position herself on the gurney and strapped her in.

She tested the tightness of the belts by trying to lift her hips. She wasn't going anywhere. "Are the restraints really necessary? I promise I won't go berserk or anything and I'm not an escaped convict."

"I believe you, but we want you to be safe." He adjusted the tension on the one across her chest. "How's that?"

"Nice and cozy," she joked, finally starting to feel a little less panic-stricken and more like herself. The heat on her face was cooling to a light simmer versus a raging boil.

He grinned and it was only then that she realized how young he looked. He was a child, couldn't have graduated junior high. Since when did they hire children to be paramedics?

"I realize this might sound a little disrespectful, but are you sure you're qualified to do this job?" she asked as she watched him record her vitals on a piece of paper.

"I've had all the necessary training."

"But, no offense, you look like you're twelve."

Smiling as he checked her blood pressure a second time, he said, "I hear that all the time." When he finished, he pulled off the cuff. "I assure you I'm older than I look."

"That's a relief, not that I have anything against kids. I like them just fine. Just wouldn't want to have to rely on one to save my life."

"You'd be surprised how adept children can be. Just the other day, we picked up a mother who'd given birth at home. Her six-year old daughter delivered the baby."

"No kidding?"

The rest of the way to the hospital she rode in silence, ruminating the irony of having been stung by a bee and having to spend her first official date with Jason in the hospital emergency room.

When they arrived at the hospital, the paramedics wheeled her inside, rattled off all the pertinent information and then gave her a smile and a "good luck" before leaving her in the care of the hospital staff. A nurse, who looked no older than the paramedic had, double-checked her blood pressure, pulse, and temperature—like she couldn't trust the paramedic to have gotten it right—and then gave her a gown to change into and left, saying, "The doctor will be with you shortly."

Jason arrived soon after. He didn't have flowers this time but he did give her a great smile. "You look better. What did they do?"

"Gave me a shot of something. You mean to tell me you didn't like my new look? I was thinking of paying a plastic surgeon a visit and making it permanent. I've heard they can implant rolled-up pigskin into your lips to give them that just-been-stung-by-a-bee look. What do you think?"

He stood just inside the curtain that partitioned off her area from the next one. "I don't think that's such a good idea. I prefer the natural look."

"To each his own." She shrugged then added, "How about this get-up?" She smoothed the lovely—gag!—blue hospital gown over her chest. "Isn't it sexy?"

He nodded, waggled his eyebrows suggestively and purred, "Incredibly."

Oh! That reaction did some great things for her heart rate. Did he have a thing for playing doctor? If only!

"Really?" she asked, her imagination running wild and delving into territory she probably shouldn't have let it. In her mind's eye she could see herself lying on the bed, a crisp white sheet the only thing between her body and his fingertips… Um hum. He could give her a thorough workup anytime.

The heat returned to her cheeks.

He chuckled. "No, I'm teasing. I swear. Don't look so worried. I just didn't want you to feel bad."

"Oh believe me, I wasn't worried but I was beginning to wonder. By the way, you can come closer. I swear I'm not contagious."

He took two steps closer but still stood outside of her reach. "Sorry, I get a little nervous in hospitals. I always feel like I'm in the way."

"In the way of what? There's no one in here but you and me. I doubt a doctor will show up for at least a couple of hours."

"That long?"

"Yeah. Why? Do you need to cancel some reservations? By the way, I'm really sorry for wrecking everything tonight."

"It's not your fault. I was the one who brought you bug-ridden flowers. I almost killed you."

"How silly. Flower homicide. Just think. There might have been a scandal and you could have been pegged the Infamous Flower Murderer."

He chuckled, the low rumbly sound rippling through her body in waves of arousal, and looked at his wristwatch. "I need to make a call." He pulled his cell phone from his pocket.

"I don't think you can do that in here. You should probably go outside."

"Okay. I'll be right back."

No sooner was he gone than Doogie Houser, MD entered. Man, either she was getting old, or hospitals and medical facilities were hiring kids right out of high school. "Hello," Dr. Houser said, offering his hand and a friendly smile. "I'm Dr. Herner. What brings you to the emergency room today?"

Feeling a little smart, since he was holding her chart in his hand and therefore knew darn well why she was there, she said,

"Well, I thought it would be interesting to see what would happen if I got stung by a bee and almost died from anaphylactic shock." If there was one thing that irritated her, it was when someone asked an obvious question when they knew the answer.

His smile wasn't so bright anymore. "I see." He flipped the top sheet of her chart and read something then lowered it again. "How are you feeling now, madam?"

"It's Miss Starke. Much better, thanks. Can I leave?"

"No, not yet. Your symptoms could return. We'll need to keep an eye on you for a while. And we'll give you some medicine to help keep the symptoms under control."

"More medicine?"

"Yes." He pulled a couple of rubber gloves from the dispenser on the wall and put them on. "Can you show me where you were stung?"

She pointed at her head. "Here."

He parted her hair and looked. "Mmmm. The stinger's still imbedded in your skin. We'll need to remove it."

"Yikes."

He walked around to a small cabinet against the wall and pulled out a tongue depressor.

"What're you going to do with that? You going in through my throat? Shouldn't you give me something to knock me out first?"

He looked at her, silently questioning whether she was really stupid enough to think he'd really have to do that or not. She grinned just to reassure him. Clearly not appreciating her attempts—as lame as they may be—at breaking the ice, he shook his head and parted her hair again, searching for the stinger. "This won't require surgery, I promise."

"Good. I…uh, ate a little snack a couple of hours ago. I've heard it's dangerous to go under general after eating."

"By any chance did you have a few drinks with that meal?" he asked as he worked on her head, scraping her scalp with the wooden stick.

"Not unless you count diet cola as a drink. I'm perfectly sober, if that's what you're asking."

"Just wanted to make sure. We need to know if you have any substances in your bloodstream before we prescribe medications." He thought she was stoned! Just because she'd cracked a few stupid jokes?

"Sure you do."

He stepped back, dropped the stick in the trash and removed the gloves. "All right. The nurse will be in to give you that medication. Do you have any questions?"

"Yeah, just one. When do I get to leave?"

"In an hour or two. We want to make sure you won't have another attack. Your reaction was severe. You wouldn't want to leave and have another one."

"True." She turned her head when she heard Jason's voice outside the curtain. He was evidently speaking to a nurse.

"Can I go in?" he asked. Within a heartbeat he was standing beside the doctor.

Dr. Herner introduced himself and asked, "Are you Mr. Starke?"

"No, there is no Mr. Starke, at least none that I know of. I'm Jason Foxx, the guy responsible. Brought her a bouquet of flowers infested with bees. How's she going to be?"

"She'll be fine. We're ordering some blood tests and medication to prevent the symptoms from returning. She's a little bit anxious to leave so I hope you'll be able to convince her to sit tight for a while."

"I'm starving," she interjected.

"I haven't been able to convince her of anything but I can try," Jason answered the doctor, ignoring her comment.

"That's all I ask."

"Can I eat?" she asked, hoping he wouldn't be so cruel as to let her starve.

The doctor turned his attention back to Jenny. "It's probably not a good idea for you to eat yet. We'll let you know as soon as you can. Okay?"

"Why did I know you'd say that?" When she nodded, he smiled, pulled the curtain aside and stepped through.

"The nurse will be in shortly to give you that medication and draw some blood," he said just before turning away.

"What's the blood for?" she called out, hoping to catch him before he disappeared for the next six hours. Blood tests meant a longer wait. The hospital lab was notoriously slow. "I had an allergic reaction. What more do you need to know?"

Glancing over his shoulder, he answered, "Just trying to be thorough, Miss Starke." And then he closed the curtain.

She looked at Jason and shook her head. "We'll be lucky to get out of here by morning. I think they're running a drug test on me to make sure I'm not stoned. Can you believe it?"

"They are not."

"Then what else could it be? Who heard of a blood test for an allergic reaction?"

"Maybe they want to make sure it was the bee sting that caused your attack and not something else."

She sighed, wishing she was a million places besides stuck in a hospital. In Jason's bed was at the top of her list, even though she knew that even if she wasn't in the hospital, that was one place she couldn't visit, at least not with a good conscience. "This stinks." Those two words summed up a whole lot more than the present situation.

He walked closer, and she curled her legs up to let him sit on the foot of the bed. He rested a hand on her knee. It felt warm, even through the cool sheet covering her legs. Her heart stuttered a few irregular beats in her chest when he gave her leg a subtle squeeze. "Maybe it won't be as bad as you think."

Giddy, even though it was an innocent touch, certainly not very erotic, she held in a shudder of delight and expectation. Was it time to play doctor? "Do you know something that I don't?"

His crooked grin gave her the answer she wanted. "Maybe."

Fighting another shudder of pleasure, she asked, "What?"

He lifted his hand, and she nearly screamed with bitter disappointment. "It wouldn't be a surprise if I told you, would it?"

"But I want to know."

"You'll know soon enough." He stretched his arms overhead, the motion setting all those scrumptious muscles on his arms, shoulders and chest rippling and flexing under his snug T-shirt.

He had to know what that was doing to her.

She swallowed a groan. This just plain wasn't fair. Not only was their evening ruined, but she was trapped in a six by eight cubicle with a man who could practically elicit an orgasm with a smile and a how-do-you-do.

Damn you, Monica. Why couldn't your zillionaire jewelry broker be ninety years old and ugly?

Why did he have to be so good-looking, and kind, and generous, and sexy, and…tempting. Jason Foxx was nothing but six-foot-something of extreme temptation. And she couldn't do a darn thing but charm him with her wit.

It was like having fasted for a month and then sitting down to a mountain of your favorite ice cream and not being able to eat it.

Couldn't I have just one little taste?

Chapter Eight

ꟷ

Uncomfortable, Jenny shifted her weight, resting it on her other hip. "Thanks for hanging around and keeping me company. This isn't exactly a rockin' place to spend your Friday night."

"At least the company's good."

She couldn't drum up an appropriate answer quickly and was grateful for the interruption when the nurse arrived to draw her blood and administer her medication. But she quickly retreated to the world beyond the pink curtain, leaving Jenny to try to untangle her tongue. "Sorry," she finally managed after several bloated minutes of torturous silence. "I guess I'm not much of an entertainer."

"Actually, since I'm the healthy one, I should be entertaining you."

Images of not-so-wholesome forms of entertainment flashed through her mind. "Good! What's in your repertoire? Do you sing? Dance?"

"Nope. Can't sing a note."

"I happen to know you're a fine dancer." She lifted her arms and folded them behind her head, using them as a makeshift pillow. "How about showing me some of your moves?"

A hint of a blush stained his cheeks. "I can't dance without music."

"I can sing for you." She bellowed out a few lines of Prince's *International Lover* in her best falsetto, including the little high-pitched ohhs and ahhs for effect. It seemed fairly appropriate.

Unfortunately, Jason didn't seem to agree, at least it seemed that way based on the disgusted look on his face, which did nothing to detract from his charm. "What is that?"

"*International Lover* by Prince. A 1980s classic in my opinion."

"Not in mine."

"Okay. I can give you an alternative. How about...*Like a Virgin*? She sang the first line in her best Madonna impersonation. The lyrics were accompanied by a half-hearted attempt at some seductive dance moves, well the best she could manage in a hospital bed.

Clearly not impressed, he scowled and shook his head. How could a man look so cute scowling? "That isn't much better."

Feigning insult she dropped her arms to her sides. "Well, pooh! You're making this difficult. My repertoire is limited, you know. I don't frequent karaoke bars."

"That's okay. I wouldn't want a nurse or doctor walking in and catching me shaking my groove thang. It might be a bit embarrassing."

But I'd sure love it. "Take my word for it, if they're female, they'll appreciate the view. You'd probably get a standing ovation and a few dollars tucked in your drawers."

He grinned, the sparkle in his eyes doing a host of heavenly things to her insides. "As pleasant as that sounds, I think I'll find a less embarrassing way to pass the time."

"Like make love to me?" *Shoot! Did I just say that aloud?*

"In here? You're kidding right?"

No. Well, maybe. Well, no. "Of course I am." She leaned closer and whispered, "But don't you wonder if anyone's ever tried such a thing? The doctors and nurses leave you alone here for hours...with nothing else to do." She nudged his backside with her toe and winked. "What do you say? Come on?" she said, knowing full well what his answer would be.

"No way."

No surprise there. But how much willpower did Jason Foxx possess? Willing to give it a small test—how much would that hurt?—she pulled at the tie holding the back of her gown closed. "I'm not wearing any undies. Easy access." She lowered her voice, aiming for a seductive whisper, "Wanna see?"

"No." His ears were turning redder by the minute and she had to concentrate really hard to keep from cracking up.

Swallowing to keep from laughing, she reached down and pulled on the sheet covering her legs. The bottom inched higher and higher, exposing her feet then shins then thighs.

His eyes glued to her exposed legs, Jason's hand trembled as he ran his fingers through his hair. Without a word, he caught the sheet with the other hand and gave it a sharp yank, covering her up again. "What are you trying to do to me?" He sounded breathless, definitely a step in the right direction. She figured he was dangling from the end of his proverbial rope at the moment. Would he fall?

"Drive you crazy?"

He chuckled nervously and stood, backing toward the curtain. He swiped an arm over his glistening forehead. "Well, it's working, you little fiend. But just wait until we get out of here."

"Promises, promises. Are you running away? Don't leave me here alone."

"I'll be right back. I need to check on something." Before she could say a word, he slipped out of sight behind the curtained partition.

"Well, so much for that." Sure she'd be alone for a while as he found a cure for the case of stiffness she'd given him, she turned on the small TV suspended from the ceiling and settled back to take a catnap. The medicine the nurse had given her was sure making her sleepy…

Moments later—or what seemed moments later—a small commotion outside the curtain woke her. Still half-asleep, she lifted her heavy eyelids and focused her eyes.

A broadly smiling Jason, who had clearly regained his composure, was pushing a cart heaped with foam carryout containers. "Since I couldn't take you out to dinner, I brought dinner to you."

What a sweetie! Can I keep him? Please? "But didn't the doctor say I can't eat?" She scooted up and straightened out the sheet that had somehow tangled around her knees.

"He cleared you for solid foods."

"Lucky me." She rubbed her hollow stomach.

"I wanted to bring in the fiddlers too, but the door Nazi wouldn't let them in."

Violins? How romantic. "Unromantic bastard."

"Tell me about it." He scooted the full cart next to her then opened the top foam container. "I didn't know what to order for you after the last meal I saw you eat. So I went for surf…and turf."

Her eyes swept over the scrumptious hunk of beef in the container and her mouth instantly filled with saliva. Next to the sinfully thick steak curled a steamed lobster tail.

The aromas of grilled meat, onions and lobster filled her nostrils and she inhaled, wishing to fill her entire being with the delectable scents.

"Don't just sit there and sniff. Eat." He handed her a plastic fork and knife wrapped in a paper napkin. "This isn't exactly the elegant setting I'd planned but it's the best I could do." He sat on the edge of the bed. "I have candles, but with the oxygen I figure that's not such a good idea."

"Probably not. This is wonderful, perfect." Starving, she set to work slicing the meat and savored the first bite. Her eyes closed, she merely moaned and chewed.

"I take it you approve?"

She swallowed then carved off a second bite. "It's absolutely delicious," she said around the second piece of meat. Suddenly aware of the fact that he wasn't eating, she motioned toward the other containers with her plastic knife. "What's in those? Aren't you going to eat?"

"That's all for you. Salad, baked potatoes with the works, a seafood pasta dish, and an appetizer."

"Holy smoke. I can't eat all that. She'll kill me if I gain another pound."

"Who'll kill you?"

"Er..." *Duh! That was a stupid thing to say.* She took another bite of meat as she thought of a logical answer to his question. "...my personal trainer?"

"You won't gain any weight from one meal. You'd have to eat over three thousand calories to do that."

"You're right. I'm going to enjoy this."

He looked pleased as she dug some of the flaky white meat from the lobster shell and dipped it in the plastic container of butter. The sweet sauce coated her lower lip as she opened her mouth and closed it around the fork. Her tongue jutted out to lick away the delicious wetness as she chewed and she couldn't help feeling a little self-conscious. He was watching her every move.

"Besides, I like a little softness on a woman," he said, his gaze riveted to her mouth. "No offense, but if I wanted to date a hard body, I'd date a guy."

"No offense taken. But I'm curious. How much softness?" She couldn't help asking. He'd never see her as plain old Jenny, but she had to know if he'd find her more voluptuous figure repulsive—not that she'd ever get the chance to do anything about it even if he didn't.

Jason was Monica's ex-boyfriend, she reminded herself for the umpteenth time. And it was painfully clear, despite his claims to the contrary, he was in love with her, wanted to take her back. He had that look, the one she'd never seen a man have for her. Still, it couldn't be mistaken. Something of a cross between the look a man would give toward a Lamborghini or a movie screen-sized flat screen TV with surround sound and multi-feature remote and the look a boy would give his new puppy. It was darn cute.

"Let's not go there now." He handed her a foam cup with a straw protruding from the plastic top. "Diet soda?" After she accepted the proffered drink, he added, "We're having a nice time. I don't want to wreck it. I'd much rather talk about something else, something safe."

"I'm fine with the subject matter. You can tell me the truth." She sucked, drawing some of the cold liquid into her mouth. The carbon bubbles tickled her tongue and throat as she swallowed.

Looking quite firm, he shook his head. "No. I'd rather talk about other things."

"Like what? Like…marriage?" She followed a second bite of lobster with some more beef, her gaze not once straying from his adorable face. The dimple that appeared every now and then on his left cheek was just too cute. She wanted to kiss it. She wanted to kiss all of him.

There it was again!

Grinning, he said, "Well, it's a little soon to be talking about that, considering it's our first date."

"Maybe officially, but we've known each other long enough to broach this topic I think, unless you're scared." She offered him a bite of steak but he declined with a shake of his head.

"I'm not scared of anything." The way he made that proclamation reminded her of a little boy who'd just been teased by a group of kids. She wondered what he'd been like as a child. What his children would look like. What it would feel like to carry his child…what it would feel like to make his child.

A little warm all of a sudden, she fanned her face. As much as she didn't want to, she forced her mind out of his bed and back to the conversation. "I didn't think you were scared. So, what do you think about marriage?"

"You've never asked me that before. You were dead set against it, end of subject."

Why did that not surprise her? What was wrong with that woman? Who wouldn't want to marry Jason? He was incredibly sexy, sweet, caring, giving...the list went on. "That was before."

"Yes, before this unbelievable transformation. Is that really you inside of there?" He leaned forward and tapped on her head.

"Oh yes, it's me all right. I'm afraid you'll have to take my word for it. There's no such thing as a personality transplant."

"If there was, I'd be highly suspicious." He shifted his weight as if he was uncomfortable. "Okay, so what about now? What do you think about marriage?"

"I'd like to be married...someday." *To you!* "Have kids." *Your kids. I'd name the oldest Jason Junior, assuming he was a boy.* "A family. I think about those kinds of things more and more these days, especially with the holidays coming up. Not that I'm unhappy with my life the way it is, er...was," she added. "Lately, I've learned to appreciate what I have."

"Okay. I have to know. What made you learn that lesson so suddenly?" If he'd written it in black ink on his forehead, his curiosity couldn't have been plainer on his face.

"Well..." She struggled to come up with an explanation that he would accept but wouldn't really explain much of anything. Kind of like what politicians did. "Recently I had the opportunity to see what a friend's life is like, to practically walk in her shoes. I've always envied this person, thought she had things so much better than me. But I learned she didn't. And she taught me a few hard lessons, really helped me open my eyes. I wasn't living right. I needed to make some changes."

"That's interesting." He shifted again, this time moving closer.

A mere fraction of an inch of air was between her leg and his rump. She fought the burning urge to close that gap. The need to touch him blazed through her body.

Aware of the slight distance between them, she picked up the food carton and leaned forward until the back of her hand pressed against his shoulder. "Won't you eat something? Please?"

"No." He gently pushed her hand back.

"Why not? You bought enough food for an army." She pointed at the mountain of containers on the cart.

"Because I know how you are about stocking your fridge. I figured whatever you didn't eat now you could take home and eat later."

"Oh! But I went shopping. I have all kinds of food at home. Enough to feed a small nation, in fact."

"You didn't." The disbelief in his voice was unmistakable and comical.

She laughed. "Don't look so surprised. I bought meat, vegetables, fruit…even some ice cream. I can prove it to you. Once they spring me from this place, how about coming over for some dessert? That's the least I can do. But before you can have any sweets, you have to eat something solid. How about some steak?"

He laughed, a sound so delightful, she couldn't help laughing right along with him. Then he opened the container and polished off the remaining steak and lobster.

By the time he'd finished, the nurse returned with Jenny's discharge instructions. Jason left the room while she dressed and within a half hour, they were on their way back to her place.

The minute they walked inside, she led him straight back to the kitchen, threw open the refrigerator and freezer doors and displayed the contents with pride. "See? You didn't believe me, did you?"

"No, I didn't but I do now." His eyes were wide as he nodded. He didn't move, so she rearranged a few things in the fridge and took the containers stacked high in his arms and put them inside. After closing the door, she went for the ice cream.

As she dished out their dessert, she watched him move about the kitchen, opening the cupboards, evidently to see if there was food inside, and inspecting the baked goods sitting on the counter.

"You did all of this because of your friend?" he asked, standing next to the full pantry.

"Kind of."

He closed the cabinet door. "Someday I'd like to meet her."

A bit of regret tugged at her gut. That would probably never happen. And even if it did, she'd have to pretend she didn't know him, didn't like him, didn't care for him…wasn't falling in love with him… How could she hide her feelings from Monica? "Maybe you will, someday."

"She sounds like a terrific person. What's her name?"

"Jenny." Jenny handed him a bowl and motioned toward the living room. "Want to eat in there?"

"You never let anyone in your living room with food."

"I do now."

They sat on the undoubtedly expensive leather couch. The leather was so soft, it reminded her of silk. But it was about the only thing in the room that was warm, comforting—outside of the man sitting on the other end of the couch. The rest of the furniture was hard, metal, cold with sharp lines. Nothing like the furniture in Jenny's living room.

He was too far away for her comfort, but she did nothing to close the distance between them. She feared another touch, no matter how innocent, would completely obliterate her failing self-control.

There was no doubt about it, she was not only falling in lust with Jason Foxx, she was falling in love with him.

"Where'd you meet this friend, Jenny?" he asked.

"Work." She spun around, facing him and sat cross-legged. It was fun watching him eat. The way he captured the spoon between his lips. The way his tongue darted out to lick away the droplet of ice cream that sat in the center of his lower lip.

"Maybe we can plan a get-together? A foursome for golf?"

"Oh, I don't know. I don't think she's much of a golfer."

"Please. I'd like to thank her for whatever she did. We had our problems in the past but you've changed. It's…incredible. Maybe that couldn't happen if you weren't ready for it, but she still had a part in it and both our futures may be changed. I need to thank Jenny…what's her last name?"

"Brown. I'm sure she realizes how much it means to you."

"I don't think anyone does, including you." He took her bowl from her and set both of them on the coffee table. Then he palmed her cheeks and gazed deeply into her eyes. "Monica, this is what I've been waiting for. You've become the woman of my dreams overnight. I'm falling in love with you all over again, and this time it could be forever."

Jenny sat mute, not knowing what to say, what to do.

The words, *I'm falling in love with you too,* sat deep in her throat but she refused to let them come out. For one thing, if she said them, she would be admitting something she wasn't ready to accept yet.

Then he tilted his head and lowered it, and knowing what he was about to do, she reached up, her hands flat on the backs of his and pulled, hoping he'd release her face before their mouths made contact.

No, no, no! she screamed in her head.

Oblivious to her inner struggle, he chuckled and closed the distance between them. His mouth touched hers in an erotic but very soft kiss. His lips were moist, pliable as they moved over hers.

She was in heaven.

Before she knew it, she was kissing him back. But she knew her kiss wasn't as patient as his had been. She opened her mouth and explored his, sighing when his tongue slipped inside. He tasted wonderful, sweet. She felt her hands shake as she slid them down his forearms then up over thick biceps to his chest. Her fingertips traced the line of his developed chest muscles through his shirt. She felt his hands fisting, gripping hair on either side of her head.

He groaned when her right index finger found the tight nub of his nipple and circled it. His tongue darted in and out of her mouth in a quick rhythm that brought to mind another kind of thrusting.

Heat slowly uncoiled low in her belly and wound its way down…

A firm but surprisingly gentle tug on her hair made her tilt her head back. With a growl, he set upon her neck, kissing and nibbling. She reached up and dug her fingernails into the hard flesh of his shoulders as chills warred with mini-blazes for control of her body. Goose bumps erupted on flesh that felt stinging hot. A steady throb began between her legs and she yearned to rub it away.

Her eyelids closed, shutting out the visual world, yet she still found herself overwhelmed by too many sensations. The sounds of his groans, the scents of man and tangy aftershave, the feel of his weight pressing over top of her, his chest grazing her tight nipples, his hands roaming up and down her torso.

"Monica, oh, Monica," he murmured into her ear. His words, the name he'd called her—Monica—acted with swift effectiveness, cooling her heating libido.

She pushed against his chest and lowered her head, opening her eyes. "Stop. Please. I can't."

"No, you don't understand—" He leaned back and ran his fingers through his tousled hair. It fell right back where it had been, in slight disorder. Sexy, rebellious, perfect.

"I'm sorry," she said, glancing down to see if any of her clothes had been misplaced. "I just…I can't…shoot! I don't know how to explain."

"No, I'm sorry. I don't know how to handle this, what to think of it. This has to sound strange, but I feel like I'm falling in love with an entirely different woman. How can this be?"

"It's strange for both of us."

"Glad to hear I'm not the only one suffering." Still looking a little uncomfortable, he winked.

Her face warmed as she saw the shimmer of love in his eyes.

This wasn't fair! She'd never seen that expression in a man's eyes before. Now that she had, she couldn't be sure who it was meant for—the Monica he saw with his eyes or the Jenny he saw with his heart. If only it were meant for the latter…

He glanced at his wristwatch. "I'd better get going. How about we go to the orchard next weekend? Get some cider and donuts."

"Sounds wonderful! Do they have a hayride? I love hayrides."

"You do?" He shook his head. "I don't know if I'll ever get used to this new Monica. You're so different."

"Is that bad?"

"Heck no! And to answer your question, yes. They have a hayride later in the evening. We can get some hot cider and take it with us."

"Sounds wonderful," she said, imagining herself curled up in the hay with Jason, a blanket wrapped around them both, a sky full of sparkling stars overhead. Her whole body tingled. It had been eons since she'd last gone on a hayride. And never had she been snuggled close to a guy as hunky and sweet as Jason.

"Good. See you next Saturday." He leaned forward and kissed her forehead. "Have a good week," he whispered. Then he left.

* * * * *

The workweek dragged by. Jenny felt like a kid waiting for Christmas as she prepared for her big date with Jason. That Saturday, she dressed in her cutest blue jeans, took extra long to fix her hair and makeup and bundled up in a sweater and jacket. Just in case she got cold—Monica was always cold—she folded a warm wool blanket to take along.

Jason showed up at six on the dot. Her heart rapped as loud against her rib cage as his fist did on the door. Nervous and giddy, she opened the front door to let him in.

His smile was warm and oh so sexy. "Hi," he said as he stepped inside. One hand was noticeably hidden behind his back.

"Please tell me you didn't bring flowers again," she teased as she stepped aside to let him enter her living room.

"Oh no. I won't make that mistake again." He drew his arm out from behind his back, displaying a small paper bag. "Brought something safe instead." He looked extremely proud of whatever it was.

Curious, she reached out and took the bag in her hand, reaching under its bottom. She knew what it was immediately, thanks to the cold that seeped through the paper and into her skin. "Mmmm… What flavor? Do I need to guess?"

"Chocolate Therapy of course. I know we might be too chilly after the hayride to eat some but figured it was worth a risk anyway."

"I'll put it in the freezer. With that blanket," she pointed at the green wool Army blanket folded into a neat square on the couch, "I expect we'll be plenty warm."

"Excellent." He clapped his hands together and rubbed them. "Hungry?"

"Not really." There were far too many butterflies in her belly to leave much room for food.

"That's just as well. By the time we get to the orchard, it should be dusk. We can take the wagon ride out to the woods. They have a bonfire. We can roast hot dogs, toast marshmallows out there. They have a little store where we get everything we need beforehand."

"Sounds like a plan!" Extremely nervous and feeling awkward, she bent to grab the blanket and gathered it to her chest.

Jason followed her to the door, reaching around her side to pull open the door.

She glanced over her shoulder to thank him but before anything came out of her mouth, she found herself kissing him.

His lips slid over hers so slowly she thought she might scream in protest. It was sheer torture. She'd never been kissed with such skill, such patience. This was not the kiss of an inexperienced man. Not sloppy, or hurried, or vulgar, it was pure seductive ecstasy. It took her breath away and left her legs wobbly and weak.

The blanket dropped from her arms as she turned her body toward him and lifted her hands. Her fingers tangled in his soft hair. Her body pressed against his wide, hard bulk. The stiff bulge of his erection pressed against her belly. Heat crept through her entire body.

He broke the kiss and looked down into her eyes with such profound affection she wanted to cry.

Who did he see when he looked at her like that?

"We better get going," he whispered, "or we won't leave at all."

I wouldn't object. Shoot! What am I thinking? "Yes. Good idea." She let her arms fall to her sides.

He bent his head and pointed at the floor. "Better not forget that."

"Huh?" Her gaze dropped to the floor and found the green blanket lying in a heap at her feet. She laughed nervously. "Oh, yeah. That."

He bent low and picked it up, bundling it into a ball in his arms. "After you."

She walked out the front door, double-checking to make sure she had her house key in her pocket before allowing him to pull the front door closed behind them.

They walked to the car. The air was crisp and cool, touching the tip of her nose. Good thing she'd thought to wear layers.

She settled into the passenger seat and tried like heck to sooth her jittery nerves as she waited for him to walk around the car and take his seat. He tossed the blanket into the backseat then got in, shut the door and started the car.

"Ready?" he asked.

"Ready."

"Let's go have some fun." He put the car into gear and they sped off down the road.

Chapter Nine

ࢻ

The drive to the apple orchard/cider mill was short but very enjoyable, and not only because of the doll of a man sitting next to Jenny. The scenery changed quickly as they drove, going from spacious sprawling suburban homes to empty farm fields, to bundles of trees cloaked in green and gold leaves. There wasn't a single cloud to spoil the cool hue of the clear sky. Picture-perfect. To the east, the beginnings of a deepening color—closer to purple—hovered near the horizon as the sun squatted low to the west.

Jason parked the car on the dirt lawn that served as a makeshift parking lot for the orchard and got out. After collecting the blanket, he opened her door. "Careful. The mud's pretty deep here."

"Yikes. You weren't exaggerating." No matter how she wished to avoid it, the deeply rutted mud was everywhere. It wasn't looking good.

As she feared, when she stepped out of the car the heel of her ankle-high book stuck in the thick muck. She tried to pull it out, but the harder she struggled, the deeper her boot seemed to sink, threatening to pull her with it. Finally, her foot slipped out and she teetered on the other, flailing, expressing her concern in mild expletives, and grasping any part of Jason she could reach to steady herself. Her fingers grazed something on their way up to his arm and she heard him gasp sharply.

With the distinct feeling in her clumsy, undirected flailing she'd touched a sensitive spot or two, she glanced his way the minute she'd managed to steady herself on one foot—as steady as one could be standing on what could best be described as an oil slick.

He looked surprised…or pained, she couldn't be sure which. "What can I do to help?" he asked.

"Rescue my boot?" She pointed at the defenseless, expensive shoe that was in danger of being sucked out of sight at any moment. "That's no normal mud. I'm quite certain it's quickmud—you know, like quicksand."

"There's no such thing." He chuckled and carefully bent to retrieve the sinking article before it was lost forever. Supporting her with one arm, he helped her sit back in the car without putting her stockinged foot in the muck then went to the trunk. "I think I have some paper towels in here."

"Is there anything you're not prepared for?" she joked as she waited for him to return.

He slammed the trunk and handed the roll to her. "Sure, plenty. I'm not ready for you to dump me."

She felt her cheeks flaming. He was worried about her ditching him? He had that backwards in her opinion. She'd be out of her mind to dump him. There had to be dozens of women standing in line waiting for their chance at dating Jason Foxx, women who wouldn't sell his grandmother's art glass to junk dealers or rack up attorney's fees for auto accidents. "You're just saying that to be funny."

He stooped so his eyes were level with hers. "Oh no I'm not. I mean it. I can't believe how things have changed between us. Practically overnight. I don't want this to end. Tell me it's for real and I'm not going to wake up tomorrow morning and learn it was all a dream." He took her shoe from her then pulled a paper towel off the roll she'd forgotten she was holding. Without looking down, he began rubbing the dirt away.

"If you're dreaming, then I am too. We're sharing the same dream and I don't want to wake up either."

He wadded up the soiled paper and tossed it into the car then took her foot in his hand and eased it into the boot. "There you go," he whispered. His gaze never once left hers. It delved deep, beyond her body to the furthest reaches of her soul.

This was the most amazing, erotic moment. She felt like he was literally bound to her—mind, body and spirit—for a brief, heavenly instant.

"Thanks," was all she could utter. She licked lips that suddenly felt very dry and stared deep into his eyes. What did she see there? Fear? Hope? Uncertainty?

A child screamed nearby, slowly breaking the spell and gently nudging Jenny back to the world around them. She looked up and caught sight of a woman and man both struggling to subdue an angry toddler and strap him into the vehicle next to theirs.

Still trying to gather her wits and find a footing as she stood, she motioned toward them. "Will that be us someday?"

"Probably," he answered, supporting her with an arm. "With our tempers we're bound to produce a houseful of hotheads."

Her heart did a couple of back flips with a twist. He said probably! They would probably be married and probably have kids. That was almost as good as a promise.

Back-stepping, he pulled her with him until they were both standing on firm ground. Even though he no longer needed to hold her, he didn't release her.

She didn't mind. Being in his arms was like being in heaven, it had to be. Although she'd never actually been to heaven—never had a near-death experience, outside of a close call ages ago when she'd accidentally turned the wrong way down a one-way road and hit a cab head-on—she was sure nothing outside of sitting before God himself could be better than being held in Jason's arms. "You? I haven't seen any sign of a bad temper in you."

"You have a short memory." He pointed at the red-faced parents who seemed to have finally won the battle, declaring victory by shutting the car door and taking their places in the front seats. "I wonder if you were a little hellion as a kid. I know I was."

"I wouldn't know," she answered honestly. "You'd have to ask my folks."

"I just might do that. But for now, let's see if we can get further this time before you start losing pieces of clothing." Loosening his embrace, he slid one hand down her arm until his fingers entwined with hers. He started walking down the driveway. "By the way, does that mean you'll finally let me meet your parents?"

He hasn't met Monica's family yet? Why not? "I'll do my best. Promise."

"Do your best at what? Keeping on your clothing or introducing me to your folks?"

"Both."

"Hmmm…I've heard that promise before. But I learned long ago that revisiting old arguments with a woman is plain stupid."

"You're a wise man."

Holding hands, the blanket wadded up and tucked under Jason's arm, they continued toward the barn that served as restaurant and store. They purchased some hot dogs, caramel apples and hot cider then stood in a long line for the wagon ride to the bonfire. From their position, they could see the gold glow of the fire cutting through the trees in the distance.

The wagon rumbled up a few minutes later and they settled into the loose strewn straw. Jenny leaned back against Jason and covered them both with the blanket. She inhaled deeply, relishing the combination of scents. Straw, burning wood, that familiar autumn scent that hung in the chilly air and the tangy smell of Jason's aftershave.

Could she stay there forever?

During the ride she just sat in silence, snuggled as close to Jason as she could get. The cold air nipped at her cheeks and nose but the rest of her remained toasty warm. Jason produced enough heat to qualify him to moonlight as a blast furnace. She could just imagine trying to sleep next to him on a sultry summer night.

She wondered if she'd ever get the opportunity to find out for herself if her suspicions were correct about that.

She felt his fingers comb through her hair and her nerve endings got all tingly and jumpy. She wanted to turn around and plant a good, long kiss on those lips, which she guessed were probably curled up at the corners in a playful smile. Unfortunately, the wagon was full of riders. And based upon the songs they were singing, snazzy adaptations of gospel tunes, she'd guessed they wouldn't appreciate a round of tonsil hockey amongst their midst.

That was probably for the better anyway. The way she was feeling tonight, she feared if she got started with Jason she'd never have the strength to stop. Monica's body or not, making love with Jason was out of the question.

After touring several empty fields, an apple orchard and finally a crop of woods, the wagon dropped them off at a clearing surrounded by more trees. The huge bonfire lit the entire area, and even from a distance Jenny could see the shadowy figures of people as they moved around, evidently preparing to catch the wagon back to the barn.

When the tractor stopped, Jason helped Jenny from the wagon. They found a cozy seat on a fallen log close to the fire.

"This is wonderful," Jenny said as she took in the sight of the raging red and gold fire, the deep shadows of the woods, and the clear, deep ebony sky with zillions of stars. "Absolutely beautiful."

"I agree," he answered in a deep voice full of promises that produced both waves of heat and goose bumps at the same time.

She glanced at Jason and he smiled. "You're teasing me."

"No, I'd never do that." Jason unwrapped a hot dog and handed it to her. "Ketchup?"

"Yes, please."

He dug around inside the paper bag and produced a plastic packet of the condiment. He handed it to her before removing the foil from a second hot dog. He buried his under layers of mustard, pickle relish and ketchup then he held it up. "Shall we toast? To a date where the highlight is not a trip to the emergency room?"

"I'll second that." She bumped her hot dog against his then took a bite. It was fresh-from-the-icebox cold.

He wrinkled his nose. "Weren't these supposed to be cooked?"

"That's what the sign said." She forced the mouthful of cold meat and bun down her throat.

"This is not the best food I've ever eaten."

"We can warm them up in the fire," she suggested.

"That sounds like a good idea." He looked around. "Um…we don't exactly have the proper tools though."

"That's okay. We can improvise." Jenny handed her hot dog to Jason and stood, making sure to brush the dirt off her rear end. Walking around with dirt on one's butt had to be a major date faux pas. "Weren't you ever in the scouts?"

"Nope."

"Me neither. But we can figure it out anyway. A couple of long sticks ought to do the trick. There are probably some over there by the woods."

They rewrapped their cold hot dogs in the foil to keep them from getting dirty and left their seats to search for fallen branches to use. None lay at the outskirts of the woods so they were forced to wander deeper into the woods. They found success about a hundred yards from the warmth of the fire.

Each carrying a stick, they returned to their seats.

The fire warmed Jenny's face as she scooted closer to toast her hot dog. And the rest of her warmed as Jason settled snuggly close next to her.

"This is wonderful," she repeated for the umpteenth time. A city girl at heart, she still appreciated the beauty and quiet of the country. Especially when it was shared with a hunk like Jason. If she had to describe her dream date, she'd describe a night exactly like this one.

"Yeah. I could get used to this real fast." He wrapped his free arm around her shoulders and gave them a squeeze and she tipped her head and let it rest on his shoulder. Oh yes, a dream date indeed. "What do you think about getting a place like this someday?" he asked.

"An orchard?"

"Maybe not an orchard, but a house with some land."

"I've never considered it. I'm not exactly a farm girl. Wouldn't know a crop of wheat from a crop of corn," she answered, trying to think of how Monica might answer his questions. Monica on a farm? It was as ridiculous as notion as hiring Paris Hilton to milk the cows.

"I wouldn't either," he confessed. With his free hand, he rubbed her arm. "Are you warm enough?"

"Sure am. Could you just imagine us on a farm? It would be like that old show, *Green Acres*. Did you watch that one when you were a kid?"

"Sure did! Yeah, we would probably look like the stupid city kids who don't know what they're doing. But I promise I won't have a pet pig in the house. Oh and we can have a phone inside." He kissed the top of her head. "I would hate to see you fall from that pole. Then again, if you landed on that cute butt of yours, I might have to kiss it to make it all better."

She glanced up at his face and he waggled an eyebrow.

Her face flaming, and not because of the fire, she gave him a playful nudge.

"Okay, maybe not. I'm scared of heights."

She chuckled and turned her hot dog. The underside was nice and toasted. "And think about how dangerous it would be to make a phone call during a thunderstorm."

"Good point. So, assuming I forgo the pet pig and outside phone, are you with me?"

She scanned the darkness and marveled at the sky. Amazed by how many stars she found overhead, so many more than she saw at home, she sighed. And fought with the temptation to say, hell yes! This was Monica's life she was talking about here, not hers. Monica's future husband and future home. "Don't tease me. I don't want to get my hopes up and then be disappointed."

"I don't ever want to disappoint you." He cupped her chin in his palm and lifted until her face turned toward his. Then he lowered his head.

Knowing what was coming, she closed her eyes.

His kiss was soft, erotic, but not demanding. His lips slid softly over hers and she held her breath and turned her body toward him. Determined to get closer, she dropped her stick to lift her arms and wrap them around his neck. Her breasts pressed against his chest and she gasped as his tongue slid into her mouth to taste her. Her fingers gripped soft, thick hair at his nape.

A sudden round of loud crackling and hissing in the fire made her break the kiss before it went any further. Still, even though the intimate contact had been brief, she was dazed a little and giddy. Focusing as she followed the line of her dropped stick to the fire was a challenge.

Eventually, her gaze got there and she realized her hot dog was gone.

"Oh drats! I lost my dog," she said, laughing. She picked up her stick and poked at a log, and brilliant red and gold sparks drifted into the night sky.

"I'll share mine." He carefully pulled his from the flame and together they wrapped it in the bun. Jason slathered one end with ketchup, the other with what relish, mustard and ketchup he could squeeze out of the mostly empty packets.

Jenny held the bun at the center between them and said, "Let's both take a bite on the count of three. Just promise you won't take my hand off."

His eyes glittered in the dim light. The flicker of the fire danced in them, making them lively and playful. "I may want your hand, but not to eat."

Did he mean what she thought he meant?

She didn't know how to respond, other than to count, "One, two, three." She leaned forward and bit into her end of the hot dog. It was warm, toasted, delicious. As she chewed, she closed her eyes. "Mmmm…"

He laughed and she opened her eyes to enjoy the sight. His whole face lit up when he was amused. He looked young and sexy and utterly adorable. She loved his dimples, the way his husky chuckles rumbled through her body like a deep tremor, the love she saw in his eyes as he looked at her.

"I've taken you to all of Detroit's finest restaurants and never have I seen you react like that."

"There's nothing better than a wiener cooked over an open fire…well, except for a steak—"

"With grilled onions?"

"Yeah. And lots of steak sauce. Oh, and a baked potato with the works."

"You're making me hungry," he teased.

She grinned and stuffed the rest of the hot dog into his mouth. "Then eat." His cheeks ballooned out as he accepted hot dog, bun and condiments and chewed. A smudge of ketchup clung to his lower lip and she wiped it away with her thumb. "Full now?" she asked between giggles.

His answer was a jumbled mumble.

"What was that?" She couldn't stop giggling. Being with this man made her feel so alive…and carefree…and wonderful. She hadn't felt like this since she was a kid. She wanted to skip, to jump, to shout with glee.

He swallowed. "Not quite. Do you want to get something else to eat?"

"Maybe in a bit. I don't want to leave yet. Can we stay a little longer?"

"Sure."

She moved from her perch on the log to the ground in front of him so she could lean back against his chest. He wrapped the blanket around them both, and warm and content, she gazed up at the sky. "Have you ever made a wish on a star?"

"Nope."

"Never? Not even when you were a little boy?"

"Heck no. I was raised not to believe in that silly stuff. Magic, wishes, dreams. My old man always said that kind of thing was for losers, guys who couldn't make things happen for themselves. He said you could either waste time dreaming about life or you could do something." He smoothed her hair away from her forehead with a broad palm.

Appreciating how a spoiled kitten might feel, and wishing she was capable of purring, she sighed. "He sounds tough. I don't think I'd want to be raised by a man who was so hard-hearted. And I know I wouldn't want to be married to one."

"He was one hell of an example, though. He knew how to take the most miserably failing company into the black. Hard worker, loyal, brilliant."

"I think there's a middle ground in there somewhere. Dreaming is good if you eventually stop thinking and start doing. Right?"

"Maybe. Dad might not have known how to be mushy, but he loved us the only way he knew how. He provided the best life he could." Jason gathered her hair into a ponytail then wrapped it around his hand.

"Us?" she asked, enjoying the slight sting on her scalp as he pulled slightly.

"Yeah. I've never told you this. I have a younger brother."

"Really? Why'd you keep him a secret all this time? Is he a wanted felon or something?" She reached both arms up and back over her head. Her hands stroked either side of his nylon ski jacket.

"No, nothing like that. He's a great guy. Lives in France. I never see him. He never sees me. We're very different."

"What about your mother? What's she like?"

"I swear I told you. She died…in childbirth," he said in a low voice. "I honestly don't remember much about her. Though Dad says she was the best mother a boy could have. Of course, knowing him, even if she'd been the worst mother in the world, he'd say that."

"Oh, I'm so sorry your mother is gone. I should've remembered that." She tapped her forehead and smiled up at him. "I'm a space case tonight. Forgive me. Is it painful to talk about her?"

"No, not at all." Looking very thoughtful and intense, he traced the line of her jaw with a fingertip. "So, now that we're talking about our families, you want to tell me about yours? We've been dating five years and I still haven't met them."

Distracted by his tickling, exploring touch, she said, "That is kind of strange. Does it bother you?"

"Yes."

"I don't blame you. I'd wonder what was up if I was dating a guy who wouldn't talk about his family. In fact, that happened to me once. I had this boyfriend and he wouldn't introduce me to his parents. Now that I look back on it, I'm sure he was ashamed of me for some reason."

Jason scowled. "For what?"

"I don't know. Maybe I wasn't blue-blooded enough for him. No big deal. I certainly don't care now. And rest assured, I'm not trying to hide you. I would never be ashamed of you."

"That's good to know. I'm not ashamed of you either. Quite the opposite. I'd like to show you off to the whole world. But you know, I'm an old-fashioned guy at heart. There are a few things I need to discuss with your folks before certain other things can take place," he hinted with a nod.

No way she could misunderstand what he was getting at.

"I'll see about giving them a call." She didn't know what else to say. Where was Monica's legendary rich father?

Did there even exist a rich father or was he another one of Monica's imaginary characters? It wouldn't be easy but she had to play it safe and answer Jason's questions with vague generalities, at least until she could get some more information. One thing was certain—since becoming Monica, she hadn't heard from a single family member, father, mother or sibling.

"I don't speak to them much at all. Can't remember the last time, to be honest. Daddy's always traveling," she added, recalling the stories Monica had told her once about her father's travels to the far east. "And Mother's usually either in a spa somewhere or spending Daddy's money in Europe. The woman's house is like a gallery but she can't resist the temptation of finding the next prized piece for her art collection."

His expression was very solemn as he nodded. "I guessed as much. Your folks were a lot like my father. They meant well, I'm sure." He bent lower, slid his hands under her armpits and wrapped his arms across her chest.

"Yeah," she half-spoke, half-sighed.

"I spent my childhood in boarding schools. I saw my father once a year, at Christmas."

"That's terrible." She couldn't imagine giving birth to a child and then handing him off to someone and not seeing him but once per year. It was a miracle Jason had grown into the gentle, caring man he was and not a cold jerk. Since he'd been robbed of years of love, she figured he was due more than his share as an adult.

She was eager to give it to him. Unfortunately, she had no idea if she'd have the chance. "My folks are no better than yours, I suppose. They have their lives and I have mine, not that I'm ungrateful for what they did for me. I have a terrific education, thanks to them. And a good job."

"So," he asked, stroking her cheek with his thumb, "when you told me all these years you were visiting your family during the holidays, were you lying?"

Oops! "Not…exactly." The sound of the tractor in the distance caught her attention. The timing couldn't be better. "Are we going back now?"

Jason tipped his wrist and rested his chin on the top of her head as he read the numbers on his watch. "I think this is the last wagon of the night. We better catch it just in case."

"Okay."

Jason didn't release her as he stood but pulled her to her feet with him. She leaned back for a moment, enjoying the way his strong bulk felt pressed against her. Then she bent to gather the blanket and trash.

Jason wrapped a protective arm around her shoulder as they walked and whispered into her ear, "I know we're supposed to be starting over, but how about going home and making love? It's a perfect way to end this perfect night."

Jenny's heart jumped into her throat. Tingles and heat waves zigged and zagged through her body in an instant response to his suggestion.

How could she say no? That word was the last thing she wanted to say.

Jason rested a possessive hand on her thigh as he drove them back to her place. With the frequent flirting glances and slight squeezes to her leg, his intentions were clear. Jason wanted nookie.

Jenny wanted nookie.

Neither one of them would get it. At least not if Jenny could somehow manage to resist. As his fingers inched higher, tickling her inner thigh, her ability to think quickly dissolved.

"I've been waiting all night. I want to make love to you under the stars," he murmured. His hand slid higher until it reached the juncture of her thighs. Through the thick fabric of her jeans he stroked her until she was a mass of spineless jelly.

She felt herself parting her legs, giving him more access to the sensitive area. Waves of pleasure pulsed through her body as he rubbed harder. She moaned and let her eyelids drop over her eyes.

Cloaked in darkness, she wallowed in the sweet joy of his touch and of the promises he muttered as he drove.

"I've missed you, Monica. Missed you so damn much. I want to make you cry out my name as you come. We'll come together like we used to."

The car stopped and she opened her eyes, surprised to see they were already at her house. Jason got out and opened her door for her. As she unlocked the front door, he stood behind her, his full length pressed against her. She felt the bulge of his erection pressing against her butt.

She fumbled with the lock, dropped the key twice. When she bent over to pick it up, Jason held her hips in his hands and rubbed that bulge against her butt suggestively. She felt every bit of her resolve melting away.

A little voice inside her head said, *No, no, no! I can't!*

A louder voice inside her head said, *Yes, yes, yes you can!*

When she finally got the lock to work, she shoved open the door and practically ran through it, barreling through the living room in a desperate last-ditch effort to get away from him long enough to gather her defenses.

He didn't give her much time. After closing and locking the door behind him, he turned and grinned. "Oh yeah. I love this game! We haven't played it in a long time. I thought you'd forgotten. Run, you little tease. I'll catch you. I'll make you pay for what you've done to me tonight."

Good God! What had she gotten herself into? What kind of kinky game was this? He was acting so different. So…aggressive. She liked it.

Despite her rising temperature and the steady throb between her legs, she waved her arms and shook her head. "Oh, no. I'm not playing."

His grin was wicked, sexy, disarming as he took long, slow strides toward her. "You're doing a fine job of acting. Been taking more classes?"

Backing herself into a corner, she muttered, not so much because she was intimidated but because she was tempted, "Seriously, Jason."

He didn't stop until he was standing inches away from her. He lifted his arms and pressed his palms against the wall on either side of her head, trapping her between the wall and his bulk. Then he leaned closer and kissed her.

Sensation, sound, touch, taste, amplified until her brain was unable to register them. His tongue stroked and prodded. His hands explored her body. He unzipped her jacket and pushed it down her arms then kneaded her breasts and pinched her nipples through the remaining layers of clothing. They felt both too thin to protect her skin from his touch yet too thick to allow it to penetrate to her deepest nerve endings.

Her throat constricted, blocking any words of resistance that might have tried to escape. She could merely moan. And that she did. More than once. The sound echoed in their joined mouths.

One of his hands reached to the top of her head and gathered a fist full of her hair and tugged slightly, urging her to tip her head to one side. He trailed kisses and licks and nibbles down her neck until her entire upper body was blanketed in gooseflesh and her legs were so wobbly and weak she was forced to cling to him in order to remain standing.

The little voice in her head—the one that was growing more distant by the second—made one final appeal before declaring defeat. *You can't do this. It's not fair to Monica or Jason!*

It was no small feat to speak whilst Jason performed magic with her body, but she managed to whisper, "Stop, please."

Jason paused for a moment, his gaze searching her face. "Are you still playing?"

"No."

"What's wrong?"

"As much as I want to, we can't do this right now."

"Why? Is it that time of the month? I mean, I completely understand if—"

"Yes!" she said a little too enthusiastically. She sobered her voice as she explained. "I mean, I'm very sorry but I'm having terrible cramps this month. You don't mind waiting, do you? We could…talk for a while longer if you like."

"No, that's okay. I should probably get going." He glanced at his wristwatch. "I'm catching an early flight tomorrow morning."

A chill crept over her arms and shoulders. "You're leaving?"

"For a few days. Will you miss me?"

A deep ache settled in her belly at the thought of not seeing him. Maybe it had been only a short time, but to her it felt as if she'd always known him, as if he'd always been there. She knew there would be a huge empty void with him gone, no matter how long or short it was. "Yes, I will," she answered honestly.

"I'll miss you too. But it's business. I'll be back Tuesday. I'll bring you a surprise."

She took a second to wonder what kind of surprise a man like Jason would bring from a business trip. She guessed it would be better than an uneaten package of airline peanuts. That had been the one and only gift she'd ever received from a boyfriend before. And she'd thought it had been quite thoughtful. After all, it had been a meal-less flight and five hours long. The poor guy had gone hungry all that time for her.

"That sounds very nice, but unnecessary," she said, slumping onto the couch and reaching for the throw slung over the arm. She wrapped it around her shoulders.

"I want to." He sat next to her, leaned forward and, hot again, she threw off the throw and braced herself for another one of those soul-searing kisses. Unfortunately, or fortunately depending upon how she looked at it, all he gave her was a slightly longer-than-normal peck on the cheek. "I can't wait to see your face when you open it."

"You're very sweet." She rested her palm against his jaw and tried to burn the expression she saw in his eyes into her memory forever. If she did eventually return to her old life as Jenny Brown, she wanted to remember how it felt to see that look on a man's face—of genuine, undisguised love—for the rest of her life. It might be the only time she'd ever see it.

"I'll call you Monday night," he said, standing.

She forced herself to her feet and leaned into him, wrapping her arms around his middle and pressing her ear against his chest. His heartbeat was a soft, steady thump in her ear. The sting of tears burned her eyes.

It was only going to be a few days. She couldn't really understand why she was getting so emotional. It wasn't like she'd never see him again…unless…

Trying hard not to look like a clingy, whimpering whiner, she followed him to the front door, gave him a breathy "goodbye and thanks" and watched him get into his car and drive away.

And then she went to bed.

Sunday dragged by as she sat by the phone waiting for his call. By eleven Sunday night she gave up, assuming he wouldn't be able to call her until Monday like he'd promised. Monday, she went to work and she and Monica worked together on their projects. They swapped what-I-did-over-the-weekend stories. A little guilty, Jenny intentionally left out Saturday night's date. For some reason, it just felt wrong telling Monica about the date, kind of like she was cheating or something. However, she did mention that Jason was keeping in contact and left it at that.

She wasn't exactly sure how she'd proceed. Falling in love, marrying, having Jason's children. That sounded like heaven. The perfect life. If it meant living out the rest of her life as Monica, then she was willing to make the sacrifice. She wondered if Monica would ever forgive her.

Monday night, after a short phone conversation with a jet-lagged Jason, she tossed and turned, restless. Her face and hands itched which didn't help. Desperate for some sleep, she smoothed on some calamine lotion and returned to bed. But like when she was sick, what dreams she had as she drifted in and out of a shallow slumber were strange, vivid and lifelike. Sometime after three in the morning, she peered at the clock one last time before falling into a deeper sleep.

Tuesday morning, she woke to the sound of morning rush hour barreling down the nearby freeway. At least the burning itch was gone.

Chapter Ten

ꟻ

"Damn it!" she yelled before she'd even opened her eyes. No doubt about it, she was back home—in Jenny Brown's apartment. The loud traffic and scratchy Army blanket had been dead giveaways long before she'd bothered to look.

Everything else was probably back to normal too.

Ready to confirm her suspicions, she threw off the covers and glanced down at her chest.

Back to barely-there double As, thighs that were a tad too meaty to be considered sexy, and a tummy that was a little soft and lumpy to be seen in the light of day. Ultra-white from lack of sunlight, it reminded her of a slightly molten marshmallow. "Hello there," she said to her less desirable parts, not exactly clear how she felt about being back to her old self and old life.

There were reasons to celebrate—like her lighter workload and hopefully solid financial status, assuming Monica hadn't maxed out all her credit cards and buried her under a heap of debt already.

But then there was also the obvious drawback, and it was a biggie—a whopper.

Jason.

Not in a hurry to get to work, for the first time since she'd started there, she took her time dressing, checking out the new clothes Monica had stocked her closet with, and fighting to style her new haircut after an extra-long, extra-hot shower.

Thanks to the switch, she figured she'd be facing an exuberant Monica at work this morning. Although Monica had stopped complaining about Jenny's less-than-glamorous home and lifestyle, she knew Monica had to be relieved to have her beautiful home and boyfriend back.

Of course, that meant Jenny had a little explaining to do, even more reason to drag her feet.

Resisting the urge to call in sick, Jenny finally forced herself out the front door. Her new car wasn't a Lexus, or a Honda, but it rode reasonably well and it had a certain sex appeal. The heater worked great too, blasting toasty air after the car had been running only a few minutes. Nothing rattled or clanked when she went over the speed bumps in her apartment complex. That was a bonus.

When she got to work and settled into her cubicle, she missed the spacious office a little bit, but not too much. Thankful for the fact that Monica hadn't come gleefully screaming the minute Jenny had arrived, she set to work immediately. Evidently, Monica had some more important matters to attend to.

But there was one small drawback—she sure missed their morning brainstorming sessions, having Monica to toss ideas back and forth with. Over the past week, they'd become quite a team and she'd produced some of the best work of her career. Everyone, including herself, had been impressed. Would she be able to continue without Monica forcing her to really exercise her mind and come up with original and exciting layouts?

Resolved to do her best, she set to work on her first project, a coupon advertisement for a pet store, but right away she found her mind wandering.

Where was Jason? What would he say when he called tonight? She missed him so much even her teeth ached. Her innards felt hollow yet heavy at the same time.

Then another thought occurred to her. Monica would be the one to welcome him home with a hug and a kiss, not her. That thought did nothing to lighten her gloomy mood.

Shit! She had no right to be jealous but she was anyway. Even though she'd assumed someday she'd return to her life, a part of her had hoped… Oh, there was no use dwelling on the impossible.

Monica's life was Monica's again…and so was Jason.

"Hey, we need to talk," Monica whispered from behind her, reminding her of where she was.

"Maybe later. I'm pretty busy right now." She moved the mouse around and pretended to be hard at work, knowing full well Monica could see her screen was blank.

"It might be just me, but I've found it's easier to use the software when it's running," Monica teased. "What's wrong? Aren't you happy to be back to your life? After all the crummy things you said about mine, I figured you'd be dancing in with bells on."

"Sure, I'm very happy." Even to herself, her voice sounded dead flat. She decided to look busy for real and at least get her design software loaded. It took a few minutes for it to open.

"You could at least say thanks for all the hard work I've done with your hair, makeup and clothes," Monica said, sounding hurt. "It wasn't easy losing those five pounds, you know. I swear your body is addicted to sugar. I had to throw away practically everything in your cupboards to keep from bingeing."

Funny, she'd completely forgotten to eat this morning.

"Thanks," Jenny said. "That was very kind of you, making such a painful sacrifice." She turned to glance over her shoulder. Monica's face was swollen, red and covered with terrible-looking oozing blisters. "My God! What happened to your face?"

"Doctor said it's a delayed reaction to poison ivy. You wouldn't happen to know where I came into contact with that, would you?" Monica dragged a spare chair up and positioned herself in it, crossing her long legs and swinging a designer shoe-clad foot. "He said it's going to take a couple of weeks for the itching and swelling to go away."

At the moment, Jenny couldn't think of a time in her life where she'd been more regretful. "I'm so sorry. I went hiking in the woods this past weekend. It was dark and I couldn't see… Gosh, I can't believe you came to work like this."

"Yeah. Brings to mind the Elephant Man, doesn't it?" Monica raised a hand to her grotesquely swollen cheek. "But what else could I do? I can't afford to miss two whole weeks. You know what my finances look like. By the way, thanks for doing such a nifty job with my checkbook."

Jenny slipped her feet out of her pinching shoes. She sure missed those Manolo Blahniks! "No problem."

"Seriously, no one's ever bothered to teach me how to balance my checkbook. I appreciate it. It felt wonderful looking at my caller ID this morning and not seeing a single 'private call' or collection agency. I can't tell you when that's happened last."

"It wasn't such a big deal."

"Maybe not for you."

The software finally up and running, Jenny opened a new document and stared at the blank white screen. "You're welcome. I'm truly sorry about the poison ivy."

"Don't worry about it. I'll get over it. Say, I wanted to ask you a couple of things."

Oh no. She had a sneaking suspicion she wasn't going to like the questions Monica was about to ask. For one thing, Monica was being mighty understanding about her hideously disfigured face. Was revenge on her agenda? "Oh?"

"First, would you like to continue to meet every morning to brainstorm our projects like we have been? I really enjoyed that."

So far, so good. "Sure. I enjoyed it too."

"Excellent!" Monica crossed her arms over her chest. "Second, I was wondering…what's Jason calling and leaving messages on my answering machine about surprises and last Saturday's date all about?"

Uh-oh! "He did?" She tried to look surprised.

"Yeah, he did." Monica did not sound so thrilled, not that Jenny could blame her. Jenny could imagine the assumptions she would make if the roles were reversed and she'd returned to find her ex-boyfriend leaving friendly messages on her answering machine if last she recalled they hadn't been speaking.

Here goes! "Well, I thought you'd be happy…"

Monica leaned closer. The blazes igniting in her eyes weren't reassuring. "What did you do?"

"I honestly felt I was doing you a favor. I mean, you said you wanted him back, wanted to marry him someday. It started the night he had the car repossessed. I went there to give him a piece of my mind and we started talking…and then we bumped into each other at a nightclub…and next thing I knew it he was asking me—I mean you!—out on a date."

"Just tell me, did you—I mean, I—sleep with him?"

"No. I swear, I would never do that to you."

Visibly deep in thought, Monica leaned back and blinked several times. Her left eyelid kind of hung there at half-mast, thanks to the swelling. She nodded. "So what happened?"

"He said he was falling in love with you all over again," Jenny answered, hoping that might cast a rosy-colored light on the situation.

It worked. A hint of a smile bloomed over Monica's disfigured face. "He did? What else did he say?"

"He said you've changed."

Monica scowled. "How have I changed? What did you say to him?"

"Well…I told him I wanted to get married and have kids. I didn't know you'd told him you didn't want those things until after I said it," Jenny lied.

"Shit. What else?"

"Oh, I don't know. I can't remember all the details. Oh…um…I ate some red meat." She cringed.

"You didn't!"

"And ice cream. But you have to believe me. Nothing happened with Jason. Our first date was spent in the hospital emergency room, thanks to your allergy to bees, and so all we could do was talk—"

"I was stung? Where?"

"Yeah. On your head. But as you can see, you're fine now. Well, sorta fine. The poison ivy was from your second date. We…er, you…went to the cider mill and a bonfire. Jason seems to be coming round. He brought flowers and said the nicest things."

"He's so sweet, isn't he?" Monica sighed. "I'm just worried that he isn't in love with me. It sounds like he's in love with *you*."

Hearing those words made Jenny's heart skip more than a beat or two. She attributed her reaction to several things. "No way. He loves you. He's a guy. He believes what he sees. How could he love someone like me? We look very different." Jenny knew darn well who she was trying to convince and it wasn't Monica.

"In case you haven't noticed—and I believe you have—he's a little deeper thinking than your typical shallow-minded guy."

I know. He's perfect. "Still, I'm plain. You're…stunning. I saw the way he looked at you. There was something—a glimmer—in his eyes, like in the movies. It was very romantic."

"Sounds like you've fallen in love with him too."

"No. Absolutely not." Jenny said with far more conviction than she felt.

"Are you sure?"

"Positive."

"He's a cutie. I wouldn't blame you."

"Nope. Through the whole thing I reminded myself he's your boyfriend, not mine. Like I said, look at me. I don't compare."

"Hey, with the new clothes and hair, I'd call you a babe."

"You're being kind."

"I might even be a little jealous of you. I didn't tell you this but I went to one of my favorite hot spots last weekend and a guy I've seen around here and there—a guy who'd never give me the time of day—flirted with you!"

"He didn't. You're lying."

"I have his phone number to prove it." Monica motioned toward Jenny's purse. "May I?"

"Sure." Jenny handed it to her and watched as Monica rummaged through the contents.

"Aha! Here you go." Looking quite pleased with herself, Monica produced a business card with a smudgy phone number scribbled on the back. She looked down at it, her fingertips toying with the edges. Her expression was a little forlorn. "His name is Bill and he's an absolute babe. We talked all night long." With a smile that looked forced, she handed the card to Jenny. "But this belongs to you now."

Jenny shook her head. "No thanks."

"Seriously, take it. He's very sexy. And who would've thought a man who works with his hands could be loaded? He drove a Beemer."

"Business must be good."

"Real good." Monica tried to hand Jenny the card again. "Even if you don't want to date him, he's an electrician. You never know when one of those might come in handy."

"I live in an apartment."

"So?"

"You're the one who has a house."

"That doesn't matter. You have electricity too."

Jenny shook her head. "Never mind. Guess you've never been a renter before."

"I've never dated a man who works with his hands before—unless you count the banker. I have to admit, dating a working man holds a certain appeal."

Like she could take the card now! Not! "You keep it. Maybe if things don't work out with Jason you could—"

"No. I mentioned myself and he said he knew me, thought I was too high-maintenance." Monica giggled. "Can you just imagine?" She wound a lock of hair around her index finger.

"Nope."

"Me? High-maintenance."

"Never."

Monica drew the card closer, obviously preparing to tuck it away somewhere safe, a pocket or in her bra maybe. "Are you sure you won't take it?"

"Positive."

"Okay," Monica said on a sigh. "You can't say I didn't offer."

Jenny merely nodded. This was weird. She didn't have a claim on Jason, who thought she was Monica. She didn't have a claim on Bill either, who thought she was Jenny, but the Jenny Monica had been, who couldn't be anything like the Jenny she was now…

Things couldn't be any more confusing!

"But he likes you," Monica said, still holding the card.

"It doesn't feel right for some reason," Jenny admitted.

"I know. But neither does me going out with Jason. It isn't fair if I get both of them." She giggled. "Listen to me. That sounds silly."

"What else can we do?"

"I don't know."

"Do you still care for Jason?" Jenny asked, hoping Monica would say she honestly didn't.

Still, what would that do for her anyway? Jenny wasn't the tall, skinny bombshell Monica was. What hope did she have that even if given the chance Jason would be able to see past her plain-Jane features?

"Yes, I do care about him. He's a very sweet guy. Attractive, giving, caring."

That wasn't what she'd wanted to hear, but that was probably for the better anyway. She nodded and bit her upper lip in an effort to keep it from quivering. "Have a great time tonight."

"I'm sorry," Monica said, standing. "I can tell this is upsetting you."

"It's not your fault. I knew what I was getting into when I decided to get involved. I could've stayed out of it and let you work it out later."

Monica leaned down, took Jenny's hand in hers, and gave it a slight squeeze. "I owe you. Big time. Any favor. You name it."

Jenny forced a smile, even though her insides felt like they'd been yanked from her body and run over by a Mack truck—no, a whole fleet of Mack trucks. "How about starting right now and helping me with this project? I'm having a hard time coming up with a decent layout."

"Fair enough." Monica sat again and scooted the chair beside Jenny's. "What do you have so far?"

"An empty screen?"

Monica smiled. "Well, that's a good start."

The rest of the day dragged by, and by seven that night, Jenny swore the minutes were lasting at least an hour each. Time had slowed to a snail's pace.

Hour after hour she sat alone in her little apartment staring at the TV but not comprehending the images playing on the screen. Her mind was on one thing and refused to budge from it.

Had Jason called Monica? Were they together now? Were they making love?

Lying on the couch, she curled into a tight ball and drew the throw up over her shoulders, clutching it tight to her chest. The apartment was dark, except the blue-tinted glow of the TV screen. And silent except for the tinny-toned voices coming from the junky TV's half-blown speakers.

"Damn it," she called into the night. "Why did I have to come back now? I wasn't ready yet."

Chapter Eleven

ജ

Jason flipped open the black velvet-covered box again, to admire the gorgeous platinum setting and even more beautiful brilliant cut five-carat diamond nestled between two half-carat natural rubies on either side. The ring was one of a kind, a true work of art.

He was proud to be able to present it to Monica. But outside of pride, he felt surprisingly void of emotion. He'd always assumed this moment he'd be an emotional wreck, not his cool, calm self.

Part of his lack of enthusiasm he attributed to Monica's seeming reversion to her old self the past few days. While she wasn't exactly the self-centered, spoiled girl-woman she had been previously, she wasn't the warm, caring, genuine woman he'd spent the last couple of weekends with either. How could her personality yo-yo back and forth so drastically? Was it hormonal? If so, he could only imagine what she'd be like when she was pregnant.

But he wasn't about to let a few doubts hold him back now. He'd made a promise to her Tuesday and by God, he'd live by it. She had greeted him with so much enthusiasm when he'd returned from his most recent trip. She acted like she hadn't seen him in weeks, made promises he'd never thought he'd hear spoken from her lips and then told him she was ready for marriage and asked if his last proposal was still good.

What other response could he give?

It had taken him a few days to see she'd changed again, but he couldn't break a promise over a little bit of moodiness. She'd said she missed him, needed him, couldn't stand being without him. What more could he want?

He stuffed the box in his pocket and knocked on her front door. It was time to make the commitment he'd waited five long years for.

When Monica answered the door, it was clear she knew exactly what was coming. Her smile was dazzling, her clothing, hair and makeup perfect, exactly the way he'd come to expect. She didn't wait for him to enter before she lifted her arms and looped them around his neck. Yet her lackluster embrace stirred little response from him, not even mild lust. She brushed her lips over his cheek and he made no effort to make the kiss more intimate.

Chemistry, or rather lack thereof, did not mean a marriage was doomed.

"Hello, sweetheart." She dropped her arms, captured his hands in hers and walked backward into the house, pulling him in with her. "You said you had something to ask me?"

Knowing he had no reason to delay, he dropped on one knee in the middle of her living room, extracted the box from his pocket, and asked, "Monica Starke, will you marry me?"

She looked as happy as he'd expect any woman to be as she watched him flip open the box and pluck the diamond ring from it. "Yes, I will."

He slid the ring on her finger. It was done.

* * * * *

Monica didn't show up for work for the rest of the week, not only leaving Jenny to wonder what had happened with Jason on Tuesday night but also struggling to complete her projects without the benefit of her brainstorming partner. She did the best she could at work—the results a far cry from spectacular—and nights she made every effort to keep busy. Spending hour upon hour imagining what was happening between Monica and Jason got old after one torturous night. She had pride. Allowing herself to succumb to pointless what-ifs just wasn't acceptable.

Instead, she took a second look at her finances and discovered she could finally afford buying a house of her own. Scouring the homes for sale on the Internet was a very potent salve, though it didn't obliterate the pain of losing Jason completely.

That Sunday, she even hit a few open houses nearby and found a very personable, down-to-earth real estate agent to work with. Her quest to buy a home was in full gear. Fall wasn't the best time of year to house shop, with fewer homes on the market. But the ones that were tended to be sold by more motivated sellers, meaning a better opportunity to find a deal.

Monday morning, she headed to work with spirits lifted and her eye on another raise. Come hell or high water, she'd prove to Mr. Kaufmann that she could deliver!

Unfortunately, her mood soured shortly after arriving when Monica pulled her into her office and flashed a rock the size of Mt. Everest and a smile so bright it put the sun to shame. The ring was noticeably positioned on her left ring finger.

"He proposed," Monica said in an excited voice as she urged Jenny to sit. "And I know what you're thinking—"

"What do you think I'm thinking?" Jenny asked as she reluctantly lowered herself onto the chair.

"That I said I didn't want to get married." Monica rounded her desk and took her seat.

"Right." *Not even close, but that's okay.* "So, what about that itty-bitty, insignificant detail?"

"Well, I did some soul-searching after Jason popped the question—he did it at my house, couldn't even wait until we got to our favorite restaurant. It was so romantic." Monica clasped her hands together and closed her eyes, visibly sighing. The sight was a bit sickening but Jenny struggled to maintain a smile. "I got caught up in the moment and without thinking said yes."

Thank God, she's doubting her decision. Shoot, what am I saying? This is what I wanted for her, isn't it? "So you don't really want to marry him?"

Monica nodded enthusiastically. "I think I do. I mean, I spent the rest of the weekend considering it and I have to say I'm excited."

"Really?"

Monica produced a thick wedding magazine from somewhere under her desk and began flipping through the pages. "I've never been a sappy romantic, but a fancy wedding with all the best—caterers, photographers, a wedding planner—sounds really fun. I'm thinking of doing a theme wedding, maybe getting married New Year's Eve. Wouldn't that be a riot? Look here." She held up the magazine and pointed at a page of wedding attendees dressed in black, white and silver.

"An absolute gas," Jenny said dryly.

Monica set the magazine down and gazed directly into Jenny's eyes. "And I want you to be my maid of honor."

"You're kidding."

"Oh no. If it wasn't for you, Jason would still hate me for giving away his grandmother's old junk."

It wasn't junk. Jenny had to avert her gaze. Monica's direct eye contact was making her very uncomfortable. She reached across the desk and pulled the magazine closer, staring blindly at the open page. "Don't you have a sister or an old friend from college you should ask instead? I mean, shouldn't your maid of honor be someone special you've known for a long, long time? A lot longer than we've known each other?"

"Nope. Besides, we have known each other long, since high school."

"I had no idea you'd noticed me back then."

"I didn't but I take your word for it. Who cares how long it's been! You deserve this honor. Please say yes!" She stood and reached across the desk, clasping Jenny's hand between hers, forcing Jenny to look up. "Pretty please?"

Jenny wiggled her fingers, pulling her hand free from Monica's tight grasp. "I don't know. I've never been a maid of honor before. Doesn't it require a lot of work?"

"No, just a little."

Jenny glanced down at the magazine, this time really seeing the picture. The clothes were fancy, the flowers, the wedding gown… "And I can tell you're planning the wedding of the century. What if I pick the wrong flowers? Or contract the wrong band? Or sit Aunt LouLou next to Uncle Hank, the man she's hated all her life?"

"Those aren't your jobs, silly."

"See? I told you. I don't know anything about being maid of honor. Or even about planning a wedding."

Monica sat and bent to the right to reach down for something under her desk. "That's okay. I'm hiring a wedding planner. She's the best in the Midwest."

"Midwest what?"

"States, silly!" Monica slid a piece of paper across the desk toward Jenny.

Jenny skimmed the contents, a printout of a website. "You're hiring a wedding planner from out of state? Is that wise?"

"Sure it is! Don't you see? She planned Oprah's wedding for God's sake! How could I go wrong?"

"Oprah who?" Jenny looked at the web printout again, wondering what she'd missed.

"Winfrey. You know. The woman on TV, you silly goof!"

"Is she married?"

"Yep. And my wedding planner did her wedding. It was on her website. See there?" Monica pointed at the paper.

"This website? Where?" Jenny read over the contents of the website again but found no reference to Oprah Winfrey. Was her eyesight failing or was Monica imagining things again?

"Yes. I know it's there." Monica took the piece of paper from Jenny and skimmed it before continuing, "Oh. I guess I missed that page. It's on another one. She's planned hundreds of weddings, including the weddings of celebrities like Oprah."

"I swear last week I read Oprah's still single."

"You probably read it in an outdated article somewhere or in one of those celebrity trash rags. They're not exactly known for accuracy."

"Maybe. But if I were you, I'd check her references. She did provide a list of references, didn't she?"

"Are you crazy? I'm not going to ask her that."

"Why not? This is going to be the most important day of your life. Don't you think you should check her out?"

Shaking her head, Monica returned the paper to whatever file she'd fished it from. "And risk insulting her? No way! I already gave her a retainer. I'll lose it if I don't hire her now."

"A retainer? Like for an attorney? Is that standard practice?"

Monica shrugged. "She said it is."

Jenny could sense this wedding planner was not all she claimed to be. The word "rip-off" was echoing sharply in her head and even though she knew Monica wouldn't listen, she felt compelled to try to talk some sense into her anyway. She was stubborn like that, or foolish, depending upon how she looked at it. "Okay. Forget about the whole Oprah thing for a moment and think about this. How can a woman from another state possibly know where the best locations, caterers and bands are here in Michigan? Where's she located anyway?"

"Idaho."

"Idaho? Your top-notch celebrity wedding planner lives in Idaho? Where they grow potatoes?"

"That's not all they do there. Besides, if you think about it, Idaho is centrally located—"

"Centrally located between what? Two potato fields?"

Monica sneered. "Very funny."

"Seriously, I see disaster looming."

"Don't say that! You're going to jinx me." Monica spun around in her chair, facing the credenza behind her. "Anyway, I won't take no for an answer. So like it or not, you're my maid of honor. And as chosen maid of honor, it's your job to go check out this location this Friday night." She snatched up a business card and turning, thrust it at Jenny.

Jenny waved her hands. "Oh no. Don't leave this to me. The last party I planned—a simple outdoor barbeque—was a complete disaster. The food burned, there was a tornado…half the attendees ended up being blown into the lake… Anyway, I thought this was the wedding planner's job. I'm sure you're paying her good money. Don't you think she should earn it?"

"She's busy this weekend with another wedding and I need to secure a location pronto. It can't wait." She stood and shuffled around the desk then dropped to her knees. It was a very dramatic gesture and if it wasn't for the genuine expression on Monica's face, Jenny would have assumed it was merely a manipulation tactic. Long fingers tipped with perfectly manicured, red-painted nails curled around the metal arm of Jenny's chair. "Please. I'm begging you. I know I've been a total snot to you in the past and I don't deserve your help, but I honestly need it. You know I've learned a lot, thanks to our little switch, and I appreciate where you're coming from now. I swear I won't take you for granted again."

Gosh, darn it, Jenny felt the urge to say yes welling up inside. When Monica was humble, like this particular moment, she was charming.

It was easy to say no to a selfish, annoying Monica. It wasn't easy to say no to a nice one.

"Honestly, you might not believe this but you're my only true friend," Monica admitted in a soft voice. "I don't have anyone else to ask."

Jenny knew this was true and that made her feel guilty. Still, she wasn't thrilled about going on Friday. For some reason she suspected it would come back to bite her somehow. "Couldn't you go check out the location yourself?"

"I have to interview the woman I'm considering to perform the ceremony. No one else can do that. She'll want to talk to me as well, I'm sure."

That was probably true. Jenny glanced down at the card. The location wasn't far from her home. It wouldn't take long to take a quick tour. "Okay," she acquiesced on a sigh.

Monica jumped up and clapped her hands with glee. "Thank you! I'm so grateful!" She bent over and gave Jenny a strangling hug. Then returned to her seat behind her desk and looking more sober said, "Now, on to business. What projects are we brainstorming today?"

* * * * *

By Friday evening, Jenny hadn't exactly grown comfortable with the idea of Monica marrying Jason, but at least she didn't feel like upchucking every time she thought about it.

Some progress was better than none.

As she drove to the reception hall, she vowed to help make Monica's wedding as special as she could, nausea or not. Despite her feelings for Jason, or perhaps because of them, she knew Monica and Jason deserved the wedding of their dreams.

It was still semi-light outside when she pulled into the driveway but sundown was quickly approaching. The western sky was covered with brilliant shades of purple, salmony-pink and gold. The eastern sky was already a deep, dusk-blue. A glance at the clock on her dash revealed what she'd already known—she was late. She parked the car and headed inside.

Crisp leaves crunched under her feet. More, bright red and orange, clung to the tree branches arcing overhead from a row of maples lining each side of the walkway. A gentle breeze smelled fresh and earthy as it whirled around her, throwing her hair about her face. She regretted having to go inside, especially since the day had been unseasonably warm. But there was no time to dilly-dally.

She entered the building, marveling at the plush interior, white marble floor, humongous crystal chandelier that looked like it belonged in a Beverly Hills mansion, and followed the signs indicating where the office was located. The door was ajar and she could hear male voices inside. One of them sounded familiar.

Jason?

"My fiancée said she may not make it tonight," she heard him say. "But if she doesn't, I believe a friend of hers is supposed to come in her place, her maid of honor."

She reached up to knock but before her knuckles made contact with the door, it swung open, revealing Jason's very handsome, very surprised face. His lips curled into a smile and she found herself staring, breathless and dizzy. Their gazes locked. "Hi," she murmured, feeling totally out of place. She forced her gaze from Jason's brilliant eyes, so familiar, so warm, and sought out the other inhabitant of the room beyond.

A white-haired gentleman stepped up behind Jason and extended a hand and a friendly smile, "My, my. Is this your blushing bride?" he asked in a deep bass voice. "I'm George Harrington. Nice to meet you."

She almost forgot which body she was in and hence didn't deny his assumption right away. Luckily, she remembered before introducing herself as Monica. She leaned forward and reached beyond Jason to shake the gentleman's hand. "Hello, I'm Jenny. Jenny Brown, Monica's maid of honor. Monica couldn't make it today. She asked me to come in her place."

As she glanced at Jason, she caught the spark of recognition in his eyes and knew he had remembered her name.

"Jenny Brown?" Jason said, offering a handshake.

She accepted, curling her fingers around his wide hand. "Yep, that's me all right."

He reached with his second one and fully enclosed her smaller hand between his. His grip was firm yet gentle. His voice was low and husky, unearthing all sorts of naughty memories of when she'd last heard him speak in such a voice. After a kiss. "I'm glad to meet you. I was beginning to think you were a figment of Monica's imagination."

Her whole body tingled. She held back a shudder. "I can see why you'd wonder that. She does have an active imagination, that girl." Jenny felt her face heating as Jason's gaze paused at each of her features.

He chuckled and she relished the sound, willing it to permeate her pores and soak into her soul. She knew she'd missed him but until this moment hadn't realized how much. Her entire body ached with the need to be closer to him.

Just a little closer. A hug would be nice.

When he released her hand, she wanted to cry.

"I didn't expect you to be here. I figured you'd be with Monica," Jenny said.

"Oh, damn—darn! Sorry. Should watch my language." He glanced at the reception hall's manager. "I forgot I was supposed to go meet with some reverend tonight."

"You honestly forgot?" Jenny asked, not believing his claim. For one, he didn't sound the least bit sorry.

"No," he admitted. "You got me. I confess. I had to meet the woman who'd single-handedly accomplished the impossible."

"I didn't..." She sensed he wanted to say more but wasn't sure if she wanted him to continue or not. It was a rather precarious position she'd found herself in, considering her feelings for both Monica and Jason. Being in the middle was getting more complicated by the second.

"You know you did. I just want to say I owe you a thank you," he said, stuffing both hands in his pants pockets. "I figured if I didn't say it today it might never be said."

"Really, you don't owe me a thing." She tried to look casual as she shrugged her shoulders. "It was my pleasure." Wasn't that the truth! "Monica's life was…a bit of a mess and she knew it. I'm just glad I was able to help."

"She rarely listens to anyone," Jason admitted, his blatant honesty surprising her. Was he looking for an ally? Had Monica changed back to the manipulator she'd once been? He glanced back at the banquet hall manager again. Clearly the gentleman was anxious to get going. "Looks like we need to attend to some other matters at the moment, but promise me we'll talk later?"

"Sure." *About what? I can't wait. Well, maybe I can. What I really wish is we could do more than talk, share another one of those kisses…no, I can't think like that! Bad Jenny, bad! Shit, shit, shit!*

The banquet hall's manager urged them forward, leading them down the hallway and through the spacious foyer to a wide staircase. "This way, please." At the top of the stairs, he paused before a set of double doors. "This is our largest suite. It seats four hundred fifty. Linens, chairs and tables are included in the price." He pushed open the doors, revealing the room's posh interior.

It was dazzling. The décor was elegant, fancy without being too garish. But the part Jenny liked the best was the wide expanse of windows running the length of one entire wall. Damask draperies framed a breathtaking view of the gold, orange and red fall foliage outside.

"Wow," was all Jenny could manage to utter.

"In the winter we decorate those trees with thousands of white lights. It's truly magnificent," the manager said.

"Is it available New Year's Eve?" Jenny asked.

"At the moment, yes. All the other rooms have been booked. This is the only one available."

"The price?" Jason sounded less than impressed.

"Total, including the meal would be in the twenty-thousand range, depending upon your choice of entrée."

Jason and Jenny both coughed.

Their host didn't look pleased by their reaction. "You're talking about four hundred plates, sir. Surely you don't expect to pay less than forty per plate."

"Silly me. Will that be a cash bar?" Jason asked.

"Yes, but for another five thousand, I can offer a free bar with wine, beer, liquors and soft drinks."

Jason, looking a little green around the gills, shook his head. "We'll be in touch." He headed toward the exit.

Jenny did the same.

"I expect the room will be booked by the end of the week," the manager said, following them.

"We'll take our chances," Jason responded over his shoulder as he shuffled down the staircase. He waited at the exit for Jenny and pushed the door open for her.

She waited until she got outside before she spoke a word. "It was gorgeous but that price!"

He paused in the front courtyard and turned to face the building. "I refuse to pay that. She'll just have to understand."

"I'm sure she will."

He shook his head and started following a path that bent around the side of the building. "I don't know about that. She had her heart set on this place."

"There are others," Jenny followed him. The grounds were absolutely gorgeous and the weather was perfect. They wandered into a cozy, romantic clearing nestled in the center of colorful trees, shrubs and flowers. Private, beautiful, it was the perfect place to steal a kiss.

Too bad she was walking with her friend's fiancé and not her own.

"I couldn't get her to even consider anywhere else. This is the only place she's mentioned since we first started talking about getting married."

Jenny shrugged her shoulders. "Lie. Tell her it isn't available."

"No. I can't do that. Besides, she'd be determined enough to call and check. Then she'd know I was lying."

"Yeah. I can see her doing that."

He stopped walking and turned to face Jenny, his eyes searching hers. "Maybe I have no business asking this but how did you do it? How'd you get her to listen? I need to know. Heck, my future marriage may count on it."

How would she explain it without taking sides or making Monica look bad? "It's a secret. I... Uh, she was in a position where she had no choice."

"Yeah?" He leaned back against a tree trunk and crossed his thick arms over his chest. "So tell me, Jenny Brown, what's your secret?"

You don't really want to know my secrets, Jason Foxx! Do you?

There was something in her eyes that enchanted him. For some reason, as he stole as many minutes with her as he could, making whatever excuses necessary to keep her here with him, he didn't feel like he should—guilty as hell. He was engaged after all, planning his wedding with Monica. *But I'm beginning to believe I don't love her. She's not the woman I fell in love with.*

At the moment all he could think about was listening to Jenny speak. He didn't care about anything else.

Who was Jenny Brown?

In a deep, down-in-the-gut sense, he felt like he knew her from somewhere, but he could find nothing familiar about her face, hair, or features. They were soft, feminine, pretty, but not as stunning as Monica's. Not as flashy or polished. Even so, he found her incredibly attractive. She was like the crisp fall air whirling around them and tossing the leaves about. Fresh, earthy, sensual.

She was nervous, had been since the minute they'd met outside the manager's office. He could tell by the flush on her face, the way her gaze hopped around.

Why? He sensed she was hiding something, a secret. What could it be?

Her cheeks were deep red now, having stained the charming shade when he'd right-out asked her what her secret was. Her brown eyes, the color of the earth, hid her secret well but occasionally little sparks of something shimmered in their depths. Would she tell him the truth?

"I don't have any secrets," she lied.

He wanted to smile, to let her know he couldn't be so easily fooled, but he didn't. For one thing, it would draw out the game. He had all night. Monica had told him she had plans with some girlfriends.

He felt her drawing closer before she moved, almost like her spirit had reached toward him before her body did. She shuffled closer, closing the distance between them to less than a foot. Her arms hanging at her sides, she stared down at his feet for several heartbeats before looking up into his eyes again.

Her lower lip trembled and she bit it, making it stain a deep cherry red. He licked his mouth, wishing he could taste her.

"I can't tell you my secrets." Her hushed voice barely rose above the sound of the rustling leaves.

"Why not?"

One side of her mouth quirked up into a playful half-smile. "Then they wouldn't be secrets anymore," she said as she took a single step backward.

A retreat.

He wasn't about to let her get away that easily. He unfolded his arms and moved forward, diminishing the distance between them to mere inches. He still wasn't close enough, but for now he would have to be content. "They're in your eyes, you know."

"What?"

He reached forward and stroked the side of her face with his index finger. Her skin was satin smooth and warm. His gaze fixed on her eyes. "Your secrets. I can read them there."

She turned her head. "If that's true, then you don't need me to tell you."

With his palm, he urged her to look at him again. He ached to find that connection again, when their gazes locked and the veil between them was drawn away. *I don't understand it, but I need to know this woman. I need to touch her, to hear her voice.* "But I want to hear you speak it, to say what I see in those eyes."

Still looking away, she shook her head. "I can't. It's… You don't understand."

"Try me."

She finally met his gaze and his body warmed as he sensed the arousal she seemed to be trying so carefully to hide…or to douse. "You're engaged. I shouldn't… We shouldn't. Why are you acting like this? Telling me these things about Monica? Shouldn't you be telling me how much you love her? How excited you are to be marrying her? You don't sound exactly thrilled, you know."

"Maybe that's because I'm not sure how I feel," he confessed. Guilt-ridden for wanting to touch her but unable to stop himself, he reached toward her.

"Don't tell me that. You have no idea what I've gone through…" She pushed his hand away and hurried back toward the front of the building. "This isn't fair. You can't do this to me. I have to think of Monica. I've got to go. Please don't try to stop me."

He didn't.

"I'm sorry," he whispered into the cool night, to both Monica for breaking her trust and to Jenny. He couldn't seem to help himself. For some reason, he felt like he'd just met the woman he'd fallen in love with. But how could that be? Could he love a woman he didn't know? There had to be a logical explanation.

Chapter Twelve

ꕥ

That moment in the woods tormented Jenny both day and night. The entire weekend she thought about it while awake, dreamed about it while asleep. At work on Monday she did her best to act like normal around Monica but it was tough. She'd crossed the line. Regardless of how close she'd been to Jason when she was living Monica's life, this was different. Now she was Jenny.

There was no excuse. Jenny had no right to be thinking *those* kinds of thoughts about Jason.

He had no right to be tempting her either.

One thing was certain—either he was a low-life, cheating bastard or she'd been terribly wrong about one small assumption—he would fall in love with the woman he saw with his eyes.

Which one was it?

Okay, she knew the answer but she didn't want to accept it. Never had she stolen a friend's boyfriend. She feared her record was about to be dashed.

That fear amplified when later that afternoon, Monica cornered her in the break room as she was buying a soda from the vending machine. Heart racing, hands shaking, she prepared for the worst—a stream of angry expletives about broken engagements and stolen fiancés.

"How was The Hawthorne?" Monica asked. "Was it as gorgeous as I thought?"

That wasn't the question Jenny had expected. Happy to respond, she said, "If you thought it was phenomenal, then yes. But it was also mega-expensive."

"Yeah," Monica said on a sigh. "Jason told me."

"I...hadn't expected Jason to be there."

"He insisted. I didn't think he'd care where we held the wedding but as it turns out he's quite the romantic. Wants to pick the location. Isn't that sweet?" Monica dropped four quarters into the vending machine and punched the button, selecting a bottle of water. The bottle dropped into the chute at the bottom.

Sweet or underhanded, depending upon his motivation. "Yeah."

Stooping slightly, Monica retrieved her purchase and twisted the top off. "But that doesn't get you off the hook. I want you to check out every place on my list." She pointed at Jenny with her opened bottle.

"Why not go yourself?"

Monica took a drink then twisted the cap back on and answered, "Jason insisted I let him choose. He wants it to be a surprise."

Oh no. I'm not liking the sound of this. I need to find a way out. "Then why have me tag along? Won't he feel like you don't trust him? Or worse, I'll tell you?"

"Nope. It was his suggestion. He thought you could give a woman's point of view."

Shit!

"Anyway, here's the place he's visiting tonight. Six o'clock. That won't be a problem, will it? I realize it's short notice, but since it's a Monday night I figured it would be okay."

Jenny glanced down at the card. This place was local. She couldn't use driving distance as an excuse. And she knew Monica had firsthand knowledge of her weekly routine. She was trapped.

Then again, maybe it was better this way. Tonight could be an opportunity instead of a liability. She could set Jason straight right now, before things got out of hand. Friday, she'd been caught off guard, unprepared. But tonight, she'd be ready. She'd let him know what a mistake he was making by pursuing her, or flirting with her, or whatever he was doing. Monica was a prize and the wedding must go on. At least if she accomplished that much she would be miserable but content knowing she did the right thing, and life would go on.

"Okay. I'll go." Jenny took the card, finished her soda and returned to her desk. She spent the afternoon rehearsing the speech she'd give to Jason.

By quitting time, she had worked herself up into a nervous frenzy. Even though she'd gone over it dozens of times, she rehearsed her speech aloud as she drove the short distance to the banquet hall. She was a sweaty, anxious mess by the time she pulled into the parking lot. Six o'clock on the dot.

She took a look in her vanity mirror on the back of her sun visor. A mess. That was probably for the better. Then she flipped up the visor and reached for the door handle.

Before she'd pulled on the latch, the door swung open. Jason stood outside smiling.

"You look beautiful," he said, holding the door for her.

Intending to deliver her speech, she opened her mouth, but no sound came out. Well, nothing except for some strangled-sounding gurgle.

He chuckled. The sound of his laughter floated around her head and bubbled in her tummy, setting the butterflies in there all aflurry. "I'll take that as a thank you." He reached down with his free hand and captured one of hers, giving it a soft tug to urge her to her feet. "There's been a change of plans."

"Oh?" She didn't like the sound of that.

"We're going to dinner. The manager had a small emergency to contend with and can't meet with us until seven-thirty. You don't mind eating dinner with me, do you?"

"Well, actually..." She tried to lower herself back into the car seat but he kept pulling. It was no use. She wasn't going to win this battle. The way she saw it she had two choices—either remain standing or have her shoulder dislocated.

"I won't take no for an answer," he said, reinforcing what she already knew.

"I noticed that about you." She wriggled her fingers, trying to free her hand.

"We have some things we need to talk about. Don't you agree?"

"True."

"Good." He pushed the car door closed behind her. "At least we agree on that much."

"And that may be all we ever agree on."

He grinned and she tried hard not to notice how cute he was when he smiled like that. She also tried extra hard to ignore the glimmer of attraction she saw in his eyes. That was tough.

Releasing her hand at last, he motioned toward the restaurant next door to the banquet hall. "Hope you like steak."

"Love it, but—" She reached for the car door handle again.

Obviously anticipating her move, he used his bulk to block her from opening the door. He crossed his thick arms over his chest. "How did I know you'd say that? Let me guess, you like Ben and Jerry's Chocolate Therapy too."

Uh-oh! He was putting two and two together. "Well, it's not my favorite…"

"Liar. I've figured it out, you know."

Her face flamed. "Figured out what? My favorite ice cream flavor?"

"No, more than that," he said, shaking his head. He took a single step toward her and feeling trapped, even though she was standing in the middle of an empty parking lot, she back-stepped away. "I figured out what you and Monica did."

"Oh? What we did? We didn't do… I mean, I honestly wouldn't know…" She took a few more steps backward until something big and hard stopped her from going any further.

Unfortunately, he didn't stop moving forward. Well, he did, but not until he was only a couple of inches from her. Heck, if she sucked in a deep breath, her boobs would probably touch his lower chest. Considering their size—even with the Wonderbra—that was saying something.

"All weekend long it was driving me nuts," he said. "I felt like I knew you, like I'd spent time with you, not just met you on the street or spoke to you in passing. But it was impossible."

"Probably that déjà vu thingy. I get that sometimes." Her hands behind her back, she explored the surface of whatever vehicle she'd backed herself into.

"I couldn't sleep. I had to figure it out," he continued.

She pretended to listen while planning her next move. If she could shuffle up around one end of the car, she could make a quick getaway. How lame! To be even considering running away. *Spineless coward! What happened to your plan to set him straight?*

"And then it came to me when I was watching an old movie on HBO," he continued.

"A movie?"

"How'd you do it? Wireless receiver?" He leaned forward, trapping her shoulders between his outstretched arms as he pressed his palms against the car's roof.

The second he made contact with the car, a loud shriek sounded in her ear, making her leap forward.

That was not the best direction to move. Her body smashed up against his, she raised her hands to cup them over her ears. That did little to shelter her eardrums from the obnoxious bellow of the car's alarm. Her nose pressed into his chest, and the scent of Jason and tangy cologne filled her nostrils. "Alarm!" she shouted.

Without speaking a word, he crammed one hand in his pants pocket and pulled out a keypad. He punched a button and the noise ceased.

But it was too late for her to make a safe getaway. Before she had her senses back, he wrapped both arms around her waist and held her tight against him. She felt every point where her body made contact with his. And there were many! Here and there, little blazes erupted, sending sparks of arousal through her bloodstream. She felt a trickle of perspiration run down her temple. She needed to lighten the mood. Pronto! Or she was going to melt.

"I know it was you," he said, capturing her chin and holding it so she couldn't look away. His gaze drilled hers. It was intense, demanding, troubled. "You coached her, told her what to say that night at my house. And at the nightclub too."

"How would I do that? What movie are we talking about anyway?" she asked, trying like heck to look casual.

"You know which one. The chick flick about cats and dogs." His fingertip traced the line of her jaw. The innocent touch sent more sparks flying through her system. Meltdown was now imminent if something wasn't done immediately!

She shrugged her shoulders and tried to pull out of his embrace. With one hand she caught the index finger that had made its way to the base of her throat and pushed it away. "You've got me there. I'm totally lost."

"Something about truth and cats and dogs…has that tall blonde, Uma Thurman, and the other one, Janeane somebody in it." Seemingly undaunted, he took that naughty finger and plunked it right in the center of her chest, where it traced the little bow in the center of her bra. It seemed a few buttons of her shirt had sprung open. "You know, where the plain-looking one is too scared to talk to the guy so she lets him think the good-looking one is her."

Almost mindless with need, thanks to his roaming hand and the heat in his gaze, Jenny tried to ease the tension by cracking a joke. Humor always helped her get through tough times. And this was one of the toughest she'd ever had to endure. "I'm not following you. Hey, are you trying to say I'm the Janeane somebody? You can't even remember her name. It's no wonder women like me who don't have legs up to their armpits feel like we don't stand a chance with men." She knocked his hand away again. "Would you stop doing that?

This Janeane somebody doesn't care to be manhandled in public."

"Please. Quit joking around and tell me the truth. I need to know. I deserve to know," he pleaded as his gaze fixed on her eyes. "Which woman have I fallen in love with? Monica Starke or Jenny Brown?"

"That's a no-brainer. You're in love with Uma."

"Damn it, Jenny. Don't you understand? I have to know." His fingers dug into her shoulders as he gripped them tightly. His brows drew together and dipped down low over his expressive eyes, eyes that spoke of passion and confusion, wanting and fear. "I'm about to marry one of them. I can't marry the wrong woman."

Marry? He would marry me? I would be Mrs. Foxx? All the clever comebacks that had been bouncing around in her head vaporized, disappearing like fog on a sunny morning. Speechless, she dropped her head, allowing her forehead to rest against his chest.

What had she done? She'd messed up not one, but two lives! Jason was confused—not that she could blame him. He was an innocent party in this.

Monica would be devastated.

She was quite certain that whoever had made the whole switch thing possible had not intended for things to end like this, no matter how great it seemed to be for Jenny!

"Honestly, Jason. I don't know what you mean. You love Monica. I'm certain of it."

"At least one of us is."

"It's probably just pre-wedding jitters. All men have those. Now, please," she said, pushing against his chest. "Let me go before someone sees something and word gets back to Monica. She's my friend and your fiancée. I can't do this to her. She's so happy about your proposal."

"But she's not acting—"

"She has a strange way of showing people how she feels sometime. You should know that by now." Jenny finally extricated herself from his embrace and half-ran back to her car. "I'm sure there's a logical explanation for whatever change you've seen the past couple of days. Take my word for it, she's thrilled."

"I honestly feel like—"

Finally within reach of safety, she opened the door then turned to face him. It was now or never. She had to convince him that it was Monica he loved, no matter how much it killed her.

"Just stop it," she said in as stern a voice as she could muster. "You know how much this would hurt her, don't you? You have to stop it now. I haven't known you for long but I get the impression you're not the low-down woman-chaser you're acting like at the moment. Of course, I've been wrong about those kinds of things before. Just tell me you're not a player who's going to propose to a woman one day then seduce her best friend the next, are you? Because if you are, then Monica and I need to have a long talk."

"No, of course I'm not. I just need to know—"

"Good. I was hoping you'd say that. Let's get back to focusing on what we came here to do—choose a venue for your wedding." She made sure to emphasize the last word in that sentence before continuing, "I'm willing to forget all the other stuff if you promise not to mention it again."

"But I can't—"

"Okay, Jason. It's your decision. I'm leaving. Choose your banquet hall on your own. I won't let this…whatever it is…continue another minute." She sat, slammed the car door and started the car, ignoring Jason's persistent rapping on the window. Not allowing herself to glance his way, she tapped the horn to warn him to move away from the car then put it into reverse, backing out of the parking spot.

As she drove through the parking lot, she peeked in the rearview mirror.

He was stooped, crouching low to the ground, holding a foot in his hands. His head was tipped down, his forehead resting on a bent knee.

I ran him over? Damn it! Why didn't he move?

Terrific! Now, she was not only guilty of fiancé-stealing but also assault with a thousand-pound—or thereabouts—racy, red, sporty coupe.

Chapter Thirteen

ꕥ

Over the next several weeks, Jason did what was right—he kept his distance from Jenny Brown and focused on planning his wedding and nursed his terribly bruised foot. Luckily, Jenny had just bumped the outer side and hadn't broken any bones.

Thanks to Monica's wish for a New Year's Eve wedding, there were plenty of details to get in order in a short period of time. While Monica took care of most of them, he was still busy with the few items she'd entrusted into his care.

Yes, being busy was a good thing. It left him little time to wonder about Jenny, where she was, what she was doing. Who she was with.

He had no explanation for why he felt so close to her right from the moment they'd first met. He'd never felt that way about someone before, not even Monica. At first, he'd suspected Monica and Jenny had somehow joined forces to trick him. But now, as he and Monica settled into the comfort of a stable but uninspiring relationship, he began to doubt that had happened.

One thing he didn't doubt—it was frustrating, unnerving how thoughts of Jenny came up at the most inopportune times, like during dinner dates with Monica. Fortunately, Monica didn't seem to notice his straying attention. If she did, she was uncharacteristically quiet about it.

He struggled night and day with the fear of marrying the wrong woman, of making a mistake and forcing Monica to pay the price.

Yes, they were getting along fine. The dramatic change of almost a month ago now had mellowed into something a little more stable. Monica was still Monica. She hadn't shaken all her weaknesses. But she'd gained a handful of new strengths. He respected her for the growth she'd shown. He admired her creative mind and go-getting attitude regarding her career. It was obvious Monica Starke would someday be a huge success.

But was admiration and respect a strong enough foundation for marriage? God, he hoped so.

He felt he must keep his uncertainties to himself, at least for a bit longer, until he was sure they weren't just a case of pre-wedding jitters. Of course, it didn't help that he had no one he trusted to talk to.

He bet Jenny would be a good listener.

"Honey, what's wrong? You look like you'd rather be a million miles away than celebrating our anniversary," Monica asked, instantly reminding him of where he was and what they were celebrating.

Five years. They'd had their first date five years ago. It seemed like both yesterday and a lifetime ago.

"Nothing, babe. I'm fine. Just tired. Jet lag," he offered the excuse he knew he'd recently started overusing. The past few weeks he'd taken several business trips to Europe and one trip to the Orient. To his credit, the excuse was somewhat warranted. He normally traveled that much in a year's time, not a month. He'd recently found a new outlet for his goods. However, this particular retail outlet was frequented by very selective customers who had an eye for the rare. He'd been forced to travel to find pieces unique and expensive enough to capture their interest.

He'd profited quite nicely. At least Monica's wedding wouldn't put him in the hole.

"You need to stop traveling so much," she said, her eyebrows furrowed with worry. She reached across the table and took his hand in hers. "I know this wedding is putting a lot of pressure on you. I feel a little guilty."

"Don't. It's your big day. Every woman deserves to have the wedding of her dreams."

Her smile was genuine. "You're such a sweetheart. That's why I'm marrying you, you know." She pushed her still-full plate away and audibly sighed. "I'm stuffed. Can't eat another bite."

"I'm just a working schmuck, nothing special." He didn't say a word about Monica's uneaten food. Recently, he'd learned Monica's eating habits were not a safe topic of conversation.

"That's a matter of opinion."

The waiter slipped Jason the check then silently stepped away.

"Did you want anything else, babe? Dessert maybe?"

"Oh, no. I'm fine. Want to make sure I fit in my dress. Only a little over ten weeks. I can't believe it's coming so quickly."

"Me neither." He filled the leather folder with enough cash for the bill plus a nice tip and set it on the edge of the table.

"Did you make the reservations for the honeymoon?"

"All set."

"I can't wait. I've always dreamed of going to Germany. It'll be so romantic."

"Yeah." He returned his money clip to his pocket and drained the remaining champagne from his glass.

"You're awfully quiet tonight. Are you sure it's just jet lag?"

"Yep. Are you ready to go?"

"In just a minute." She finished off her champagne then stood and let him help her into her coat. Her diamond ring flashed brilliantly, the muted overhead lights reflecting off the facets as she reached her arm behind her back and slid it into her coat sleeve. As they walked through the restaurant's dim interior, he caught all the appreciative glances she collected from both male and female diners.

Going out with Monica was like going out with a local celebrity.

He had no doubt there were dozens of guys who would love to be in his shoes. But that did nothing to ease his doubts.

After dropping Monica off at her place, he shut off his cell phone and stopped at the bar down the street for one last drink before turning in. A trendy hotspot full of Metro Detroit's up and coming. Jason liked to stop in occasionally for a beer and some wings.

Jason had no way of knowing Jenny Brown would be there tonight but the minute he saw her, he knew he wouldn't be able to leave without speaking with her.

He heard the bartender's jovial greeting as he hurried past the bar, but he didn't slow down. His heart pounded in his chest as his gaze took in every detail of her clothing, her hair, her face.

The more he saw, the more beautiful she was in his eyes.

In the bar's warm, mellow golden light, her hair was a shiny, deep mahogany. Smooth and straight, it hung over her shoulders, reflecting the light of the candle on the table. Shorter pieces framed her face, making her eyes look very large. Doe eyes.

Her makeup was soft, her lips a muted red, just deep enough to emphasize their fullness. Her eyes sparkled as she chatted with a woman sitting in the chair next to her at the round table. As he drew nearer, he noticed how the deep V of her red top showed just enough cleavage to stir his interest.

Her friend noticed him before Jenny did. He didn't miss her questioning stare as he stepped up to their table. Nor did he miss her obviously approving smile.

"Hi," the woman said in a low voice.

Most likely curious, Jenny followed her friend's gaze, halting when she saw him. "Hi," she said in a cold tone that was clearly meant to scare him off.

"Hello, Jenny. I swear I didn't come here to find you. But now that I have, I owe you an apology."

"Apology accepted."

Clearly surprised by Jenny's behavior, the other woman gave Jason an apologetic smile then leaned closer to whisper in Jenny's ear.

"Sorry," Jenny said. "I'm being rude. Jason, this is Lori. Lori, this is Jason, Monica's fiancé."

"Nice to meet you," Lori said. "Won't you join us? Where's Monica?"

"She decided to turn in early. I'd love to join you, but only if it's okay with Jenny. I'd like to buy you ladies a drink."

"Actually, we're meeting someone here," Jenny mumbled.

"We are not. Jenny, where are your manners tonight?" Lori shook her head. "I'm sorry, Jason. I don't know what got into her all of a sudden. Please, have a seat."

Jason looked to Jenny for some kind of reaction. She didn't give him much encouragement to join them but her expression didn't exactly scare him off either. "Thank you," he said as he pulled up a nearby chair and sat. "What'll you ladies have?" He glanced over his shoulder, looking for a waitress.

"A glass of white wine for me, thanks," Lori answered.

"Nothing for me, thanks. I'm fine," Jenny said.

After waving down a waitress, Jason noted Jenny's empty glass but didn't push the issue. She wasn't about to make it easy on him. But that was okay. He'd taken the best Monica had to offer over the past five years. He had a feeling what Jenny Brown could dish out would pale in comparison.

Content for the moment to sit tight and weather out the Jenny storm, he ordered a beer for himself and a glass of wine for the chatty woman on his left. While Lori talked his ear off, Jenny remained quiet and withdrawn. She didn't seem to be angry or go out of her way to be difficult. She was simply…distant. That was the best word he could come up with.

When the waitress delivered Jason's beer and Lori's wine, Jenny ordered a beer for herself and paid the waitress cash.

Although Jason could have easily been offended by an action that could be seen as rude, he wasn't. She had accepted his apology. She wasn't obligated to accept a drink from him. She was being polite but not over-friendly as she watched him chatter with her friend.

She drank her beer very fast, draining it within minutes of receiving it. In the dimly lit room, he could see the start of an alcohol-induced flush stain her cheeks.

Lori filled his ears with friendly banter about jobs and houses, cars and nightclubs while Jenny added an occasional comment. As she drained a second then a third beer, the slight pink turned to a deeper red.

He hoped she wasn't driving home tonight.

"I need to go to the ladies room," she said, sliding out of her chair and standing on wobbly legs. She gripped the table to steady herself. "Be right back."

He found her slightly rumpled, clumsy appearance adorable.

"Are you okay? I'll go with you," Lori offered. She motioned toward Jason to stay put with an index finger, grabbed Jenny's elbow and half-led her, half-carried her toward the rear of the bar. She returned a few minutes later without Jenny. "Jenny's had a little too much to drink. She's fine but we should probably go. The problem is, she was our designated driver. She never drinks. I never would have thought… Anyway, I've had too many to drive too."

"Not a problem. I can call a cab for you," he offered.

"That'll take forever. You only had one beer and that was a while ago. Couldn't you drive us home? Jenny and I can come back for her car tomorrow. Please? I'll pay for gas."

"Sure."

"Good. I'll go collect Jenny from the ladies' room and meet you outside."

"Okay. Do you need some help?"

"No. She can walk. She's just a little unsteady." Lori smiled. "I've never seen her drunk before. Heck, I can't remember the last time I've seen her drink alcohol. She won't even touch cough medicine with alcohol in it. Now I'm beginning to see why. You wouldn't believe the stuff she's saying. She's hilarious. I'm going to have to get her to do this again sometime. Oh, and make sure you drop me off first. You'll want to hear what she has to say to you without me there." She gave him a knowing wink then walked back toward the bathroom.

He was left wondering exactly what a potent truth serum, like alcohol could be with some people, would bring out of Jenny Brown. He had a feeling he'd find out very soon.

After paying his tab, he went outside and drove his car up to the front entrance. Jenny was half-draped across Lori as they stood, or rather swayed, next to the security guard positioned at the door.

Jason got out to help them both into the car. Jenny settled into the front passenger seat and tipping her head back, closed her eyes. Jason eyed the unfastened seat belt then looked for Lori who had already secured herself in the backseat.

"Jenny, you need to buckle up," he said before rounding the front of the car and getting into his seat.

She didn't move.

"Jenny, you need to wear your seat belt," he repeated as he got in and fastened his own.

Still no reaction.

Either she was going to ride without a seat belt or he was going to have to fasten it around her.

"Okay. I'm going to do it for you then," he warned. "Speak now or forever hold your peace."

"Oh, for heaven's sake, just buckle it!" Lori said from the backseat. "She's probably passed out."

After unclipping his, he leaned way over to reach for the shoulder strap. That put him in a very interesting, though somewhat painful, position.

Nose-to-nose with an intoxicated, sleeping Jenny Brown was a temptation hard to resist. Her breath warmed his lips as she slowly exhaled. He wanted to kiss her so bad his whole body ached, especially when the corners of her mouth lifted into a hint of a sleepy smile. Was she still asleep or was she messing with him?

"Jenny?" he whispered.

The smile broadened. Her eyes still closed, she lifted her arms and looped them around his neck. "Jason," she said in a low voice that was like a soft caress over his body. "You came back for me." She pulled him closer and planted a soft kiss on his cheek.

He stiffened, not sure if she was aware of what she was doing. Jason Foxx never took advantage of drunk women, no matter how beautiful and sexy they were. "Came back?"

"You went on a trip, silly. Remember?"

"Huh?" he asked, thoroughly confused. "I just went outside to get the car." Straining, he grasped the buckle and pulled the seat belt over her chest. With his urging, it clicked into place next to her hip.

"She's talking in her sleep," Lori explained. "Last time I heard her do that was when she was sick one time and took too much Nyquil. Just wait 'til later. It'll get better. Last time she started talking about little green men in spaceships visiting her in the middle of the night. That girl has one active imagination."

"Wow." He started the car and let it warm up for a few minutes.

"You know, until now, I'd forgotten all about that night. I was so tempted to tape-record her, especially when she denied everything the next morning. To this day she thinks I'm lying."

"I believe you."

"Thanks. That's one person who doesn't think I'm totally nuts."

"Well, I didn't say that," he joked. He put the car in gear and drove across the parking lot. "Which way?" he asked before turning onto the street.

"Turn right. I live a few miles down the road. Not too far."

"At least you don't have far to go home," he said, making small talk.

"Yeah. I planned it that way. When I'm loaded I get terribly carsick. Wanted to make sure I didn't mess up Jenny's cute new car. It's a beauty, isn't it? I nearly died when she told me she'd bought a new car. And her hair and clothes are all different too."

"Really?" Had Jenny also done a complete one-eighty like Monica?

"Yep. Oh. Turn left here."

"Shoot." Caught in the wrong lane and surrounded by cars on all sides, he missed the turn and had to go down several blocks and turn around.

"Sorry. My bad. Anyway, I didn't hear from her for a week or two and then next time I saw her, she'd been magically transformed."

"Really?" He was repeating himself, but something about Jenny's "magical" transformation was fishy. "How long ago was that?"

"A while back. September, maybe."

Same time as Monica's. "How has she changed?"

"She used to dress…well…how can I say this? Uh, very plain. Her clothes didn't fit her well at all. They were all dark, dull, did nothing for her. Sort of frumpy. Her hair was plain too. Usually just pulled back into a sloppy ponytail. And you should have seen the car she drove."

"Oh yeah? Bad?"

"Rust on four wheels. I've tried for years to convince her to buy a new one but she said she couldn't afford a new car. Now, out of the blue she can. I wonder if she's moonlighting somewhere…" She whispered the last sentence conspiratorially.

"How long have you known Jenny?"

"Only a couple of years but we're best friends. We do almost everything together." She paused for a moment then added. "Turn right at the next light. My house is at the end of the street."

"Okay."

They rode the remaining distance in silence. Jason dropped her off and insisted on leaving Jenny at Lori's house. Lori was politely stubborn, declining a houseguest for the night. She gave him concise directions to Jenny's home then stumbled inside and closed her front door.

Jason followed the directions, pulling up to a quaint house converted into a multi-family. He found her door around the back. After returning to his car, he tried to wake her but when she remained unconscious, he rummaged through her purse for her keys then walked around to unlock the door before carrying her inside. When the door swung open, he found a long, extremely narrow staircase. That would be a bear to navigate with a limp woman in his arms.

Curious, but not wanting to leave Jenny snoozing in the car for long, he dashed up the stairs and opened the door at the top. He found a cramped but homey apartment. Traditionally furnished with soft chenille couches and feminine draperies and rugs, it was exactly what he'd imagined her home would be like. The kitchen was tidy but used. Baked goods and a bowl of fruit sat on the counter. Back in the living room, he noticed the French door opening to what looked like a terrace overlooking the front of the house.

He stepped outside and checked his car, parked almost directly below. Everything looked okay. He could take just a minute more to snoop…no, find the bedroom. He would need to turn down the bed so he could put her right to bed when he carried her up.

Yeah, that was it.

Back inside, he opened the only door off the living room, finding a small room with only two pieces of furniture—a small dresser and the largest four-poster bed he'd ever seen. There was almost no space to walk around it and ultra-feminine, it wouldn't normally be something he'd appreciate. But he had to admit it was beautiful, romantic. Dressed in filmy white sheers with tiny red ribbon roses embroidered throughout, it beckoned him. He sat and ran his hand over the ivory satin comforter.

A person's bed, especially their pillows, usually held their scent. He lifted a pillow to his nose and inhaled.

Heaven and lavender.

"Jason? What are you doing in here?" Jenny slurred as she staggered into the room, bouncing off of walls and furnishings like a pinball.

He dropped the pillow and, totally awkward and uncomfortable for being caught on her bed, he jumped to his feet. "I was going to turn down the covers for you."

"Oh, that's sweet." She smiled and staggered toward him, looking like she'd fall over any moment.

He reached out and caught her before she did and supported her as she took the last few steps toward the bed. As she hobbled around him, she stomped on his healing foot and he bit back a cry of pain. Even after three weeks, it was still a little sore.

She dropped onto her bottom then fell backward, leaving her legs hanging over the side. He forgot his pain.

Bent backward like she was, her short skirt barely covered her vitals and he had to force himself to look elsewhere. She was wearing black lace panties. He loved black lace.

Her eyes closed, she said, "I don't feel so good. I think I had a little too much to drink. I hate being drunk. Why did I do this to myself?"

"You'll feel better tomorrow."

"Oh, I remember now," she said, answering her own question, or so he assumed. She drew her legs up onto the bed and rolled to her side. The neckline of her top slid down, exposing her matching black lace demi-bra and the tantalizing swell of one breast. "You aren't leaving right now, are you?"

A mountain-sized lump formed in his throat as his gaze glued itself to that smooth ivory skin. He could even see the pink of her nipple through the lace. It was erect. So was one particular part of him. "I should be going."

"Won't you stay for just a little bit? I'm tired but I need to tell you something. I know I won't have the nerve to tell you later."

"Okay. I'll stay for a short time." He looked around the room for a chair. Of course there wasn't one.

Jenny patted the bed. "Do you want to sit?"

"No thanks."

"Please? It's making me dizzy looking up at you like this."

"All right." He sat on the very edge of the mattress as far as he could from that exposed breast. To further remove temptation, he pointed at her chest. "Your top."

"Yeah. It's new. Do you like it? It's a very bright color. I don't usually—"

"No, I mean it's a little…needs to be fixed."

"Oh." She glanced down and quickly made an adjustment. A soft pink stained her cheeks. "My goodness. You weren't lying. Better?"

No. "Yes. Thanks."

"Anyway. I wanted to tell you something." She rolled over onto her stomach.

"Yes, you said that."

"You're probably going to think I'm crazy," she said, picking lint off the soft blanket. "But I swear I'm telling you the truth."

"I would never think you're crazy."

"We'll see about that. Um…I don't know how to say this."

"Just spit it out," he suggested, noting how nervous she appeared. Her gaze was fixed on the blanket she was practically picking apart.

"Okay. It's about Monica and me. You remember when you asked me about the time at your house?"

"Yes." He wondered where she was going with this.

"Well, you were right. It was me. I was there."

Ah ha! I knew it. I wasn't going crazy. "How? Was she wearing some kind of wire?"

"Oh no. Nothing like that. I was her. I mean, I was the one at your house that night. You were talking to me."

Huh? "Oh?"

She looked up, her watery, bloodshot eyes searching his face. "I don't blame you for not believing me. It's pretty much impossible."

"I'm trying to understand."

"I'll go back to the beginning. Do you remember my question about wishing on stars? We were at the cider mill."

"I remember that night with Monica, yes."

"That was me then too. I asked that question for a reason. One Monday night a while back I made a wish on a falling star…or a meteor…or something. Anyway, the next morning I woke up in Monica's bed."

That sounds…kinky…but what does it have to do with anything? "Really?" he asked, not able to disguise the doubt in his voice.

"Yep. I swear it's the truth. I don't know how it happened. I've always been jealous of her. Of her fancy cars and rich boyfriend and what I thought was her sheltered life. I thought she had it so much better than me and I envied her. Anyway, somehow some fairy godmother or pissed-off god or someone switched us by magic and I was her and she was me for a while. Kinda like that *Freaky Friday* movie. Did you see that by any chance?"

"No."

"Me neither. I was wondering how they were switched, thought it might shed some light on how it happened to me."

"You think it was your fairy godmother?" he asked, recalling his earlier conversation with her girlfriend, in particular the part about the green spacemen.

She chuckled. "Sounds silly, doesn't it?"

He shook his head. "Oh, no. Absolutely not. I believe in fairy godmothers too."

Her smile was broad. Her eyes sparkled, despite the dilated blood vessels making them look blood-red. She rolled over onto her back and settled her head on a pillow. Her hair fanned out around her face like liquid mahogany. Her eyelids fell to halfway cover her eyes. "You do?"

"Sure." Despite the almost excruciating urge to curl up with her in that bed, he drew the covers up over her and stood. "Thanks for explaining. Now how about going to sleep?"

Still on her back, she raised herself on her elbows. "Are you humoring me?"

"Absolutely…not. Go to sleep. I'll see myself out."

"But doesn't this mean anything to you?" She sat up. He swore her eyes were sloshing around in her head like an ice cube in a stirred glass of water. She'd feel like heck tomorrow morning. He wished he could be here to take care of her, give her some aspirin, an ice pack for her pounding head.

"Sure." He patted her knee.

She caught his wrist with one hand and held her head with the other. "Yikes. Can't move too fast right now. Stop moving so I can focus, would ya?"

He remained motionless for a moment.

"That's better. Thanks. Now I can ask you, don't you see what I'm trying to tell you?" She tipped her head and looked up at him with round eyes. Her expression was so serious, so innocent. Her lips were soft, glistening wet, tempting. He wanted to hold her. He wanted to kiss her.

He needed to leave. "Yes. I understand. It was you. Now, lay down. You need to get some sleep."

She gave his wrist a sharp yank. "But I was the one eating the ice cream and talking about babies and farms and marriage and all that other stuff. So I need to know…which one is it?" He gaze searched his face and he could read the desperation in it.

"Which one what?" he asked, knowing what her answer would be but unable to face it.

"Which one of us do you love, Jason? Monica or me? I need to know."

Jason couldn't answer her question. Not at the moment. There were too many peoples' hearts at stake. Too many lives potentially shattered. He had to think things through. He had to do what was right for everyone. That did not involve a hasty answer to a drunk woman's desperate question. Yet, he couldn't hurt her feelings either.

A quick retreat was his best bet. Maybe her friend was right and she had a crazy imagination. Maybe she didn't know what she was saying.

Like a chicken, something he never prided in being, he headed for the door. "Jenny, get some rest and we'll talk about it later."

"Promise?" she said behind him as he made his getaway.

"Promise," he answered, hoping by morning she would have forgotten all about it. Or better yet, come to her senses.

There was no such thing as fairy godmothers. And wishes—even made by lonely little boys on falling stars or on extra-special, limited edition coins thrown in wishing wells—didn't come true.

He had indisputable proof of it.

Chapter Fourteen

ꟹ

Jenny saw neither hide nor hair of Jason throughout November and half of December. Monica didn't send her on any more excursions to check out banquet halls and he didn't make an appearance at her wedding shower.

She guessed whatever had happened the night she'd gotten tanked, both Monica and Jason had decided she shouldn't be near him any longer, or vice versa. She was almost glad she didn't remember what she'd said or done—she tended to get amnesia from imbibing too much. From the aftermath, she guessed it had probably been pretty darn stupid.

Tonight, as she did her hair for the annual company Christmas party, she tried to convince herself she'd have a good time. Again, she would probably be the only one there without a significant other, but it was becoming tradition. Why change it now? Besides, who would dance with Mr. Kaufmann's aged father? In his nineties and still going strong, the man could dance the night away with the best of them.

She made sure she had a dress she could move in without exposing anything important and heels that wouldn't make her lame in fifteen minutes then headed out to the car. She'd briefly considered sharing a ride with Lori and her boyfriend but quickly dismissed that idea as downright stupid. The last thing she needed to be tonight was a third wheel.

Tiny snowflakes, glittering like diamond chips, were falling from the sky, coating her car, the grass and the road in a thin layer of white dust. Not bothering to brush it off the windshield, she put the gaily decorated package she carried in the backseat, then got in her car, started it and flipped on the heat and the wipers.

Bone-chilling air blasted her in the face, doing nothing to melt the snow that coated the windshield. Luckily, it was light, versus the thick heavy snow that came later in the winter and accumulated by the foot. The wipers did the trick, whisking away the thin layer in one swoop. She didn't wait for the heat to warm up before she put the car into gear and drove to the banquet hall where the party was being held.

"I'll eat, dance a few with old man Kaufmann then head home," she told herself, dreading the evening and wishing it was over before it began. At every turn, she considered going back home and forgetting the whole thing, but the fifteen-dollar ticket tucked safely in her clutch kept her from actually going through with it.

Money was money. She rarely spent so much on a night out. Also, she knew Lori would not let her get away with pulling a no-show. She'd call every minute until Jenny answered the phone and agreed to come. Friends could be real pain in the you-know-what sometimes.

By the time she pulled into the parking lot, she was prepared to make her entrance. She parked, sucked in a long breath to try to wash away the last bits of regret for showing up, and walked inside.

The first face she saw was the last one she'd expected—Jason's. He was standing smack-dab in the center of the foyer, looking toward the door. Monica was nowhere to be seen but had to be there somewhere too, perhaps the ladies room. Neither had been expected to show up. In all the years Jenny had worked at the Kaufman agency Monica had never attended the Christmas party.

Why did she have to pick this year to break with tradition?

When her gaze locked with Jason's, Jenny felt her face heat up. Desire washed away the dread and she felt herself being drawn across the room toward him, as if pulled by an invisible rope. To stop herself, she gripped the closest stationary thing she could find, the door handle, and hung on, hoping the temptation to throw herself at his feet and beg for a hug would pass.

Just one little hug. That would be enough to last a while, at least a week…okay maybe not.

Someone outside rapped on the door and she reluctantly released it so they could enter the building.

Forcing a smile, she walked toward Jason and nodded. "Hello, Jason. It's good to see you again."

"Hi, Jenny. You too."

As she continued past him, she forced herself to look straight ahead, toward the room at the opposite end of the hallway and the sign sitting on the easel that read, "Kaufmann". She felt his gaze on her back, whisper-soft and warm, like a caress.

She sighed. "Well, if that wasn't awkward!" she murmured to herself. This night was going to be even worse than she'd thought. Even more reason to eat and make an early escape—and above all avoid alcohol.

She saw the usual characters as she paused just inside the door and scoped out the scene. The people who rarely saw each other during the normal workweek chattered with each other like old friends. Mr. Kaufmann junior was sitting at the bar, tilting a little to the left already, nudged by a few brandies, she guessed. His father was on the dance floor, practicing his moves to the mood music playing on the speakers. The DJ wouldn't start playing the dance music until after dinner, but the elder Mr. Kaufmann was always anxious to get his groove thang loosened up early. For that, he needed a partner. Jenny knew her goose would be cooked the minute he saw her, so she tried a stealth maneuver toward the closest seat, at a round table about ten feet from the door.

Right away she spied a familiar purse sitting on the chair. This was not the ideal table to sit at. She glanced up to see if the dancing man had spied her yet.

Nope. But his gaze was headed in her general direction. If she dared try for another table, he'd see her for sure. She was not about to get out there and dance to orchestrated 1980s tunes in front of the entire office…again.

She hunched over a little and headed to the next chair she could find with no purse or napkin signifying possession by some roaming individual and sat in it. Determined to make this temporary and find another seat as soon as possible but suffering a throat as dry as the Mojave, she tucked the wrapped gift for her Secret Santa under the table and reached for the metal pitcher of ice water.

"Over here, honey," she heard Monica say.

Jenny's mild case of dread developed into a severe one. She guzzled the water, which seemed to miss the dry spot in the back of her throat as she swallowed and frantically searched the room for another empty seat.

Maybe dancing to the elevator-music version of *Like a Virgin* wasn't such a bad thing.

Monica sat beside her and smiled. "Jenny! I'm so glad you made it. And I'm glad you decided to sit with us. You remember Jason." She pointed over her shoulder at a red-faced Jason who was standing behind her, playing the gentleman by pushing in her chair for her. The huge rock on her left ring finger glittered in the light from the table's centerpiece candle as she pointed. Even after all this time Jenny couldn't help noticing it.

"Yes, I remember. We bumped into each other out in the lobby when I first came in," Jenny said, trying hard not to stare at his handsome face. Was it possible he'd gotten better-looking since she'd last seen him? Her heart ached as memories of moments shared alone with him buzzed through her mind. "I was surprised…to see you came this year. This has to be the first time, isn't it?"

Jason took his seat on the other side of Monica, too far away yet not far enough.

"Yes. I usually avoid these kinds of gatherings like the plague. But every year I hear all the stories about this party and regret not coming, so this year I decided no matter what I'd have to come. Have you had a drink yet?" Monica asked, stirring a tall glass of something with a swizzle stick that looked like a candy cane. "I can send Jason to the bar for you."

"Maybe later. What're you having?" Jenny asked, eyeing the glass with suspicion. "That's not your usual water with lemon."

"Long Island Iced Tea. I've heard they're fabulous." Monica took a sip and wrinkled her nose. "Whoo. Strong."

"More like lethal," Jenny summed up as she tried to get a glimpse at Jason. He seemed to be hiding behind Monica.

Monica took a second drink. "Well, I wanted to have something a little stronger than the usual since tonight's a special night. You know, we'll be getting married exactly three weeks from tomorrow. I never thought I'd say this but I can't wait."

Jenny merely nodded. "I know."

Monica turned her head toward Jason. "What's wrong, honey? You're mighty quiet tonight."

Jason whispered something in Monica's ear then excused himself and left the table.

Monica turned toward Jenny again and shrugged. "Says he's not feeling well. Poor baby." She took several long swallows of her drink then set it down. "It's probably jet lag again. He's been traveling a lot lately."

"That must be hard on you too."

"No, not really," Monica answered, coolly. "I've never been the dependent, clingy type. In fact, I like a little space. It's good for a relationship."

Jason returned a minute later, smiled at both Jenny and Monica and sat. Either Jenny had been imagining his dark mood or something had made it do a sudden one-eighty. He looked downright chipper. He leaned forward, resting his elbows on the table. "So, what are you ladies talking about?"

"Men, of course," Monica answered. "That's what all women love to talk about. Can't live with them, can't live without them, as they say."

He chuckled. "I should've guessed. So, what did I do this time?"

Monica patted his knee. "Nothing, sweetheart. At least nothing bad."

That last part made Jenny feel a little ill. She did not want to know about their sex life—correction, any more about their sex life than she already knew. She knew enough as it was. She recalled the chasing game and the look on Jason's face the night of the hayride.

Then she felt a little sicker.

"Are you okay, Jenny? You don't look so good," Monica said.

"I'm feeling a little under the weather. Must be all those last-minute wedding plans I've been taking care of," Jenny suggested, adding, "since someone's hoity-toity wedding planner decided to pick up shop and move…out of the country."

"That's not my fault." Monica crossed her arms over her chest and grimaced. "Who would've thought she'd lie about Oprah, for God's sake? I thought that was illegal." Her frown changed suddenly into a smile. "Thank God you've really come in to save the day. I owe you so much. I don't know how I'll ever repay you."

"Maybe you can introduce me to your brother-in-law someday," Jenny suggested.

Monica scowled. "My brother-in-law? I didn't know I had one of those. Honey, you have a brother?" She looked at Jason.

Jenny looked at Jason.

Jason looked at Jenny with very wide eyes and visibly swallowed. "Sure, I told you the night of the hayride. You remember that, don't you? You must have told Jenny, or she's a private investigator," he joked. He smiled and winked but the alarm Jenny had seen was still plain on his face.

Had he just realized she was the one who'd been with him that night?

"Sure," Jenny said, making certain to keep her voice light and her tone joking. "That's it. I moonlight as a private investigator. And since I was so concerned for Monica's welfare, I did a little bit of snooping, Mr. Foxx."

Monica looked convinced. "How handy. What did you find out?"

"Oh, the usual things. He pays his taxes," Jenny said, looking at Jason. Should she say more? Gauging by his intense stare, she was sure she had his captivated attention. But what would she gain from it? So what if he knew it was her that night? He was happy with the Monica he had now. They'd switched back some time ago. Since then, they'd become engaged and planned a wedding. He clearly wasn't having any doubts about which woman he loved, at least not anymore.

It would be unforgivably wrong to break them up now…unless he was still searching for the truth.

He couldn't be!

"What else?" Monica asked. "You look like you've found some deep, dark secret. Jason, dear. What sorts of skeletons have you been hiding in your closets?"

"Mmm…I'm not going to say. Let's let Jenny tell us. What else have you learned?" Jason prodded. "You've piqued both our interests. What sorts of secrets have you discovered?"

"Oh nothing… I shouldn't," Jenny mumbled, not sure she was doing the right thing. What if she caused them to break up and Monica was devastated? Could she live with herself? Heck no!

"Yes, you should," Jason stated firmly. The way he looked at her spoke volumes. He was still searching. He needed to know the truth.

Jenny looked at Monica for some help, a hint, anything. Monica nodded. "Pretty please? I want to know what you found out too."

"Well, let's see," Jenny tried to recall the other private information he'd shared with her. "His mother died during childbirth…and…his father is a hard-nosed workaholic who…taught his boys to never believe in wishes."

Monica's eyes widened in alarm as she finally seemed to understand what they were talking about. "How could you possibly know…" She didn't finish the sentence. Instead, she turned to Jason. "Oh, I remember now. You were right. I told her. Silly me. I'm so ditzy sometimes. You know I'm a natural blonde…"

Jason didn't look at Monica. His gaze was razor-sharp and fixed on Jenny. "I…I… Shit. I'll be right back." He stood and hurried from the room.

Jenny braced for Monica's wrath, or at least a few harsh words, but as Monica faced her, she realized it wasn't forthcoming. Monica was smiling. In fact, she appeared downright gleeful.

Perhaps the half of the Long Island Monica had consumed had taken effect?

"I think we've totally confused the poor man," Monica said with a chuckle. She drained her glass and stood. "Now, that makes two of us." Obviously feeling the effects of the strong drink, she half-walked, half-staggered across the room toward the bar.

Eager for some clarification—this whole confusion thing was downright…confusing…to Jenny too!—she followed Monica. But before she reached the bar, someone caught her hand and gave it a sharp yank.

Realizing where she was standing, in the center of the dance floor, she knew the person who had caught her could only be one Mr. Kaufmann, Senior, dance fiend extraordinaire.

He grinned, displaying a set of sparkling white dentures and said, "There's my dance partner. I've been waiting for you, honey. Where've you been?" He pulled her into his arms with a force much too great for a man his age and waltzed her around the dance floor.

The whole room filled with applause.

"I'm so glad you made it," he said as he led her into a spin. "That little young thing, what's her name, April, Ann? She doesn't know how to dance worth beans."

"You're close. That's Angela. Maybe you could teach her," Jenny suggested, trying to find Monica as she whirled in time to a fully orchestrated rendition of *Tainted Love*. Monica was confused? About what? About Jason?

"Nope. I tried. She doesn't have a lick of rhythm," Mr. Kaufmann said.

"She should have. She was a cheerleader in college." Jenny craned her neck, still trying to locate Monica.

"Really?" He dipped Jenny. His pale blue eyes scanned her face. Then he returned her to an upright position, and she returned her attention to searching the room for one drunk Monica who seemed to be in the mood for honesty.

"I swear." Her back to the bar, she craned her neck to try to catch a glimpse of where Monica might have gone. "She has a picture up in her cubicle at work."

"Who're you looking for, doll? Doncha want to dance with me? I live for this every year, you know."

She looked at him and smiled. "I'm sorry. I was right in the middle of something when you…I mean, a few minutes ago. I suppose it can wait. But you have to promise me you won't be disappointed if I need to take a break after this dance."

"Fair enough." He looked very pleased. "I don't suppose your date would appreciate me keeping you to myself all night."

She didn't correct his false assumption. It might lead to hurt feelings. Instead, she tried to enjoy the moment. The man really did know how to dance, unlike the guys she dated. He knew how to hold her, how to lead her in the right direction with just the slightest pressure to her shoulder or a subtle shift in his weight. It was a shame younger men didn't learn to dance like that anymore.

When the song ended, Mr. Kaufmann released her and gave her shoulder a gentle pat. "You're a good girl, Miss Brown. I've always told my son that he should treat you better."

"Well, thank you. I suppose I need to do more than be a good dancer to earn my raises, but I appreciate the thought."

She found Monica and Jason both at the table. Based on their grim expressions, she guessed they were involved in a very serious discussion. Not wishing to be an unwelcome interruption, or cause any more trouble, she decided to go find another seat and give them the chance to hash out whatever they were discussing.

Maybe she should just call it a night? The guilt sitting heavy in her belly for stirring up this whole mess tonight wasn't going to let her enjoy a minute of the festivities. Monica and Jason were arguing and it was all her fault. What had she been thinking?

She hadn't been thinking. That was the problem. If she had been using her head, she wouldn't have dared rattle off information that would set off Jason's suspicions. Then again, he'd asked and Monica had encouraged her.

That was no excuse!

Of course, she'd left her purse on the table and the gift for her Secret Santa on the floor. Darn it! She had to get those.

Trying hard to quietly retrieve them while avoiding eavesdropping—a temptation she wasn't sure she could resist—she took the long way back to the table, approaching it from the opposite side of the room. She figured, since she was coming from behind them, she might be able to snatch her purse and leave unnoticed.

She was wrong.

Monica caught her wrist as she reached for her purse and held it fast. "Don't you go anywhere."

"I swear, I'm sorry for everything. I shouldn't have opened my big mouth," Jenny blurted.

"Have a seat." Monica directed her to the chair on the other side of Jason.

"You encouraged me. I wouldn't have said a word if you hadn't. Honest." Jenny stood behind the chair and stared at the back of Jason's head.

"He deserves to know the truth," Monica said, motioning toward the chair again. "I can't marry him like this, by tricking him and lying. It isn't right. It's been bothering me for weeks."

"Well..." Jenny wasn't sure what to say next.

Jason swiveled in his chair and looked up at her. "Please. This has gone on long enough. I've lost patience. Whatever you two have been up to, it's time to clear it up now, before anyone makes the kind of mistake that could ruin their life."

Jenny nodded and sat but didn't speak. She waited for Monica or Jason to begin. Her gaze ping-ponged back and forth between them until Jason finally spoke, "I want you to tell me the truth. How did you know those things about me and my family?"

"You told me," she stated. "The night of the hayride. The night we walked into the woods and roasted hot dogs and exposed ourselves to poison ivy."

Chapter Fifteen

ꙮ

If it weren't for the fact that Jason loved one of these woman so bad his insides were nothing but mush, he might have told them both to take a hike. But he couldn't. Partly because of sick curiosity and partly because of a truth he hadn't wanted to believe for weeks.

He was engaged to the wrong woman.

"No," he corrected Jenny. "I told Monica those things the night of the hayride. She got the poison ivy. I saw the aftereffects. You, on the other hand, had no signs of a rash when I saw you at the banquet hall. Your skin was flawless."

"Yeah, while I walked around looking like the Elephant Man," Monica added. "But crazy as it sounds, Jason, she's telling the truth."

"How? You had some kind of microphone on…right?" he asked.

Jenny and Monica both shook their heads.

"Not exactly," Monica said.

"What does that mean?" Jason asked, getting frustrated and annoyed. "Just tell me what's going on. What did you two do? And better yet, why?"

This time Jenny answered, "The why is something I don't think either of us have been able to figure out yet. But the what is fairly simple, if you can get yourself to believe the impossible."

"Try me," he said, not sure what to expect.

"We switched bodies," Monica said.

Huh?

"Like the *Freaky Friday* movie," Jenny added. "I don't suppose you've seen it?"

He shook his head. "Nope. You asked me that before. What's it about?"

"A mother and her teenage daughter switch bodies and learn what it's like to live in each others' shoes."

"Okay. How'd they do that? Makeup?" he asked, trying like heck to make sense of what Monica and Jenny were telling him. It wasn't logical. He didn't particularly like things that weren't logical.

"Magic," Jenny said.

He laughed. "Magic? There's no such thing."

"That's the only thing we can attribute it to," Monica said, nodding.

"This is ridiculous," he said. "You two don't expect me to believe this. There's got to be a logical explanation. Monica, you were wearing a microphone, transmitting our conversations to Jenny, who listened in and fed you lines back so you'd know what to say. Now, that makes sense. Switching bodies? That's a good one." He laughed. He couldn't do anything else.

"I don't care what you believe. I know it's true." Monica pointed at Jenny. "It's all her fault. She wished on a falling star and the next morning I was—"

"Falling star?" he repeated. *Impossible! Wishes don't come true.* He'd made a wish on a falling star many times, including not too long ago…a couple of months ago, maybe? Right about the time Monica had changed…

"Yeah," Jenny said. Her eyes were wide and round, her gaze fixed to his. She was either telling the truth or she was one of those psychopathic liars who could fool a lie detector. "I swear we're telling you the truth. Monica didn't have any wires on. You know that. You would have felt them when—"

"He would have what? I thought you said nothing happened between you two?" Monica interrupted, sounding as bewildered as she looked.

"Nothing…um, major," Jenny admitted. "It would've been weird if we hadn't at least kissed a little. Heck, you two've been dating for five years. I had a hell of a time keeping us out of bed. Jason wanted to—"

"Why do I feel like I shouldn't be hearing this?" Monica's cheeks stained a light pink. "Suddenly I feel like the third wheel."

Clearly respecting Monica's discomfort, Jenny returned to the previous subject, "Anyway, there was a meteor shower or something one night and—"

"What night?" Jason interrupted, not buying the story yet, but warming up to it. There were some intangibles that suggested they might be telling the truth, as impossible as it was. And this time he wasn't hearing it from a drunk woman known to tell outrageous stories.

"It was a Monday night," Jenny answered. "The night before you had the car repossessed. I'd had a rough day. Monica had dumped a huge project on my desk the Friday before and I got bawled out Monday for not finishing my work because I'd been too busy doing hers. I was mad, thought she always got the better deal in life. So I did something silly, childish, never expecting anything to come out of it. That night, I stood on my balcony watching the stars, and out of the blue I saw a bunch of meteors or something…and just for kicks I made a wish."

"The night before the car was repossessed?" Jason repeated, trying to remember if that had been the night he'd made the wish too. He wasn't certain, but it could have been.

What are you thinking? You're letting a couple of women make you believe in magic and wishes? How gullible are you? This was all too much! He wasn't about to believe some silly wish had come true by magic. His old man would be rolling on the floor in a fit of hysterical laughter and calling Jason a complete idiot if he heard this. The logical explanation he'd provided earlier had to be the answer.

Jason Foxx was no idiot.

But that left one unanswered question. Why were Monica and Jenny lying? He had to know the answer.

Why would Monica want to trap him? Money? Marriage? Maybe both?

"You bugged my house," he said, looking at Monica. "And you heard me."

She looked confused. "Heard what?"

"You heard what I wished—wanted—and you went to Jenny and asked for her help and she made you into that person so that I'd marry you—"

"Hold on!" Monica waved her hands in the air. "I would never do that. You know me. I'm me and no man's going to change that. Either you love me the way I am or you don't. How many times have I said so?"

"True," Jason admitted. The motivation was lacking. Monica didn't like to change, especially for someone else. "But you also knew I was miffed about the art glass and the car—"

"But I wouldn't marry you for money. I'd rather end up in bankruptcy court than do that. That's why I'm telling you the truth now. We were this close to getting married, Jason. If I'd kept Jenny from you and kept my mouth shut, we'd be waltzing down the aisle in a few weeks and then half of what you own would be mine. If this whole thing was a con, then I'm one stupid con man…er, woman…to screw it up now."

He felt tired suddenly, exhausted. "Okay. I can't think about the whys or even the hows right now. I just need to know who each of you are. I need to know which woman was the woman I fell in love with." He looked at Monica then at Jenny. In his heart he knew the answer.

Monica was the most beautiful woman he'd ever met. She was stunning, from head to toe, with thick, long blonde hair, large, round blue eyes rimmed with long lashes and a face that could easily grace magazine covers. Her body was svelte with a few surgically enhanced curves where men liked them most. But she was also the antithesis of his dream woman, of the woman he'd wished for the night of the meteor shower. Whether he cared to admit it or not, it had taken that time when she wasn't acting herself to see past her physical beauty and accept what he'd been denying for five long years.

And then there was Jenny. As earthy as her last name, she was everything Monica wasn't. She was the woman he'd, in anger, shouted to the stars for. Beautiful in body and mind, gentle, intelligent, loyal, trusting, caring, she was the woman of his dreams.

Monica spoke, "Only you know the answer to that, Jason." She looked at Jenny then at him again. "I think it's safe to say we both love you, in our own ways. You need to choose."

Shit. "I don't want to hurt anyone."

"We'll live." Monica reached out and took his hand in hers. "Jason, if there's one thing I know about you it's that you've always known your mind...and your heart. Trust your instincts. Make your choice."

His gaze zig-zagged back and forth between the two women as he tried to sort out the mountain of thoughts and emotions that were clogging his insides. His sense of loyalty to Monica and his wish not to hurt her. His respect for her intelligence and independent spirit. His new and unexplored feelings for Jenny. "I can't do anything. Not now. Not tonight. I need some time to think."

"Fair enough." Monica nodded. "Jenny? Can you take me home later?"

"Sure."

"Jason, thanks for coming tonight. You're free to leave if you want."

He shook his head, adamant. "No way. I don't ditch my dates at parties."

"Please," Monica said. "Go think about things, figure out in your heart what's best. You need to take some time for yourself. You haven't had that, thanks to the wedding. I'll be fine. Jenny isn't drinking. She's a safe driver."

"I shouldn't…" He slid his rump to the edge of his seat but didn't stand.

"It's fine," Jenny said with a nod. "I don't mind driving Monica home. I won't be staying here long anyway. I'll make sure Monica gets there safe and sound. She can call you when she gets home if you like."

"You really don't want me to stay?" he asked, directing the question to Monica.

"No. This whole thing is very awkward and uncomfortable and I would just as soon not let it get worse and have all our coworkers know about our personal lives. Outside of Mr. Kaufmann, who's clearly three sheets to the wind, everyone else looks sober enough to remember what happens tonight. I'm not fond of being the subject of Monday morning water cooler rumors."

"Okay," he said on a sigh. "I'll go. But only because you insisted. I'll call you tomorrow."

"Better make it late. I fear I'll be slightly hung over," Monica said.

He didn't kiss her before he left. His parting was awkward, tense.

Wishes, magic, or whatever, things had just gotten more complicated than ever.

* * * * *

Throughout dinner there was no mention of Jason. Lori and her boyfriend sat at their table and provided plenty of lively chatter to distract Jenny. And three or four Long Island Iced Teas seemed to do the job for Monica. Thanks to the alcohol, Monica became the proverbial life of the party and Jenny was hard-pressed to drag her away from it after a couple of hours.

A handful of party tunes, including the Birdie Dance, Secret Santa gifts exchanged and names revealed, and two hours of Monica at her best…or worst, depending upon how one looked at it, and Jenny was past ready to leave. She said goodbye to everyone who mattered, including her half-conscious boss and his charming father then went to gather Monica, who was telling everyone in her path how much she loved them.

Monica complained the entire way out to the car. She didn't stop as they drove back to her place. By the time they pulled into her driveway, however, she was thanking Jenny profusely for dragging her out of the party before she made an ass out of herself.

Then she threw up in the front yard and, crying hysterically, begged Jenny to stay the night with her so she wouldn't be alone.

Jenny was in no mood to nurse a barfing grown woman but since she was undoubtedly the source of some of Monica's misery, she felt she owed her at least that much. She agreed to spend the night on the living room couch. Monica insisted she take the guest bedroom upstairs.

Naturally, thanks to Monica's frequent stumbling trips to the bathroom, Jenny got no sleep that night. But with Monica's tongue loosened up, thanks to the alcohol, she learned what she had long suspected.

"My father's a bum, running from the law," Monica confessed sometime in the wee hours of the night. "I didn't know it when I was a kid, but I learned later he wasn't the business tycoon I thought he was, but a crook."

"I'm sorry, sweetie," Jenny said as she helped Monica get back into her bed. Monica's face was an odd mixture of crimson blotches on a field of sickly white. Her eyes were red and watery, the lids hanging over them as if they were too heavy to be lifted completely. "There. You just lie down and be still."

"I am. The freaking bed just won't stop moving." Monica closed her eyes. "My entire life's a big lie. I'm nobody. The daughter of a fugitive with no money, no future, no fiancé…"

"Jason hasn't broken up with you."

"Not yet. But he will." She lifted her eyelids just long enough to look Jenny in the eye. "He loves you, you know. He has since the switch. I had to say something. I couldn't stand it any longer. I'm not you. I can't pretend to be."

"Oh, Monica. You have so much going for you. You're beautiful and popular. You have a terrific home. Look at this place." Jenny motioned around the room at the expensive furniture. "Not to mention you're intelligent and have a great career—"

"I'm alone."

"It's better to be alone than to be with the wrong person..." She gave Monica the same line she'd repeated to herself too many times to count.

Monica sighed and blinked. A fat tear slipped from the outer corner of her eye and dribbled down the side of her face. "But you're not alone. You have friends who truly like you, not just want something from you. You have parents who call and leave worried messages on your answering machine if they haven't heard from you in a while. All I have is a grandmother in a nursing home who occasionally remembers who I am. I pay her bills every month but half the time she screams for the police when I visit, claiming she's never seen me before."

"That's where all your money goes?"

Monica's watery gaze fixed on Jenny's. She whispered, "Grammie is all I have left. Medicaid won't pay for her to stay at Sparrow Court but I didn't want her moved. The owner is an acquaintance of mine. I know Grammie gets the very best treatment, isn't stuffed in a corner and forgotten. It's the least I can do."

"How very sweet and generous of you."

"It's killing me financially but if Grammie knew the truth, that all her money was gone, it would kill her. Years ago, dad talked her into signing over her assets to keep the nursing home from taking it all...and then he cleaned out every account! He even used her money to pay for my graduation gift. I tried to stop him but I couldn't."

"I'm so sorry."

"How could he do that and live with himself? I feel guilty and all I let him spend on me was the money for the trip to Europe," Monica said, sobbing. Her eyes were even redder now and deep red splotches stained the skin around them. "He stole from his own mother and I couldn't stop him." She sniffled and Jenny handed her a tissue from the box on the nightstand.

"Is that why you changed your mind about marrying Jason?" Jenny asked, putting two and two together.

"At first I was ready to smack you for getting involved in Jason and me. I mean, what nerve!"

"Sorry. I thought I was doing the right thing."

Monica nodded and slid her a smile. "I know. Your heart was in the right place. And that, along with the knowledge that if I didn't marry him, I wouldn't be able to afford to pay Grammie's bills any longer, kind of squashed any thoughts of me inflicting any physical harm on you. By getting Jason back for me, you did me a huge favor. You know what those bills are doing to my finances. My house is near foreclosure. Since Jason cosigned the mortgage for me, his credit will be ruined too if I don't make the payments."

"Have you told Jason about your grandmother?"

"No."

"Okay. I need to ask you then, and maybe I shouldn't be asking you this now when you're clearly…"

"Blitzed?" Monica supplied for her.

"Yes, blitzed."

"Ask away. I'm in the mood to be honest. Ask me about my deepest darkest secrets."

"I just want to know about one. Forgetting for a moment about your grandmother, about the money aspect, do you love

Jason?" Jenny held her breath as she waited for Monica's answer.

"That's the thing. I do love him. Very much. But not the way I should. He deserves to have a wife who is crazy about him, can't stand to be apart from him for even a minute. Who dreams about him at night. Who can't stop thinking about him throughout the day…" she mumbled, her voice getting lower and lower. "I do love him. I just can't…love…him…enough…" A soft snore buzzed from her throat.

Careful to be quiet so she wouldn't wake Monica, and lost in her thoughts, Jenny tiptoed from Monica's room and returned to the guest bed. Her thoughts, about Monica and Jason, about Monica's grandmother, and about wishes and stars, kept her company as she watched night turn to dawn.

Chapter Sixteen

ℌ

The next morning, Jenny woke up with a start. Either someone had pulled another switcheroo on her again or she was sleeping in the Arctic.

She opened her eyes.

Neither seemed to be the case. There were no icebergs in sight and she recognized her clothes and the room in which she'd dozed off a short time ago. But in that time, it appeared, Monica's furnace had gone kaput. Either that, or she hadn't paid her gas bill.

She knew she had a couple of options. She could go home and let Monica figure it out…but that one wasn't very nice. Or she could bundle up and do some investigating. It was a chilly alternative, but the better of the two. Already feeling the effects of the cold on her nose and fingers, she wrapped the comforter around her and walked to Monica's bedroom. After knocking and receiving no response, she opened the door and poked her head into the dark room. The shades were drawn. The room was deathly quiet.

"Monica?" she said in a hushed voice. "Are you okay?"

She got a groan for a reply.

Deciding it was better to wake up a hungover Monica than to leave said hungover Monica in a house with no heat, she walked to the bed and tapped Monica's shoulder. "Monica, either your furnace died last night or you owe somebody some money."

Monica groaned again and slowly lifted a hair-tousled head. "What time is it?" she grumbled, turning her head toward the nightstand.

"I don't know." Jenny noticed the clock's red numbers weren't lit. "The clock isn't working." She went to test the light switch on the wall. The overhead didn't turn on. "Did you pay your electric bill?"

"Yes. Two weeks ago."

She kept flipping the switch, knowing it probably wouldn't all of a sudden work but willing to keep trying anyway. "Are you positive?"

"Yes. It's winter. I'm not that stupid. I can't live without lights and heat." She sat up and dropped her head into her hands. "Ohhh…my head is killing me. That Long Island stuff is trouble."

"I warned you." Jenny lifted the blind and glanced outside. From her vantage, she could see the corner of the neighbor's garage. The motion detector-activated light was on. "Your neighbor didn't lose power."

"I paid the bill. I can show you the check stub to prove it."

"Maybe you mailed it too late?"

"It cleared the bank."

"Well shoot! I don't know what's wrong then."

"I know what to do." Moving slow, like a zombie rising from the dead, Monica sat up then stood. Her head hung low as she shuffled across the room and opened the top drawer of her dresser. She held out a business card. "Call this man." When Jenny took the card, Monica dragged her miserable frame back to her bed and laid down. "Let me know when he's coming. Please? Thanks."

"Okay. But do you have a cell phone? I don't think your cordless is going to work."

"My purse." She pointed at the chaise in the corner.

Jenny rummaged through the contents of Monica's purse until she located the phone then left the room to make the call to Bill the electrician.

Recognizing the name, Jenny introduced herself as the woman he'd met at the club a month or so ago, gave him Monica's address and explained their dire circumstances. He said he would be over within the hour. She reported her success to Monica, who suddenly seemed to have made a remarkable recovery. She bounded out of bed and ran to the shower, ignoring Jenny's suggestion she wait. As expected, she returned from the bathroom a little while later with dripping wet hair and a scowl. "I can't dry my hair. He can't see me like this."

Jenny chuckled. "I tried to warn you. Just let it dry naturally."

"I'll have icicle dreadlocks."

Jenny shrugged. "Maybe that'll turn him on. You said he thought you were too high-maintenance. This oughta prove you're not." She tugged on a soggy lock of hair.

"Hardly. It'll just make me look scary."

"You couldn't look scary if you tried." Jenny nudged Monica's shoulder then walked to the door. "Better hurry. According to the clock on your cell phone, he could be here in as little as ten minutes, maybe sooner."

"Okay, okay!" Monica ran to the dresser as Jenny left the room and closed the door.

Hungry, she headed for the kitchen, hoping to find something edible. It had been a long time since the switch back, so all the goodies Jenny had bought would be long gone. She could only hope she'd find something that would fill her stomach without making her ill.

The refrigerator was empty.

The cupboards were empty.

The freezer was empty.

Drats! She put on her coat and collected her purse and keys. "Monica, I'm headed up the road for donuts," she shouted up the stairs. "Want anything?"

"No, I'm fine. Thanks anyway."

"Suit yourself!" She hurried out into the cold, surprised to find almost a half-foot of snow on the ground and more falling. Unlike last night's snow, these were the big, soggy flakes that accumulated by the inch. The road was covered, with little more than two dirty ruts wandering through the quiet neighborhood. The air was still. It was eerie.

She got in her car and white-knuckled it to the donut shop where she picked up a dozen donuts and a dozen bagels, just in case she was forced to stick around Monica's for a while. At least she wouldn't go hungry. Then she headed back.

A big white van was parked in Monica's driveway. She parked her car next to it and went inside.

It was still freezing inside, and dark. Her arms full of paper bags with donuts and bagels, she walked to the kitchen, shouting, "Monica?"

"We're down here," Monica answered from the basement.

Jenny took a bite of a custard-filled donut before venturing down the stairs at the rear of the kitchen. She followed the moving beam from a flashlight either Monica or the electrician was holding in the rear of the basement. It was dark down there, but not pitch-black, thanks to several long but narrow rows of glass blocks letting in faint daylight. "How bad is it?" she asked as she approached them.

The electrician's back was turned toward her, and his flashlight was directed at the circuit breaker box on the wall. "Looks like the main breaker tripped off."

"Why would that happen?" Jenny asked.

"Hard to say."

She heard a click then the lights in the basement turned on.

Monica grinned. "Yay! That's all it was?"

"Sure looks that way." Bill the electrician shut the panel door and turned around to face the ladies.

Jenny smiled. "Thanks a lot for coming on such short notice."

"What about the furnace?" Monica asked. "You wouldn't leave two helpless women here during the middle of a snowstorm to freeze to death, would you?"

Jenny couldn't miss the twinkle she saw in Monica's eyes as she smiled at the hulking electrician.

"Helpless? Hardly." He chuckled and returned Monica's smile. Then he grinned and winked at Jenny too. Jenny couldn't miss the fact that there was more than one kind of electricity happening in that basement. The air around her was charged with nervous energy, fed by the looks Monica was giving Bill and he was giving Jenny. "The furnace should come on in a minute. The blower can't operate without electricity."

Monica giggled and twirled a soggy lock of hair around her finger. "Oh, how silly. I knew that, of course." She stepped closer, her wide eyes fixed on his face. "Thanks so much for coming out here so quick. I don't know how I'll ever repay you."

"Not a problem. Give me some time and I'll think of something. Two beautiful women…I'm sure there are one or two possibilities." He smiled at Jenny, and growing more uncomfortable by the second, Jenny failed to respond.

Was he suggesting…a ménage?

Bill was one handsome devil of a man, no doubt about it. Tall and solid, he was built like Atlas, his arms thick and muscular, his shoulders broad, his chest wide, his waist narrow. And his face was ruggedly handsome with deep brown eyes and sexy dark stubble over his chin and jaw. There was a naughty spark in those eyes. That man was trouble with a capital T, perfect for Monica. Not perfect for Jenny.

"How about a donut?" suggested Jenny, knowing that was a far cry from what he was looking for.

"That's a good start but I was thinking more along the lines…" He stepped closer and Jenny found herself back-stepping away. "…of a home cooked vegetarian dinner." His chest inches from Jenny's chin, he tipped his head and whispered, "What do you say?"

Monica stepped in, catching Bill's arm as he lifted it, no doubt intercepting his touch to Jenny's face. "Jenny there's had a change of heart and has gone all Atkins on me. The good news is she gave me all her old cookbooks, and with power, I can get my way around a kitchen with the best of them."

His attention diverted, he backed away from Jenny enough to allow her to breathe again. "Can you make a decent Reuben?"

"The best!" Monica said exuberantly. She took him by the hand and led him upstairs. "I'm on a first name basis with the delivery boy for Mike's Market down the street. I can get the ingredients here in two snaps." She illustrated with a couple of saucy finger snaps.

Several steps behind them, Jenny pondered her getaway, choosing the moment Monica dialed the market to gather her donuts and bagels and break the news that she was leaving. Monica mouthed, "Thank you." And waved. She didn't look the least bit put out.

But Bill did.

Certain he wouldn't be sorry for long, Jenny made an excuse about a dog she didn't really own needing to be let out, and made good her escape. Just before she headed out the door, Bill cornered her and whispered, "I'll call you." A little bit guilty for using him the way she had, but not interested in feeding his interest, she simply smiled and said, "Enjoy your meal with Monica. She's nothing like you'd expect when you first meet her."

His knowing nod suggested he understood exactly what she was implying.

Satisfied she'd set him straight, Jenny trudged into the snowstorm, started her car, and swept off the inch or so that had accumulated on the windshield in the short time since she'd returned from the donut place.

Top speed as she drove home was about ten miles per hour. A self-proclaimed snow wimp, she fought to keep her zippy new car on the road as all-wheel-drive trucks barreled past her, blinding her with the mud-tinged slush they threw off their wheels. Thanks to a fear of freeway driving during snowstorms, her trip home was long and exhausting, and thanks to getting very little sleep the night before, she was ready for bed the moment she pulled into her parking space.

Safe, warm, and prepared to hunker down and ride out the storm, she carried her goodies into the kitchen, took the most direct route to her bed she could find and, after changing into her favorite sweats, climbed into bed and buried herself in the blankets. It took her no time to fall asleep.

As she drifted off, she heard Jason's voice. He was calling her name. No, he was doing more than that.

Unclothed from the waist up, he was bent over her, whispering, "Jenny, let me show you how beautiful I think you are."

Instantly tingly and breathless, eager to feel his weight pressing upon her but equally guilty and confused, she asked, "But what about Monica?"

"You know as well as I do that we're through. We have been for a long time. Neither of us wanted to admit it, even after we broke up." He sat back and gathered her hands in his. His grip was warm, firm, his expression sober. "It took something extreme for us to sever the last bonds."

"But I'm her friend." She wiggled her fingers in his hands, not really wanting to pull them free but knowing she should. "Even if you've broken up, I don't date my friends' ex-boyfriends. It's just not right."

"But I love you. And so does Monica. She wants us both to be happy." He kissed each fingertip then released her hands. He bent lower and kissed her, his tongue teasing the corners of her mouth before plunging inside. She heard her breathing quicken, felt the rush of warmth wash up her chest and over her face. A slight but steady throb began between her legs as his hands plunged under her shirt and found her breasts. He pinched her nipples between his thumb and forefingers and she moaned. He nibbled on her neck and she squirmed with pleasure. He pressed a knee between hers, and she rocked her hips back and forth, rubbing away the ache of need growing by the second.

"Oh God," she moaned, surprised by the swiftness of her reaction to his touch. She couldn't stand waiting any longer. She wanted him. All of him. "Please make love to me."

He pulled off her sweatpants and knelt before her, a hand on each knee. He gently pressed, urging them apart. Just before he lowered his head for his first taste, he whispered, "I think you're the most beautiful, intelligent, perfect woman on earth."

"Now I know I'm dreaming," Jenny said aloud, waking herself. Blinking and horny from her dream, she looked at the window on the opposite side of the wall. "Perfect? Me? What a joke. What am I thinking?" Recognizing it was dark, and curious to see how long she'd been sleeping, she turned to look at the clock. Eight o'clock. In the evening, she assumed. She found the remote on her nightstand and turned on the TV, not surprised to see weather updates on all the local channels.

Today's storm had dumped over a foot of snow in most parts of the city and more was expected. Several thousand people were without power.

She wondered how Monica was doing.

More than that, she wondered what Jason was doing.

* * * * *

Jason watched the white van, marked Bill's Electric, pull out of Monica's driveway as he turned the corner of her street. Was Monica having electrical problems? Why hadn't she called him like she usually did?

Out of habit, he eyed the guy driving the van as their vehicles passed. In passing, the guy looked young. He had a smart-assed grin on his face, which made Jason feel uneasy. Had he taken advantage of Monica somehow? Anxious to find out, he pulled into her driveway then shut off the car and took long steps through the deep snow to her front porch. Vowing to clear the front walk and the empty half of the driveway after he made sure she was okay, he rang the doorbell.

She answered the door in her bathrobe. Her hair was a tangled mass of waves, dry but tousled like she'd just gotten out of bed. Her expression quickly changed from glee to surprise. "Oh my gosh! Jason."

He didn't miss how her gaze hopped from his face to over his shoulder and he turned and looked back to see if someone or something was behind him. "Hi, Monica. Were you expecting someone else?"

"No…I…uh…the electrician just left. I didn't have power this morning. Jenny called him for me."

"Jenny? Is she still here?" he asked, still standing on the porch because Monica hadn't invited him in yet. He glanced at his watch. It was almost seven.

"No. Why? Are you looking for her? She left a…while ago." Monica lifted a hand and started chewing on a manicured nail. That was a telltale sign that something was wrong.

"What's going on here?"

"Nothing." She crossed her arms over her chest and lifted her chin.

"Then why haven't you invited me in?"

"Oh!" She pushed open the storm door and stepped aside. "Sorry. I'm just a little slow today. Hangover. You remember last night."

"Yeah. I came to check on you." He walked into the living room and feeling like he might find someone there, looked to the left and right. "I wanted to make sure you're okay." The room was empty but he couldn't shake the feeling that Monica was hiding something.

"That's very sweet. I'm fine. As you can see." She tightened the belt on her robe.

"Actually, I can't."

Her eyes got huge.

"But I'll take your word for it," he added. "So, you say you didn't have power this morning? What was wrong?" He walked through the living room toward the kitchen.

"Um…something about the main breaker being tripped," Monica answered, following him.

"That's all?"

"Yep. Only took the electrician a minute to switch it back on, thank God. It was frigid in here with no heat. He said a surge might have triggered it. He checked everything else and said it looked fine."

"And that took…what? Ten hours? He must have been very thorough."

"Yes…he sure was," she said tensely.

As Jason neared the kitchen, the scents of toasted bread and pickles filled his nostrils. "And you cooked while you were waiting? You never cook for yourself."

Something was fishy here, and it wasn't in the fry pan.

"I was hungry?" she suggested with a shrug.

He noted the set of two plates, two glasses and two forks in the sink. Turning, she followed his gaze. "I…had seconds."

"Corned beef? What are you not telling me, Monica?"

She sighed and ran her fingers through her tangled hair. "I'm eating red meat these days?"

He answered her quip with a scowl.

"Okay." She sighed. "We need to talk."

"Let me guess. You slept with the electrician?" he said, summing up his suspicions. He was shocked by how little those words hurt as he spoke them.

"Yes I did."

He was even more shocked by how little her confession bothered him. It was as if he didn't care an iota. "I see."

"But that's not what we need to talk about." She pulled out a kitchen chair and sat at the table. She motioned for him to take a seat across from her. "Do you want something to drink first?"

"No. I think I should be sober when I hear this." He sat and waited for her to speak. He wasn't overly anxious. In fact, he realized he became more emotional during business transactions than he was at the moment.

"I think we both know by now that the wedding is off," she said.

"I'm gathering that, although it would've been nice if you'd told me before sleeping with someone else."

Looking guilty, her gaze lowered, she nodded. "I'm very sorry about that. Honest. It was a thoughtless, impulsive thing to do, you're right." She bit her lip and pulled at a fraying edge of her placemat. "But in my defense, I wanted to tell you last night. I just didn't know how to. And you looked so hurt…and we were at a party…I didn't think it was the right place…and I was sloshed…I'm sorry." She looked as forlorn as she sounded, and he knew she wasn't putting on an act for once. "There are so many things you don't know about me."

"Like what? We've dated for a long time," he reminded her. "Up until recently I thought I knew you pretty well."

She shook her head. "It doesn't matter now. I want you to go on with your life. I've manipulated you long enough."

"You got away with manipulating me only because I let you," he admitted. He wasn't exactly proud of it, but it was the truth. She'd used his sense of pride and stubborn determination to stand by his word to force him into doing things he probably normally wouldn't have done.

"Maybe. But I feel like a creep. I can't hold you to a promise that neither of us wants you to keep. I lied. I don't want to be married, at least not for the reasons I'd told you."

Her confession didn't surprise him. Deep in his gut he'd known that all along, but a man of his word, a man who lived by a promise, he couldn't allow himself to back out. It would've gone against everything he believed himself to be.

But now, as she sat before him, offering him the freedom he'd secretly longed for, he felt guilty. Would she be okay? "What're you going to do? Continue sleeping with the electrician?" he asked, needing to hear some reassurance she wouldn't be alone, unhappy.

"It doesn't matter. At least I won't be hurting you anymore. We don't work, Jason. You know that. I know that. Why can't we just accept it and move on? Just because we've invested five years in this doesn't mean we can't let it go. Love isn't something a couple thinks about and plans…it's something they feel—"

"Bull. Love isn't a feeling. It isn't some silly, here-today-gone-tomorrow emotion. It's a commitment to take care of one another and respect each other forever. That's what's wrong with people these days. They follow the whims of their hearts, act on feelings that are prone to change as quickly as the weather."

"Let yourself be free," Monica pleaded.

"Free? Of what?"

"Of logic, and should-be's, and must-do's." Monica sighed and met his gaze. "You're a human being, not a machine. Let yourself act like one. Let yourself feel, believe in the impossible, act on an impulse. It's the only way you'll get what you're looking for out of life."

"That's nonsense. A cop-out. Only children or people afraid of responsibility believe you should act without thinking. Where would our world be if everyone acted like that? There would be mass confusion. No order. No law."

"I have thought about this. A lot, for your information. And I don't believe for a minute that—"

"Okay. Then tell me, where's the logic in your decision? Don't tell me you actually thought about it before you climbed in the sack with your electrician."

"Yes. Of course I did. I thought about it and decided to follow my heart."

He laughed. "You thought about it for all of three seconds, I'm sure. Don't get me wrong. I'm not upset about what you did. If you say we're over then we're over. What bothers me is how you're preaching to me that I need to change when you clearly need to get a handle on your own life. You threw away a relationship of five years for a screw with a stranger. Five years should've meant more to you than that," he said, repeating what he'd been telling himself for hours last night as he lay sleepless in bed, afraid of falling asleep and dreaming about the wrong woman. "I guess it meant more to me than it did to you."

"No it didn't. But I'm willing to accept that history is history. It doesn't have to dictate our future. We must do what's right for both of us, and for Jenny."

"Jenny? What does she have to do with this?" He sat mute for a moment, not sure what to say next. Then, an idea took shape. "Is that what this whole switching thing was? Some kind of complicated way to dump me? Because if it was, you sure wasted a lot of time and energy. We were as good as over before all this switching nonsense began."

She stood and walked to the counter, filling a glass with juice from the pitcher sitting next to the stove. "We weren't over. You were mad about your grandmother's stuff but eventually you would've gotten over it and we would've gotten back together again, like we have so many times before."

Unable to sit, thanks to the nervous energy pulsing through his body in waves of jittery heat, he stood. "So it's true? You did create this complicated farce to get rid of me." He laughed, long and hard. "You poor thing. No wonder you said you'd been thinking about having sex with that guy for a long time. You were waiting. Funny, though. It would've been a lot quicker to sleep with your electrician and let me catch you like you did today."

"No. I'm convinced the switch was for Jenny and me. We both needed to learn some lessons. It had nothing to do with you."

"It had everything to do with me." He felt the heat of frustration churning his insides and creeping up his neck. "How can you say it didn't?"

She set her glass in the sink and stepped closer to him. He could see she wanted to reach out and touch him but resisted. Her arm lifted then dropped. Then she crossed both over her chest. "We didn't mean to hurt you. Like I said last night, I think Jenny and I both love you, just in different ways. You deserve so much more than what I could give you, but Jenny—"

"So you cooked up a scheme to shove me off onto your good pal, Jenny. No guilt."

Her eyes staining pink with unshed tears, she shook her head. "No, I swear, it wasn't like that."

"I'm so tired of trying to figure out what that was all about, what you two were up to. I've had enough." Not even close to being calm anymore, he walked to the front door. Just before he opened it, he shouted in frustration, "All I want to know is who is the woman I fell in love with? Why is it so hard to figure that out? Hell, does she even exist?"

Much calmer, Monica followed him to the door. "Jason, you know the answer to that. Just listen to your heart for once and leave your head out of it. Close your eyes and think about the woman you love. But don't imagine what she looks like, imagine who she is deep inside. That is the part of her you've fallen in love with."

In the middle of Monica's foyer, he closed his eyes and tried to do as she suggested. Who was the woman he loved? If he blanked out her face and just thought about her, what was she like?

"Tell me. Describe her."

"She's funny and clever, witty and strong. Intelligent, responsible. She wants what I do in life, marriage, a family. I can talk to her about anything. She's my friend, my lover. I can't stop thinking about her. I want to know everything there is to know. And I want to share every moment with her." He opened his eyes.

Monica smiled and nodded. "And who do you think that is? We both know that isn't me." She took his hands in hers. "If you never listened to a word of my advice, listen to me now. You need to go to her and tell her how you feel. Pronto." Releasing his hands, she opened the door and gently pushed him through it. "Goodbye, Jason. Make her happy. She deserves it."

He closed the door and inhaled the crisp air. And for the first time in his life, he closed his mind and opened his heart. Yes, he knew the answer to his question and yes, he would go to her. And he would spend the rest of his life making her happy if she let him. He had the perfect gift in mind, too. One that would show her exactly how much he loved her.

Chapter Seventeen

ꟗ

Monica breezed into work Monday morning, sat her butt on Jenny's desk and proclaimed, "I slept with Bill."

"Why are you telling me this?" Jenny asked, motioning for Monica to move so she could get back to work on her latest project. It was due by the end of the day and she was just now starting it. "Forgive me, but I don't have time to chit-chat about your sex life."

"But I thought you'd be happy to hear—"

"What? Why would you doing the nasty with your electrician—and cheating on your fiancé—make me happy?"

"Because, silly. That's just it." Monica caught Jenny's wrists and pulled them away from her keyboard, forcing Jenny to meet her gaze. "Jason's not my fiancé anymore."

Jenny was both happy and confused. "What? You broke the engagement?"

"Yep."

"Wait a minute..." Jenny needed to make sure she understood what Monica had just said. She was almost one hundred percent sure she'd misunderstood. "You broke your engagement to Jason so you could sleep with Bill?"

"Yep." Monica lifted her left hand and displayed her bare ring finger to illustrate. "See? The rock's gone. I gave it back. I'm not much for rubies anyway. What's your birthday?"

"That's insane," Jenny summed up in two words the flurry of thoughts shuffling through her brain. "The sex was that good? Jason loves you. He's a good man. Generous, loyal, kind—"

"I just couldn't go through with the marriage. I told you I didn't love him like I should. He deserves so much more. He deserves someone like you, who'll appreciate him."

"What about your grandmother?" Jenny asked, recalling their conversation the night of the party.

"I'll figure that out."

"You need his money and you said you loved him."

"I won't use him. I can't believe I even considered it. And I know I told you I love him, but I don't love him like you do."

"So what are you suggesting?"

"I want you to go for it. Call him."

Jenny couldn't believe her ears. "I can't call him. I don't date my friends' exes. That's a surefire way to lose a friend. I learned that back in high school," she said, recalling the one time she had dated a friend's former boyfriend. In the aftermath, she found herself lacking both a date to prom and the best friend she'd had since kindergarten. Friendships didn't come easy to Jenny and through the past few months she'd come to appreciate the one she had with Monica. She didn't dare risk it over a man.

"Well, we're not in high school any longer, and I'm giving you my blessing."

"You'll change your mind. Now, quit with this. Okay? I appreciate the thought but it's impossible. I need to get back to work." She slid the mouse over her desktop to disengage the screensaver.

Monica caught her wrist and held it tightly. "Nope. I won't quit until you agree to call him."

"Besides, who says he wants anything more than friendship with me? In case you forgot, I don't look like you. Look at me." After extricating her wrist from Monica's claw-like grip, Jenny stood and did a quick pirouette. "I'm short, dumpy, chubby and plain. What would someone like him want with someone like me? He's absolutely gorgeous. He could have any woman he wants."

Monica rested her hands on Jenny's shoulders and gave them a soft shake. "That's just it. He wants you. He just doesn't realize it yet. Heck, he told me he was in love with you."

"He said what?"

"He said he wanted to find the woman he'd fallen in love with."

"That was you," Jenny reminded her.

"No. That was you," Monica corrected. "You're right for him. You want the same things, you like the same things. You're like two pieces of a puzzle. You complete each other. I only hope to find what you have someday. Congratulations, Jenny. You found true love. Now, are you going to be a wuss and run from it?"

"But..."

"No buts. I'll kill you if you don't call him. I'll nag you every waking moment. I'll harass you at work, at home. I'll hide out in the ice cream aisle of the grocery store and hold every pint of Ben and Jerry's hostage, whatever it takes until you listen to me."

Jenny wasn't sure if she should laugh or cry. She didn't know if she should thank Monica and confess the feelings she'd repressed for so long they were eating her alive or keep them to herself. And so she did the only thing she could. She nodded and said, "Okay."

Content with her answer, Monica pranced away.

Jenny rehearsed a dozen different greetings throughout the day, determined not to make the call until she had down pat what she'd say to him. But later that night, as the buzzing of the ring in her ear ceased and his familiar voice took its place, all words were lost to her. She quickly hung up the phone and stared at it, suspecting it would ring any second. Everyone had caller ID these days.

It didn't ring in five minutes, or six, or ten, or twenty, or thirty.

He wasn't going to call her back. Monica had been wrong. Jason Foxx had no interest in plain-Jane Jenny Brown. He was probably having a good, long laugh.

Stupid, stupid, stupid! Her face hot, her back sweaty from nerves, she pushed open the French doors, stepped out onto the balcony, and looked up at the stars. There were a few bright enough to be seen, even this close to the city. The night was frigidly cold. Very still and quiet. The distant freeway traffic was light, sending the occasional rumble of a semi-truck to her ears.

To think it had all begun like this. A Monday night when she'd been looking up at the stars, though not as cold. Had it been a one-shot deal? She hadn't thought to give it another try.

"Star light, star bright. First star I see tonight. I wish I may, I wish I might, have the wish I wish tonight." She closed her eyes and before she could stop herself, she said, "I wish Jason was here with me now."

She waited a few minutes before opening her eyes, hoping she'd hear his voice any moment.

The only sound she heard was the distant tinny blaring of someone's car alarm. Disappointed, but not surprised, she opened her eyes and looked down, expecting to see a car with the telltale flashing lights in the parking lot below her window. Morbidly curious but not seeing the car emitting the obnoxious round of whoops, sirens and buzzes, she leaned over the railing to see if it was one of the cars parked in the closer spots.

Something touched her back and, caught off guard, she jerked away, lunging forward and nearly toppling over the weak wooden railing. Her arms flailed until one hand caught hold of the decorative finial on top of a support post. No doubt the source of nutrition for millions of carpenter ants and termites, the wood snapped and Jenny's weight flew forward. The balls of her feet rolled over the edge of the porch and instinctively, she threw her arms forward and closed her eyelids, expecting to hit the ground within seconds.

A pair of strong hands gripped her waist and pulled her backward. "Oh no, you don't. I did not go through this hell to have you kill yourself now."

Instantly recognizing the voice, she spun around and wrapped her arms around his waist. Her own heartbeat still hammering in her ears, she pressed one side of her head against his chest and waited for her racing heart to find its normal rhythm. Then she remembered what—or rather who—had caused that near-fatal accident and she tipped her head up to look at him. "You darn near killed me," she teased, loosening her grip but not releasing him. It felt too good being in his arms. Sinfully good. She realized her heart rate was picking up again, for entirely different reasons. "I was just fine until you touched me."

"Sorry. I wanted to surprise you."

"That you did."

"What were you doing hanging over the edge like that?"

"Being nosy," she admitted, pointing toward the street. "Someone's car alarm was going off. Despite the relative warmth and safety she found in his arms, she released him and ventured toward the edge again. "Looks like it stopped. Hopefully the owner disengaged it and not some hoodlums. Speaking of hoodlums, how'd you get in? Did you pick the lock?"

"Didn't have to. You left the door unlocked. This isn't the worst neighborhood but it isn't the best either. You should lock your door." Looking a little nervous, he reached forward and pulled her away from the edge again. "Better stay back here until that banister gets fixed."

"I do lock my door…I mean I did. I'm positive…" she said as she followed him inside. As they walked toward the living room, she eyed the front door with suspicion. Had another wish come true? Had a little fairy flown from Neverland or somewhere and unlocked her door? "Not to be rude, but what're you doing here anyway?"

"I'm not sure to be honest. I'm still trying to figure that out."

"Did…you drive here?"

"Of course I did. My car's down in the parking lot."

She giggled at her own silliness. "Of course. It's just that…well, I made another wish and I thought since you said you weren't sure what you were doing here that you literally didn't know what you were doing here… Does that make sense?" She knew she was blabbering, but the way he was looking at her, she either blabbered or she stopped breathing. She figured nonstop yammering had to be better than having her drop cold in a faint.

"You made a wish?" His expression intense, his gaze fixed to hers, he stepped closer. "What did you wish for?" he whispered.

The air crackled between them, like tiny sparks of electricity were leaping back and forth from her to him and him to her. The hairs on her arms stood up and a tingle tiptoed up her spine. "I wished…that you were here with me."

"Why would you wish that?" he asked, taking another step closer.

"Isn't it obvious?" she asked, gasping for a breath. Why wouldn't her lungs work? And why was he torturing her like this? Maybe her wish had brought him here. She'd probably never know. But it wouldn't keep him here. He was doing that on his own. What did he want? His gaze suggested something she wasn't sure she dared believe. "What would you wish for if given the chance?"

"I don't make wishes."

Despite the sober tone of his voice, she didn't believe him. Both this time and the last, he was too…defensive. "Never? You never wished for something? Not even as a little boy? You can tell me. I promise I won't laugh."

"There was one…" Although he didn't move, he seemed to be withdrawing.

This was a moment she knew could change both their lives. "What? Please tell me. I want to know. I want to know everything about you, your weaknesses as well as your strengths. Your failures as well as your successes. Your fears and dreams and wishes." Stepping forward, she touched his face, allowing her fingertip to trace the strong line of his jaw.

He visibly swallowed. "I wished my father would come home and stay home. That was the only thing I wished for and it never came true."

She knew it had been difficult to share that, and knowing he'd trusted her enough to admit something so personal touched her deeply. Her heart broke for the boy he'd once been, craving the two things his father's money couldn't buy—time and love. At the same time, her heart soared. She had his trust. He'd admitted something to her he had probably never even admitted to himself. The problem was, she had no idea what to say.

"Silly, I know," he said when she didn't respond.

She gripped both his arms in her hands and squeezed. "Oh no, not at all. You were a child. You needed love and attention from your father. He was all you had left. I'm sorry he couldn't give it to you. It's the least a child deserves from their parents, the one thing so many children crave. Ironic, it's free yet so often ignored."

He nodded. "I won't do that to my children."

"I know how it feels. Although I didn't go to foreign boarding schools or have jet-setting parents who shopped in Milan or Japan, I was alone too as a kid. I learned to be very self-sufficient and responsible."

"You have to when you're your own parent. So, are you the woman I met the night I had Monica's car repossessed? Was that really you on my front porch?"

She nodded. "If you can get yourself to believe in something you probably consider impossible, you know the answer. I was the one in the hot tub, and at the dance club, and at the apple orchard...in the poison ivy. I was the one eating roast beef and ice cream and talking about family and marriage. Can you believe, Jason?"

He smiled, the expression warming her insides until she could do nothing but sigh. "I forgot to mention one other wish," he confessed. "I wasn't a little boy when I made this one."

That was a surprise. Intrigued, she asked, "Are you going to tell me what it was?"

"You weren't the only one making wishes the night of the meteor shower. I did too. I wished Monica would become the woman of my dreams."

Not sure how to take that, she said, "Oh? So did your wish come true?"

"In a way. I had to see beyond her outward beauty to finally accept that she wasn't the woman I could love. I was stuck in a rut, created by my own stubborn determination to make my relationship with Monica work even when I knew it wouldn't. I had to experience Jenny Brown to know what true love was like. I guess I had to learn to believe in the impossible."

"Oh?" she squeaked. Did he just say her name and love in the same sentence? "But what about Monica?"

"We had a long talk about grandmothers and nursing homes, electricians, car payments. We settled a lot of things, stuff that should've been settled a long time ago. She's one hundred percent with us on this. She wants us together. She believes we're perfect for each other." He gathered her into his arms and she sighed. This had to be a dream! Jason Foxx couldn't have just told her he wanted to be with her!

"What do you believe?" she asked, tipped her chin up to look at his face.

"I believe…that wishes come true." He lowered his head slowly and her breath caught in her throat as she closed her eyes and awaited his kiss.

She didn't have long to wait. His lips moved slowly over hers in a kiss that curled her toes and sent all kinds of giddy, happy emotions exploding throughout her body. As his tongue dipped inside her mouth, she thought she just might die right on the spot from too much excitement. Surely her pulse had to be up in the stratosphere somewhere. Her brain couldn't be getting adequate oxygen. That could be the only reason for her feeling as if she was floating... Breaking the kiss, she looked down and realized her legs were not under her.

Cradled in Jason's arms, she lifted her hands to his face. Her fingertip traced the lips that had only seconds ago been doing the most amazing things to hers. She could imagine them doing amazing things to other parts. "This is happening so quickly."

He stopped before the couch and slowly lowered her onto it. "I can stop at any time. Tell me you don't love me as I love you. Tell me you haven't been suffering the same frustrations I have whenever we've been together and I'll leave right now."

"I can't. I never believed in love at first sight...until I saw you. Some people might think I'm crazy, but I know I love you. I...want you."

His response was a crushing kiss that curled her toes and set her blood ablaze. It was as if all the pent-up passion inside him had broken free. Now, as Jenny lay below him, it was pressing upon her in the form of a trembling, tense mass of all-male, all-sexy flesh. Anxious to feel all of his weight on top of her, Jenny gripped his shirt in her fists and pulled him closer, closer, closer until his hips were nestled between her legs and his chest was grazing her breasts.

Their breaths mingled as their mouths joined, their tongues swirling and tasting in a wild dance. Jason's hands slid up her hips and over her stomach before finding the swell of her breasts. They kneaded and caressed, pinched and squeezed, until Jenny could do nothing but moan.

The sound of her voice echoed inside her own mouth.

Jason broke the kiss but didn't stop his thorough exploration, beginning at the base of her jaw and working down.

Between licks and nips, he murmured her name, repeating it over and over as if he couldn't hear it often enough.

His hands slipped inside the deep V of her T-shirt and fingertips tiptoed down the crest between her breasts. Thanks to the fact that she was wearing no bra, her nipples were readily available and he took advantage, tracing slow circles over first one then the other.

Jenny couldn't remember the last time she'd felt so overcome by need and emotion and wanting and desperation. Every part of her trembled, from her feet to her eyelids, awaiting Jason's very gentle, very thorough touch. And he clearly didn't wish to disappoint. On his journey down her neck, he didn't miss a fraction of an inch. When he sucked, she shivered. Goose bumps rose over her arms and chest. When his tongue swirled over her skin, leaving a path of cool, damp skin, she shuddered. Heat blazed through her body in waves, from the deepest parts of her body out to her fingertips and toes.

"I want to make love to you but I won't if you want me to stop," Jason said in a deep rumbly voice that made goose bumps rise up on top of goose bumps.

"Oh yes. Please do!" she said just before he scooped her up and carried her to the bedroom.

Chapter Eighteen

ꟹ

Undressing Jenny was like unwrapping the most precious gift he'd ever received. Her wide-eyed gaze was focused on his face the entire time as he slowly removed first her oversized T-shirt and then her baggy sweatpants. Underneath the bulky, sloppy clothes, he found the most exquisite female body—soft, curvy, delicate. His need to have her burned so fiercely he feared he'd go too quick. This would be the first of a lifetime of nights spent lovemaking. He was determined to make it a night she'd remember forever.

He could tell already, as she looked up at him with round eyes and kiss-swollen lips, tonight would be the ultimate test of his self-control.

Keeping his clothes on would prevent things from escalating too quickly. He held himself over top of her with outstretched arms. His hips were strategically placed beside hers on the bed, rather than on top. If there was one thing he wouldn't be able to endure it was another moment of that seductive grinding she'd performed in the living room.

Of course, her little moans and whimpers as he kissed her neck and shoulders were doing their damage to his fragile self-control. A powerful aphrodisiac, the sounds made blood rush straight to his groin. His erection was painfully engorged and his body demanded release, already.

When she reached down to stroke his crotch through his clothes, he quickly snatched her hand away. "Not yet, baby," he told her in a soft voice before teasing a nipple with his tongue and teeth. In response, she arched her back, pushing her breasts higher into the air. When he flickered his tongue over the second taut bud, her gasp filled his ears.

She was so responsive, so sexy. It seemed his every touch, light or firm, upon arm, breast or stomach, made her quiver with delight. He delighted in watching her face as need and tension, love and adoration played over her features. When he slipped off her panties and caught the scent of her arousal, he almost lost all control. He wanted her so badly he could practically taste his need as it pulsed through his body.

Again, she reached for him, her hand brushing against his jeans where they hid the firm flesh that ached to be inside her and again he gently pushed her hand away. To further discourage her from touching him yet, he slid back, away from her. Then he lifted her knees and parted them, drinking in the sight of the wet curls covering her sex.

Drawn by the promise of sweet juices, he lowered his head and inhaled her scent. Intoxicating. Addictive. He couldn't get enough. He inhaled several more times then took his first taste.

No sooner did his tongue make contact with her slick flesh than she cried out and squirmed. He stilled her with firm pressure on her pelvis and skirted her slit with his tongue. As expected, she tasted sweeter than any nectar. At that moment, he knew he could never get enough of her. His first taste was his undoing and he'd spend the rest of his life hungering for his next.

He felt her stomach muscles tighten under his right hand as he flickered his tongue over the most sensitive part of her, the tiny nub tucked in her folds. And when he pressed a finger inside as he continued to stimulate it, warm sweet juices coated it.

His erection was beyond discomfort now. He glanced up and saw the tension of her arousal on each of her features. Her mouth was drawn into a straight line. Her eyelids were clamped tightly. Shallow creases drew lines across her forehead.

"Make love to me," she pleaded. "Just tell me I'll be yours, for always."

"It took me a lifetime to find you, including a couple of the most confusing, frustrating months of my life," he said, sitting up and gathering her into his arms. "I'm not about to let you go now. Jenny Brown," he added, looking into her eyes, "you are everything I've ever wished for in a woman. Physically, mentally, emotionally. I was an idiot for not seeing that sooner. Will you forgive me?"

She grinned. "I suppose…if you let me see what's under those clothes. Don't you think you've made me wait long enough?"

"Probably." He raised his arms, enjoying the way her gaze followed the hem of his shirt as she lifted it up over his stomach, chest and then shoulders.

She gasped. "My goodness! What you were hiding under there. I had no idea."

Feeling a little wicked, he teased, "Just wait 'til you see what's under the *Jockeys.*"

* * * * *

Jenny had never even dreamed of sleeping with a guy who looked like Jason. Never, ever. Not even when she'd been a teenager. He was so perfect. Starting at the waist, he had sharply chiseled abs like the guys in underwear commercials, a developed chest that had to have taken eons and zillions of pushups and bench presses to shape…and his shoulders. Oh those shoulders! Having a weakness for wide, heavily muscled shoulders but never being this close to a set, she was in awe. There were bulges on top of bulges and they didn't end there. They carried down his arms.

And when he moved those arms…she was in heaven! She wondered if she might have an orgasm just from the sight. Still wondering if she was dreaming again, she reached up and poked his chest with an index finger then said, "Pinch me."

He pinched her forearm, just hard enough to sting.

She wasn't sleeping.

"Has anyone ever told you you're beautiful?" she asked as she let her index finger follow the deep ridge between his pecs down the center of his stomach. It stopped at his pants waistband and she shuddered with expectation, staring at the bulge front and center behind his zipper. No doubt about it, he wasn't kidding when he'd said wait until she saw what was in there!

A little bit of bravery and a lot of curiosity gave her the strength to unzip his trousers. And the steady throb between her legs was enough motivation to push them the rest of the way down his smooth-skinned, muscular legs.

The man was built like a god! And he wanted to be with her?

With his pants gone, the sheer size of the bulge in the front of his snug black cotton briefs was a little intimidating. But with a little gentle encouragement from Jason, she finally pulled the briefs down and took her first look at what was under them.

A huge lump formed in her throat. His shoulders weren't the only…oversized…part of this man. It was the size of one of those dildos she and Lori saw at the sex-toy shop. She was grateful it wasn't the size of the John Holmes model at least, but she still wondered if it would fit. Her experience being what it was—best labeled limited—she couldn't be sure of anything.

"I have a silly question," she said, feeling foolish.

"Sure."

"Um…have you ever killed a woman with that?" she asked, pointing at his tool.

His laugh was a delightful blend of amusement and wicked promises. "Not literally," he answered. "I promise if at any time you tell me to stop, I will. I don't want it to be painful for you. Okay?"

"Okay."

"That's why I want to make sure you're good and ready." He pressed on her shoulders, easing her onto her back then gently parted her legs again. His fingers found all the right spots as they drew circles on the outside of her privates, plunged in and out, and otherwise drove her to near insanity.

The sounds of his voice as he whispered sweet promises to her, the scent of his skin, the feel of his hands on her, the tickle of his hair against her thighs as he lowered his head between them, and the taste of his kiss that still lingered in her mouth and on her lips all competed with each other for her attention. It was as if her brain couldn't register it all at the same time.

At the same time, she felt her heart expanding, swelling from the gentle touches and loving words he lavished upon her. No man had ever made her feel so special, so treasured. She was the luckiest woman alive!

He got up, found his pants and produced a wrapped condom. Kneeling on the mattress, he said, "I'm going to make love to you now. If it hurts, tell me. I'll go very slow."

Her eyes closed, since she was unable to process so much sensory input, and dizzy from her uneven breathing, she waited.

His first touch was soft. He parted her outer lips and pressed his thick member against her tight flesh. Out of instinct, she flinched and tightened. But with some coaxing from Jason, both with words and gentle caresses, she was able to relax. Slowly, he slipped inside, inch by inch. He stopped when she was completely full, giving her the opportunity to enjoy the wonderful, new sensation.

"Are you okay?" he asked, sounding strained and breathless.

"More than okay."

"I love you, Jenny. I want this to be the most memorable, special day of your life."

"Oh, believe me, it has been."

She swore it could get no better than that, Jason's arms wrapped around her, nuzzling her neck, his breathing quick puffs in her ear. But then he started moving *that* part, inside her, slowly withdrawing it until only a tiny portion, the very tip, was still inside and then pushing deep again.

"Oh..." she moaned as heat poured through her body, forming a thin coating of sweat over her stomach, back and chest. With each thrust the warmth increased a hundredfold, despite the cool draft chilling her damp skin, until she thrashed and cried out.

Jason held her head in his cupped hands, making her feel cherished and secure. Wanting him deep inside when she climaxed, she tilted her hips in rhythm with his thrusts, taking every wonderful inch she could.

As the first tingles of a once-in-a-lifetime climax spread up and out from her center, she heard him call out her name. Together, they rode the bliss of orgasm in each others' arms. And when the intense explosions dimmed to little twitches, Jenny sighed, wrapped her legs around Jason's hips and kissed his slick shoulder. Giddy, she rested her head on his chest, which was rising and falling rapidly, and said, "Wow, when can we do that again?"

He chuckled, the sound low and rumbly in her ear. "Give me a chance to recover and I'd be happy to oblige. But before we do any more bedroom gymnastics, my little kitten, we have a few things to talk about."

"Oh? Like what?"

"For starters, what you think I should do with this."

"This?" Confused, she lifted her head to see what *this* he was referring to.

Smiling, he held a small velvet box in his hand. "It seems on my most recent trip to Italy I stumbled upon this little trinket which is in need of a female finger, size six, for a home. You don't happen to wear a size six, do you?" With his free hand, he twined his fingers with hers and seemed to be studying their size.

"How'd you guess?"

"Trained eye." He handed her the box. "Are you going to open it? And before you ask, no, it isn't the diamond and ruby ring I gave Monica. I'm not that much of a schmuck."

She chuckled. "I'd never call you a schmuck." With a strategically placed thumb, she flipped the top open to reveal the most beautiful ring she'd ever seen. Set in silver-toned metal was a huge square-cut clear stone. Little diamonds surrounded all four sides. "Wow," she said, muttering the only word she could summon up at the moment. The whole evening, from the moment she'd stepped outside, had been one surprise after another. It was almost more shocking than the morning she woke up in Monica's bedroom.

"Do you like it? That's a very rare diamond. And it's set in platinum. It's very old, one of a kind."

"It's the most beautiful gift someone has ever given me. I don't know what to say."

"How about yes?"

"You haven't asked me a question yet. What would I be saying yes to?" she teased, knowing full well what he was implying.

"Let me do this properly then." He slid from the bed and knelt beside it.

"Are you praying?" Jenny teased, sitting up and swinging her legs over the side. She wrapped a sheet around herself as she wiggled herself into position on the edge of the bed. Her face was flaming hot as she anticipated the moment she hadn't dared dream would ever happen.

"Yes, I'm praying. For patience. I'm going to need a lot of it with you," he teased back. Then with a smile, he plucked the ring from the box, took her hand in his and said, "Jenny Brown, would you make me the happiest man in the world by becoming my wife?"

"That depends," she said, curling her finger so he couldn't slip the ring on.

"On what?" he asked.

"On how you answer one question. Do you believe in wishes?"

He grinned. "Not only do I believe in wishes, but miracles, fairy godmothers and little green men in spaceships. There can be no other explanation for how I found you. But now that I have you I won't live another day without you."

"Excellent!" She uncurled her finger. "My answer is yes." Her heart jumped in her chest as he pushed the ring up over her knuckle and tears burned her eyes. "Yes, Jason. I want to be your wife." As he stood, she wrapped her arms around his neck and clung to him, pressing her entire body against his. Tears of joy ran freely down her cheeks. Wishes did come true. And there had to be fairy godmothers, but the little green men? Now that one was a bit of a stretch. They kissed, and touched, and explored, and played, and made love, over and over until dawn tinted the eastern sky a brilliant shade of pink.

Content, exhausted, and excited, Jenny lay in her rumpled bed and stared out the window, Jason's soft snore like the most beautiful music in her ear.

It stopped and he asked, "What're you thinking about?"

"Monday."

"Work?"

"No, the Monday night we get married. It has to be on a Monday, you understand."

"Of course."

"Just the two of us."

"You don't want a big wedding?"

"Nope. Just us, the officiate and the stars…oh, and who or whatever made our wishes come true. I have a feeling he or she is out of the office Tuesday through Sunday."

"Who? The officiate?"

"Nope, my fairy godmother. She has a cushy job, one day a week. Wouldn't you say?"

"Yes, but I'd also say she's darn good at what she does, even if she only works one day a week. Since you want a small wedding, tell me you aren't going to make me wait a year, or even a month to be married."

"Heck no! Next Monday works for me. Plus, it's a full moon. Can't get any luckier than that."

"Sure I can, and I have. Because I have you now." He gathered her into his arms and they made love again, and again and again, until daylight gave way to twilight and both of them finally succumbed to their exhaustion.

As she slipped into a shallow slumber, Jenny swore she heard the sound of a child's voice outside on the terrace, "I haven't had a day off in centuries, thank you very much. The workload for Monica alone is overwhelming. I'll be happy to wrap up her case next. But at least now my caseload is lightened by two. You can make each others' wishes come true from this point on."

That was exactly what they did.

The End

About the Author

ဢ

Sydney Laine Allan welcomes mail from readers. You can write to her c/o Ellora's Cave Publishing at 1056 Home Avenue, Akron, OH 44310-3502.

Please enjoy an excerpt from:
ASTRAL NIGHTS

Astral Nights

After midnight, Callan's astral projection stood at the foot of the bed and looked down at her earthly body. In her astral eyes, it seemed small and vulnerable in its exhaustion, lying so still, its breathing nearly imperceptible.

The tousled, newly washed hair, crowned by the halo of silver cord, seemed glossier and prettier than when she saw it in the mirror. The nose appeared more pert and less prominent than she had believed, but she hadn't realized before that her chin looked so stubborn.

The impersonal appraisal was moderately interesting, better than dwelling on the debacle earlier with Sam, but of no actual importance. Time to go. She wasn't sorry to leave that poor, worn out piece of flesh behind for a while.

Callan willed herself outside her bedroom window as Rosemary materialized above the Douglas fir on the front lawn. Her arms were akimbo as she hovered and studied the protective auras covering the Ellisons' house and Callan's.

I can hardly tell these are houses. What did you do? Suck up all the earth energy in the western hemisphere? she asked telepathically.

Not quite. Besides, after the night I've had, I need all the protection I can get.

Got man problems too? The wise aqua eyes in the young face narrowed with amusement and some sympathy.

I don't want to talk about it, so don't pick, Callan snapped back. *What's the procedure tonight? At the rate we're shuttling people upstairs, it'll be Halloween before it's finished. One person at a time is hopeless. Plus my paranormal powers aren't adequate. I forgot to tell you that Bianca broke my protective aura when she got Stephanie. Gave me a headful of boiling oil, while she was at it. Furthermore, I still don't know how to make her stop.*

Callan looked away, ashamed that she was taking out her frustration and fear on Rosemary, who was putting herself in jeopardy for her benefit.

I'm sorry, Rosemary, she said, looking squarely back at her friend. Rosemary seemed unperturbed about her outburst. *I'm scared and still so ignorant. Not even a half-baked psychic yet.*

Rosemary studied Callan for a moment, then said, *You're right to be scared. If Bianca broke your protection, she's tapped into extra power. You'll have to go to the source too. The ethereal plane has enough energy to defeat Bianca's army, although it's dangerous to take too much on at once. Overdone, it can have a harmful impact on the body.*

So what! I have no choice! I'm sick of being Bianca's equivalent of popcorn and a movie! After moving Stephanie's pillar of light tonight, can we do it, whatever it is? We have to take Katie with us too. We can handle both of them, can't we?

Certainly. It's a good idea to start taking them in pairs whenever we can. Let's get at it.

In accord they flew toward the Ellisons' house, where Callan opened a doorway in the protective shield, and they entered Stephanie and Matt's bedroom.

One glance at the bed sent Callan's eyes skittering away. Matt was naked. If he hadn't been curled spoon-fashion against Stephanie with an arm snuggled around her waist, he would have been totally exposed. Matt then rolled over onto his back, and she swallowed a gulp and felt her face grow warm. What else could she expect? Embarrassment was only justice if a person invaded someone else's bedroom in the middle of the night.

This is a horrible invasion of their privacy, Callan mumbled, as they drifted closer to the bed. She kept her eyes fastened on Stephanie's face and away from Matt.

Can't be helped. Go on, coax her spirit out. Rosemary seemed unperturbed by the ethics of the situation.

Callan's tactic to entice Stephanie's astral spirit was much as she had done with Connor, only this time she said that Katie wanted her mother. Stephanie's spirit promptly slipped from her body with an audible pop and stood by the bed. Her eyes were open, and the vacancy in them was similar to her catatonic state earlier that evening. Their strangeness gave Callan a queer shivery feeling.

Stephanie's silver cord draped over her left shoulder, gradually fading into the floor. Totally unlike her usual daytime wear of practical denim, she wore a short, diaphanous sea-green nightgown. Emphasized by the revealing gown, her figure was even more voluptuous than Callan had realized.

Oh, jeez, Callan said with a gulp, as she saw her friend's scanty nightwear, *she can't go out nightwalking like that. Where's her robe?*

She spotted a long cotton kimono lying across a chair and recreated it on Stephanie's astral form, with the belt snugly tied around the waist. Rosemary, looking on with a bemused expression on her face, said nothing.

I just thought of something. What if Matt moves and disturbs Stephanie? Won't that cause her astral spirit to snap back here? Callan asked, remembering Bianca's painful termination of her own first nightwalking attempt.

No, she's used to having her husband beside her. Unless he shoves her out of bed or tries to violently shake her awake, his movements will make no impression on her. Married couples nightwalk all the time without ill effects. Let's get the baby.

Callan and Rosemary, with Stephanie between them, appeared beside Katie's crib. Katie, in her yellow terry sleepers, slept on her stomach, her knees pulled under her and her bottom in the air. Stephanie stared straight ahead, across the crib, engaged in a dream of her own.

What now? Callan asked irritably, emotionally spent from the problems of the day. *How do we coax the astral spirit of a baby? What will move her?*

Her mother, of course. Really, Callan, you must learn to take more initiative, rely more on your common sense and intuition in these matters, Rosemary answered with dry exasperation.

Sorry.

She seemed to have spent the last few hours doing nothing but apologizing to her friends.

Katie, mama wants you to go bye-bye with her, Callan said to the baby in a barely audible mind whisper. Katie stirred and removed her thumb from her mouth.

Katie, Katie sweetie, come to mama.

Katie's astral spirit detached with a whoosh and stood by the crib's railing. Her black curls were flattened on one side. Looking from one to the other, the tiny spirit seemed fully awake and aware of them. Callan ruffled the curls so they stood out around Katie's face. She smiled, displaying her front baby teeth, and held up her arms.

Pick up Katie, Callan said to Stephanie. Stephanie obediently held out her arms, and the child rose from the crib to settle into them. Katie looked around the room as if expecting some entertainment, then popped her thumb back in her mouth.

See, easy isn't it? Since they're not long from the spiritual state, babies are natural nightwalkers, Rosemary commented, as they guided Stephanie back to the master bedroom overlooking the cul-de-sac.

Callan reopened the protective shield and ushered Stephanie through into the night. Suddenly, Rosemary wasn't on Stephanie's other side. She glanced back to check on her.

Rosemary's head and shoulders were behind the bedroom wall, invisible, while her hips, legs and silver cord floated free outside.

Whoa! The pecs and buns on that fella! Callan heard her say.

This was contemptible! Scandalized, she let go of Stephanie, grabbed a handful of leather jacket and gave a yank.

Rosemary, cut that out! she yelled. Rosemary's upper half popped from the wall. *You're disgraceful! Ogling Matt like that!*

Rosemary turned to face her, casually straightening the white silk scarf around her neck. The protective aura around the house flowed shut behind her. Rocking back on her heels on empty air, she hung her thumbs from the front pockets of her pants.

Honestly, Callan, you're such a prude, Rosemary said sardonically. *Sometimes, I think you're the old lady instead of me.*

Stung, Callan retorted, *I am not! I just respect other people's privacy.*

That's a load of crap! I see in your mind a picture of that young man half naked! You can't fool me, I'm psychic!

He mows his front lawn with his shirt off! I can't help but see him if he parades around in public like that!

Oh sure, gawking out your kitchen window, getting an eyeful is more like it!

You stay out of my private thoughts! What would Stephanie think if…where's Stephanie?

Callan whipped around, scanning the area. Stephanie, with a beaming Katie peering back over her shoulder, passed over Bernie Rabney's house and moved steadily eastward.

Why an electronic book?

We live in the Information Age—an exciting time in the history of human civilization in which technology rules supreme and continues to progress in leaps and bounds every minute of every hour of every day. For a multitude of reasons, more and more avid literary fans are opting to purchase e-books instead of paperbacks. The question to those not yet initiated to the world of electronic reading is simply: *why?*

1. *Price.* An electronic title at Ellora's Cave Publishing and Cerridwen Press runs anywhere from 40-75% less than the cover price of the exact same title in paperback format. Why? Cold mathematics. It is less expensive to publish an e-book than it is to publish a paperback, so the savings are passed along to the consumer.
2. *Space.* Running out of room to house your paperback books? That is one worry you will never have with electronic novels. For a low one-time cost, you can purchase a handheld computer designed specifically for e-reading purposes. Many e-readers are larger than the average handheld, giving you plenty of screen room. Better yet, hundreds of titles can be stored within your new library—a single microchip. (Please note that Ellora's Cave and Cerridwen Press does not endorse any specific brands. You can check our website at www.ellorascave.com or

www.cerridwenpress.com for customer recommendations we make available to new consumers.)

3. *Mobility*. Because your new library now consists of only a microchip, your entire cache of books can be taken with you wherever you go.
4. *Personal preferences are accounted for*. Are the words you are currently reading too small? Too large? Too...**ANNOYING**? Paperback books cannot be modified according to personal preferences, but e-books can.
5. *Instant gratification*. Is it the middle of the night and all the bookstores are closed? Are you tired of waiting days—sometimes weeks—for online and offline bookstores to ship the novels you bought? Ellora's Cave Publishing sells instantaneous downloads 24 hours a day, 7 days a week, 365 days a year. Our e-book delivery system is 100% automated, meaning your order is filled as soon as you pay for it.

Those are a few of the top reasons why electronic novels are displacing paperbacks for many an avid reader. As always, Ellora's Cave and Cerridwen Press welcomes your questions and comments. We invite you to email us at service@ellorascave.com, service@cerridwenpress.com or write to us directly at: 1056 Home Ave. Akron OH 44310-3502.

Cerridwen Press

Cerridwen, the Celtic goddess of wisdom, was the muse who brought inspiration to storytellers and those in the creative arts. Cerridwen Press encompasses the best and most innovative stories in all genres of today's fiction. Visit our website and discover the newest titles by talented authors who still get inspired—much like the ancient storytellers did, once upon a time...